Perfect REGRET

For Kim—

♡

A. Meredith

WD xx

a novel

A. Meredith Walters

ISBN 10: 149238223x
ISBN 13: 978-1492382232

For my daughter who gave me my life of purpose.

Chapter
1

I DIDN'T do depressed. I wasn't one to wallow when life sucked. I was the girl who picked herself up, dusted off the bullshit and kept on trucking. I doled out the advice about making lemonade out of lemons and put one foot in front of the other.

I didn't get pulled down into crappy emotion filled holes.

But that was before I got dumped.

And we're talking remove his testicles with a teaspoon dumped.

It hadn't been pretty. It hadn't been civil.

It had been nasty and hurtful and had reduced me into a giant pile of pathetic.

And instead of bouncing back and getting into the life groove, here I was, lying on my bed feeling so sorry for myself that even *I* hated me.

Riley Walker had been reduced to the sad and lonely dumpee. And that wasn't a person I had *ever* thought I'd be.

Because Damien Green and I had been perfect. Things had been fantastic. We had fit together like the proverbial missing puzzle pieces, each complementing the other just as we were supposed to.

Our relationship had been simple. Easy. And maybe that's why this hurt so badly. Because now I was forced to admit that my simple and easy relationship had bored my former boyfriend to death.

Perfect Regret

So much for soul mates and eternal, undying love. Clearly what Damien and I had couldn't make it past junior year and was causing me to question my judgment when it came to guys and dating and all that other blah blah stuff.

And I hated questioning myself. Because for a girl who always had the answers, I was finding that I had woefully failed the test.

So, yeah. Love sucks.

And to commemorate my recent descent into early spinsterhood, I had compiled a play list of the most obnoxious and annoying love songs ever written. Nothing says heartache and the overwhelming urge to disembowel yourself with a butter knife quite like an hour of Celine Dion ballads.

I picked up the remote and cranked the volume of my stereo, gritting my teeth through another round of "Because You Loved Me." If I was going to wallow, I might as well do it right.

I caterwauled along with the lyrics, adding my own tone-deaf rendition to the horrendous soundtrack off my life. I ignored the knock on my bedroom door, singing louder to try and drown it out

"Dear God, enough already!" Maysie yelled over the kitschy strains of some ridiculously horrendous One Direction song. She cupped her hands over her ears as she entered the room.

I pointed at the open door. "Get out," I told her, trying to put feeling into the words. Too bad I only sounded tired and defeated.

Maysie threw a pair of ear buds at me and I didn't bother to try and catch them. I appreciated the dramatic effect of letting them hit me on the chest and fall off my side and onto the bed. My best friend and roommate of the last year and a half rolled her eyes.

"I thought I had the market on over dramatics. Don't you think it's time to give your best friend and the rest of the people living in the building a break? Because if I have to hear Vanessa Williams sing about *Saving the Best for Last* one more time, I won't be responsible for my actions," she complained.

I picked up the ear buds and sat up. Balling them in my fist, I chucked them back at her. She caught them clumsily. "And how about you let a gal listen to cheesy music and mire in the untimely demise of her relationship?"

"And friends don't let friends listen to Chicago," Maysie said, turning off the stereo just as the beginning notes of "Look Away" started to fill the room.

"Hey, I was enjoying that," I whined.

Maysie shook her head. "I don't think anyone this side of 1985 enjoys that, Riley," she quipped and I couldn't deny her point. I hated it when she out snarked me. There was something fundamentally wrong about that.

Maysie, clearly bent on an intervention, came over and sat down on the bed. She put her arm around my shoulders and I tried to shrink away from her.

I hated the touchy feely stuff and she knew it. I wasn't the kind of girl who squealed and hugged her friends. Sheesh, I wasn't five. I had successfully avoided the stereotypical trappings of my gender and was proud of it. I wasn't some crazy fem Nazi. But I sure as hell didn't spend hours doing my hair and make up. And I most definitely didn't moan about why a guy didn't call me. I hated each and every show on E! and I refused to upgrade our cable package just because the Style network was now available.

So why, do you ask, was I subjecting my eardrums and sanity to an over-indulgence in feel sorry for myselfitis, which was a clear sign of estrogen gone wild?

Damien Green happened, that's why.

Stupid, too-cute-for-his-own-good and recent Riley dumper Damien Green.

"You're supposed to be at Barton's in thirty minutes. Maybe you should get up and get dressed. Do that whole shower and grooming thing that most people do," Maysie remarked, squeezing me tightly, with a grin. I glowered at her with every ounce of baleful irritation I could summon.

Maysie tossed her annoyingly shiny hair over her shoulder and winked. Looking at my best friend, I couldn't help but wonder for the millionth time what sort of crack fate had been smoking when it threw the two of us together, thus creating the most unlikely friendship in the history of unlikely friendships.

Perfect Regret

Maysie Ardin was my polar opposite in every way. She was girlie and gorgeous and way too into shopping and color coordination. Whereas my wardrobe was monochromatic in color and style. I didn't do skirts, I sure as hell kept all flesh from the ankle upwards perfectly covered.

Not that I was a prude. Screw that. I just hated dressing like I was headed for a nightclub at ten in the morning.

But Maysie, she treated fashion like a religion. If you need more convincing that our friendship was a result of something far more whacked than coincidence, take this on for size. She had rushed a sorority! The unholy pinnacle of the stereotypical bullshit college experience.

Though, to be fair, she had woken up and smelled the fake about the illustrious Greek system after the majority of her so called sisters had single handedly trashed her reputation last school year.

The girl had been put through the ringer. But I thought she had come out on the other side for the better. And seeing the concern and understanding on her face, I knew why we were friends and always would be. Because my girl was loyal to a fault.

"Yeah, yeah. Personal hygiene is overrated," I muttered, getting to my feet and going over to my dresser to pull together my outfit for work. Thank goodness it only consisted of a polo shirt and black pants. Given the level ten crappiness of my mood, I didn't think I'd be able to put together anything more complicated.

"Is he working tonight?" Maysie asked and I tried not to flinch. Christ, this was almost comical if it wasn't so damn depressing.

Damien was just a guy. Sure he was the guy I had dated for over an entire year. The guy who I had talked about marriage and a future with. A guy who I had been able to see in my life for the long haul. And now he was just a guy who had put me out like yesterday's trash for no real reason other than, "he needed something *more.*"

"Yeah, I think so," I answered her, feeling the heavy dread of my evening crash down on top of me like a three ton weight. Yep, a three ton weight of nasty, funky dread. Sounds like the makings of perfect night to me.

"Just try to ignore him, Riley. Jordan will be there. I know Jaz is working too. Try not to breathe the same gnarly air. He's not worth it," Maysie fumed and I appreciated her mama bear protectiveness.

I slammed my drawer shut and gathered my clothes. I didn't bother with responding and instead headed to the bathroom. I didn't want to talk about this. I didn't want to converse about what a dick Damien was. Stating facts didn't seem necessary. I sure as hell didn't need to remember how I had been completely blindsided by my former boyfriend's inner asshole. He sure as hell had kept *that* hidden.

I closed myself in the bathroom and wished I could fast forward time and be on the other side of graduation all ready.

The door pushed against my back and I stumbled forward as Maysie came inside. I arched an eyebrow at her as I reached behind the curtain to turn on the water.

"I knew you always wanted to see me naked," I smirked, dropping my clothes on the floor and grabbing a towel off the rack.

Maysie snorted and then gave me her serious look. "I'm just worried about you, Riley. This whole depressed girl act is freaking me out a bit. I don't know if I should be plying you with liquor or forcing you to go to church. Because I'm beginning to think you've been possessed."

I sighed and opened the bathroom door. I not so nicely shoved her out into the hallway. "I'll be fine. Aren't I always fine? I just need more than two days to reconcile myself to the fact that the boy I thought I loved was a complete and total assface. Now please, I have to shower and get ready to face said assface at work this evening. And I don't need to spend the next twenty minutes listing all the reasons he sucks and how I should react to seeing him. I just need to be alone, all right," I said a bit more harshly than I meant to.

I knew Maysie meant well, but right at that moment I had very little patience for well- meaning chitchat. Though perhaps I should be a bit more receptive to her advice. Because the girl did know how to do the tragic, broken hearted thing with the best of them. Lord knows I had to sit through a mountain of it last school year during the drama otherwise known as "Jordan-gate."

After getting out of the shower, I stood in front of the bathroom vanity and started to blow-dry my hair. I stared hard at the girl in the mirror and wondered how it all went so wrong.

Because, seriously, Damien and I had been solid. I'm not just saying that because I'm in some crazy state of denial. I know girls will whine "but things were *great!*" right after being dumped by their dick of a boyfriend while her friends laugh behind her back because the jerk had been boning half the campus and snorting coke off a hooker's boobs in his free time.

But seriously, we had been *solid!* Better than solid. We were the perfect package. He *got* me. Or at least I had thought so. We had been together for over a year. And even if it wasn't the crazy, passionate relationship Maysie had with Jordan, it was good. It was nice.

And my heart felt heavy without it.

My eyes narrowed as I took stock of my appearance. I was pretty. I could admit that. I didn't do self-deprecation very well, among other things. I had nice, shoulder length hair that was so dark it was almost black. My eyes were a pale blue. Everything was proportionate. My nose wasn't too big and my ears didn't stick out. I felt pretty confident that I could check off *raging case of the fuglies* on the why-I-had-been-dumped-on-my-ass list.

So why hadn't Damien been happy?

I snarled at my reflection. I was annoying the shit out of myself. Who was this girl and what happened to her self-esteem?

I was not one to question myself. I was very clear on my thoughts and opinions about things. I never deviated from course. And Damien had fit nicely into the picture I had created of my future.

So when he had come over three days ago and gave me the lame "it's not you, it's me" speech, I was left in recoil. I mean, who the fuck still gives that line of crap?

Yeah, I lost it. I'm ashamed to admit that when he had told me that he felt our relationship wasn't going anywhere and that he wanted something a bit more than what we had together, my vision went a little blurry and all I saw was red.

Some not very nice words were hurtled in his general direction. I kind of threw a lamp at his head, which he dodged, by the way.

And then I cried. Oh hell had I cried. We're talking snot all over yourself cried. And you know what my fuck nugget of an ex did? He patted my back and said, "There, there. It'll be fine."

I will repeat...WHAT. THE. FUCK?

I spent a good thirty minutes ugly crying all over his shirt and then he got up, said he had to go and left. I had been able to pull together what small semblance of pride I had left and didn't run after him and beg him to stay. So that was something.

So, yeah, I've been in mourning. Not just for a year of my life wasted. But also the death of my dignity. Because it was currently taking a long vacation with my self-respect. And I'm pretty sure my confidence and backbone had stashed away in their luggage.

I hadn't been back to work since the break-up. I had called in sick yesterday and I knew Moore, the general manager, would expect a doctor's note tattooed to my forehead if I tried to flake on my shift tonight. And of course, *he who shall not be named* would be working. Because we had purposefully coordinated our work schedules so that our shifts fell on the same night.

I really wish I could smash my former blissful ignorance in the face.

I was lacing up my black sneakers when Maysie came into my bedroom again. Girl really couldn't take a hint that I didn't feel like talking.

"You want me to do your hair or something? Nothing gets back an ex like looking fabulous," she suggested, holding up her hairbrush. I rubbed my temples, feeling the throb of a headache coming on.

"I'll pass, thanks. I could walk into Barton's with my tits hanging out and I don't think it would make much of a difference," I said blandly. Maysie tugged on my ponytail affectionately.

"His loss, Riley. Seriously. Am I gonna have to go tough love on your ass and smack the shit out of you like you so lovingly did for me?" she threatened, holding her hand up. I grabbed her by the wrist and tugged it down.

"You don't have the balls, my friend," I said, my lips quirking into the shadow of a smile.

Maysie laughed. "You're right, you scare me. I wouldn't even try it," she said shuddering and then looped her arm through mine and tugged me to the door.

I grabbed my bag and car keys and Maysie followed me out to the car. Our neighbors Raymond and his girlfriend, Cicely, were hanging out on their stoop, smoking something that looked nothing like a cigarette. Raymond was half passed out and Cicely was winding beads into her hair.

I couldn't even summon up the energy to mock them. What had my life come to when I didn't have it in me to make fun of the losers next door? I was seriously losing my touch.

Damn Damien! Damn him to hell!

Maysie waved at them and looked at me expectantly. "Nothing? No witty barb? I'm disappointed," she teased, though I could see the worry pinching her face.

I shrugged. "Maybe I shouldn't be making fun of anyone right now. It's not like I have a whole lot going for me apparently," I said dramatically with a sigh. Maysie cocked her eyebrow and I knew I was taking the depressed dumpee a step too far. And when Maysie started to laugh I had to as well. I was being ridiculous. My maudlin act was bordering on ludicrous.

"Okay, enough with the sob fest. I've got to get to work," I opened the car door and threw Maysie her school bag that she had left on the passenger seat.

"I'll be in later. Generation Rejects are playing tonight at nine. So at least you'll make good tips. And seriously, don't even talk to the douche. Jordan'll look out for you." Maysie kissed my cheek before I could stop her and hurried back into our apartment.

I got in my car and headed to work, not looking forward to my evening.

Mega tips or not.

Chapter 2

ONCE I arrived at Barton's I was happy to see that I had gotten there before Damien so I was able to clock in, deliver my mandatory hello to Moore, give my customary middle finger greeting to the smarmy dishwashers Paco and Fed before heading into the dining room. It was dead, which wasn't surprising. It was only three-thirty on a Saturday. Most of the people who would frequent Barton's were most likely still hung over from the night before. The place wasn't what you would call a "family joint."

"Hey, Jordan," I called out as I grabbed a mint from the bowl at the end of the bar and popped it in my mouth.

Jordan looked up and gave me a toothy smile. Damn, the guy really did have a nice face. "Afternoon, Riley. How's it going?" he asked as he hefted a rack of glasses up onto the counter. It really should be illegal to have muscles like that. Yes, I was ogling my best friend's man. Come on, his arms were incredible! Even I wasn't immune to the charms of Jordan Levitt.

Jordan and the rest of his band had only just gotten back from eight weeks on the road. Generation Rejects had played up and down the east coast for most of the summer. They had slowly built a solid fan base and some great contacts in the industry. Once back in Virginia, they had booked time in a local studio to record their demo. Maysie had said they hoped to get it out to more promoters in the hopes of getting back out on tour. But until then, Jordan had decided to come back and work at

Barton's. And I know that decision had everything to do with the girlfriend he could never leave behind.

Despite my staunch belief in the fact that love blows, I knew that what Jordan had with Maysie was the real deal. So even if I grew old, adopt fifty cats and became the woman with blue hair that scares kids off her porch, at least my best friend had found something worth holding onto. And I could say that without an ounce of bitterness.

Well maybe only a small amount of bitterness.

Who the hell was I kidding? I was totally freaking bitter.

"I hear you're playing tonight. Should be a riot," I commented, making Jordan chuckle.

"We'll convert you yet, Riley. Just wait and see. One day soon, you'll be our biggest fan," Jordan said, throwing his dishrag in my face. I rolled my eyes and gave an inelegant snort.

I had gone with Mays a few times to see Jordan and his band play over the summer. We had spent a weekend in Atlantic City when the guys had performed at Croctail's Tavern. It wasn't much of a secret that I kind of hated their music. Generation Rejects were the hard rock, scream so you can't understand the lyrics stuff. I'm much more of an Indigo Girls, Tegan and Sarah chick. And while I wasn't going to rush out and tattoo their band logo on my butt cheek, I could still appreciate their talent.

Because individually the guys were good. Cole, the lead singer, when you could actually understand him, had a great set of pipes. Mitch, the bassist, was pretty killer. And Garrett, when he could stand upright and wasn't stumbling around on stage like a fool, could play a mean guitar.

And Jordan, well there was no denying he was damn good on the drums. The band had built a decent following. Maysie had started a fan website and was building their social media presence. She had become their defacto public relations guru. She loved helping out, even if it was starting to eat a lot of her time.

"Yeah, that'll be about the time you start doing Sarah McLachlan covers, right?" I joked, tossing the towel back at him. He caught it easily and threw it into the sink.

"You guys should totally do Possession! I would pay good money to hear that," Lyla, the other bartender on shift said, walking behind the bar to grab the liquor inventory.

Jordan choked. "Uh, yeah, I don't think so," he said shaking his head. Lyla and I glanced at each other and started laughing. And it felt good. See, I could laugh and be normal and forget that my heart had been put through a meat grinder.

"What are you guys laughing about?"

And just like that, my heart twisted into a bloody pile of pulp all over again.

I looked over at my shoulder to find douche bag extraordinaire, clipping his employee card onto his belt loop. I hated how cute he was, with his stupid dark hair that was just a tad too long and those annoyingly pretty green eyes behind heavy, black-framed glasses. I hated how smart and together he looked. I hated that he looked fine when I felt like a barely held together wreck. I clenched my hands into fists. I was totally going to punch him.

Jordan immediately picked up on my mood and intervened. "Nothing at all," he said coolly and I gave him a small smile, letting him know I appreciated his loyalty. Nice to know Jordan Levitt had my back.

Damien smiled entirely too casually for someone who had so recently dumped his girlfriend. His eyes flickered to me and then away again as though he couldn't even look at me. "Hey Riley," he said, sounding as though he had swallowed a mouthful of thumbtacks. And I really wish he had.

"Hey," I said back, proud of how unaffected and downright bored I sounded. No one could pull off emotionless bitch like Riley Fucking Walker!

"Later, guys!" I called out, waving at Jordan and Lyla who were both watching me closely. It was obvious by the way Lyla was staring at both Damien and me that she knew we had broken up. I'm sure we would be the source of endless gossiping and speculation tonight. Maybe it wasn't too late to pretend I was still sick.

"Riley, hang on a sec." I tensed up instantly. Damien's hand curled around my wrist and I looked down at the offending appendage in shock.

Was he for real? How dare he touch me? I almost hissed at him like an alley cat getting ready to claw someone's eyes out.

I wrenched my arm away and shot him a look of pure death. I wanted him to get sucked ten feet under by the strength of my anger alone. Too bad he continued to stand there, looking obnoxiously concerned.

"How are you?" he asked in a tone that was completely patronizing. He was looking at me as though he expected me to fall apart at any second. Though to be fair, I had done just that three days ago when he evilly broke my heart.

I gave him the fakest, brightest smile I could muster. "Oh, I'm fine. Don't you worry your pretty little head about me." I patted his back condescendingly, my lip curling in disgust. "It's amazing what losing a year's worth of shit can do for your outlook on life," I said nastily, turning my back on him. I didn't wait for him to say another word. Instead I walked straight to my section and started my shift checklist.

That should have felt good. I wish I could tap dance on the eviscerated remains of our relationship but instead I just felt like icky. Because I didn't *enjoy* being nasty to Damien. But at this point it felt like an imperative necessity. I just couldn't let him know how utterly destroyed I have been. That would be like conceding defeat in some way.

And Riley Walker didn't do defeat.

"Hey Riley," a perky voice piped up behind me. I felt my shoulders tense and my teeth clench. I continued to wipe down my tables, even though they were so clean you could lick your food off them.

"Hey," I responded less than enthusiastically. Jaz Digby was not my favorite person on the planet. She was entirely too enthusiastic about the monotonous routine that defined our roles as wait staff at Barton's Bar and Grill. I don't think the girl ever got pissed off and people like that bothered me on a molecular level. There was something wrong about someone that continued to smile while being chewed out by a disgruntled customer. People like that weren't to be trusted.

The only reason I tolerated her on any level was that Maysie liked her, in that sweet, deluded way of hers.

Jaz sat down at the table I was meticulously scrubbing. She started to rearrange the salt and pepper shakers and given my current state of mind, she might as well be clubbing baby seals. It pissed me off that much. I reached over and quickly put them back the way I had them originally.

Jaz pursed her lips but wisely didn't say anything. She leaned forward and put her elbows on her knees and cupped her chin. "So I hear you and Damien are kaput," she said, dropping all pretense of friendliness. She sounded entirely too happy about it actually.

"And that's your business because?" I asked shortly, turning my back on her and started to sweep up the carpet underneath the tables.

"Because he asked me out and I wanted to make sure that was cool with you," she said, her lips twisted into a fake smile, her eyes sparkling.

I would have laughed if her words hadn't just drilled a hole straight into my gut. Was she for real? Or had she burned away the last of her brain cells with her curling iron?

Though I guess it was nice to know we were past pretending to like each other. Acting like she didn't drive me nuts was more effort than it was worth most days. Plus, I always knew Jaz was a fake ass harpy. Happy to see that my instincts were spot on.

I tried to focus on the blinding rage instead of the knot in my gut that made me want to vomit at the news that not only was Damien all ready asking other girls out, but he had in fact, asked out one of our co-workers. And one that I would have traded easily for a shirt I didn't like.

Did his asshattery know no bounds?

I held my feelings mercifully in check. I continued to sweep as though my heart hadn't been shredded to pieces at my feet. I blanked my face and turned to look at Jaz, who seemed both pleased and genuinely perplexed as to whether she had broken a sacred rule of girldome. *Thou shalt not date other girl's jerkwad of an ex within seventy-two hours of break up.*

Wasn't that standard knowledge? Did Jaz not read the handbook on how *not* to get yourself bitch slapped?

"Do what you want," I said, trying not to strangle on the words. Jaz raised her eyebrows.

13

"Really? Because I'd be devastated if the guy I had dated for over a year asked another girl out less than a week after he dumped me," Jaz stood up and flipped her hair over her shoulder. "And if it bothers you, I swear I won't do it," she lied through her teeth.

I squared my shoulders and laughed humorlessly. "It will take more than Damien Green to devastate me," I leaned in and whispered in Jaz's ear. "Maybe you're better equipped than I was to deal with his weird blow up doll fetish and the fact he needs to wear a dress while he has sex." I shrugged.

Jaz's face went a little pale. "That's not true, is it? I mean, I get that you're upset that he asked me out but making stuff up is wrong, Riley," she choked out, looking across the restaurant to where Damien was talking to a few of the other servers.

"I understand you'd think that, but here, I've got pictures…" I stated, pulling out my phone and making a show of scrolling through, looking for the non-existent photographs. Jaz shook her head.

"No!" she said sharply and I looked up.

"Are you sure? I don't want you thinking I'm *making stuff up*. That I'm just being a bitter ex." I held my phone up, waving it in front of her.

"I'll pass," Jaz muttered and left my section. I watched as she stormed into the back of the restaurant. I couldn't help but snicker. Okay, that felt good. I glanced over toward Damien again and relished in the anger and borderline hatred I felt when I looked at him.

Damien looked up just then, our eyes catching and he lifted his hand in a wave.

So I waved back…with my middle finger.

"**H**E didn't!" Maysie breathed out, taking a long drink of her Long Island Iced Tea while looking completely appalled after I had filled her in on the Damien and Jaz situation. I was perched up on a barstool beside her, waiting for Generation Rejects to begin their set. I had been cut twenty minutes ago and decided to stay and hang out with Maysie.

My shift had been mostly uneventful. After my confrontation with Jaz, she had wisely kept a healthy distance. Damien wasn't operating on the same level of mental functioning apparently, as he made a good half a dozen attempts to talk to me throughout the evening. Ignoring someone who was clearly trying to assuage themselves of some hefty feelings of guilt was pretty freaking difficult.

So by the time Maysie had arrived, I was exhausted and ready to inflict considerable bodily harm on the next person who asked for a drink refill. Patience and I were not BFFs right now.

"I can't believe Jaz would be such a butt," Maysie commented, shooting a murderous look in the direction of our co-worker. I rolled my eyes as I hopped up on the barstool.

"Really, you can't? This is the same girl who refuses to wear a bra most days because she likes guys to see her nipples. I don't think scruples, or something simple like common decency, are in her repertoire," I remarked, giving Jordan a wane smile as he passed me a soda.

"I know it's easy to be pissed at Jaz but don't forget it's Damien who's being the jack ass in this equation," Jordan said reasonably as he wiped down the bar.

"Are you seriously defending her?" Maysie asked incredulously and with more than a little venom. Uh oh. Jordan had better tread very, very carefully.

Jordan cleared his throat and rubbed the back of his neck, picking up on his snafu. "Of course not, baby. Just trying to focus your rage where it really belongs is all," he said and started backing away. "This is me leaving the conversation. I'd like to keep my appendages." I couldn't help but snicker at his hasty retreat.

Maysie patted my back. "You focus your rage wherever you want. Don't listen to Jordan. He's entirely too diplomatic. It's obnoxious," she said, though her words weren't said hatefully. And the severity of her criticism was negated by the warm and gooey look she threw her boyfriend's way. If I was up to full snark levels, I would cut through that warm fuzzy with a very sharp knife. But as it were, I didn't have it in me.

Paging Riley Walker's sarcasm…you are needed stat!

I was distracted by a loud commotion toward the front of the restaurant. Looking over my shoulder, I saw a rag tag group of disheveled guys lumbering into the bar. Each one looked as though he had just rolled out of bed, and given who was gracing Barton's with their illustrious presence, I'm sure that's exactly what they had done.

The noise level dramatically increased from bearable to pierce my eardrums with an icepick.

Because it seemed wherever Generation Rejects went, rowdiness and an inability to talk at reasonable volumes followed.

Groaning, I pulled a small bottle of ibuprophen out of my apron and shook three capsules into my palm. I swallowed them down without water, grimacing as they stuck in my throat. Maysie cocked her eyebrow at me, her lips twitching in an amused smile. My dislike for Jordan's music wasn't a secret, though I tried to curb my vocalizations.

Jordan was very protective of his band and I learned early on that it was one of the few things he would cut you off at the knees for. That and hurting Maysie in any way.

So if you wanted to be friends with Jordan Levitt, be nice to Maysie and don't diss Generation Rejects.

"Piper! My man, three pints of your finest ale," Cole, the lead singer shouted, affecting one of the worst British accents I had ever heard. His use of the misogynistic nickname for Maysie's boyfriend set my teeth on edge. Being called the Pied Piper of Pussy was not a compliment in my book. It was just sad.

Jordan immediately uncapped three beers and placed them on the bar.

"Guess I should go clock out," I said hurriedly, trying to make an escape before the horde descended. It's not that I disliked the guys from Generation Rejects. Well, not completely. I know I probably sound totally stuck up, but the truth was they annoyed the hell out of me.

And it wasn't just them, or their screamy music; it was the atmosphere that surrounded them. It so wasn't my scene. Yeah, yeah, I know, I should just take the stick out of my butt, right?

Well let's just say that my history with Generation Rejects shows or parties involved being vomited on, catching an elbow to the nose in a mosh pit, having my hair lit on fire by a crazy jealous ex of one of the band members because she knew I was "flirting with her man" (Uh, yeah, I wasn't). And who could forget about the time some scary dude that looked as though he'd wandered off the mountaintop followed me around a party because I "looked purty."

So pardon me if I tended to get full on hives when I knew my evening would involve Cole, Mitch or Garrett in any way.

"Rushing off?" a slow drawl asked just as I was about to make my escape. I glanced over my shoulder to see a decent looking guy with chin length blond hair and heavy lidded blue eyes gazing at me blankly. Meet Garrett Bellows, lead guitarist and total pothead. I can't remember a time I had seen him that he wasn't half lit and barely standing. The guy liked to party and sorry to say, had "loser" written all over him.

Yes, I was making a judgment. Perhaps an unfair one, but I had never shared more than a half a dozen words with this guy that wasn't tinged with deteriorating sobriety. He seemed like a happy guy. He was always in a good mood, except when he spoke to me.

I wasn't sure when we had become contentious adversaries. Maybe it was the night I had accompanied Maysie to one of the Reject's infamous after parties and accidentally sent the keg rolling down the hill into the creek behind Garrett's house.

I know, party foul, but I wasn't the asshole that had propped the stupid thing up on cinderblocks at the top of a steep incline. And it was totally Maysie's fault for making me wear those stupid heels that should carry warnings about broken necks and public mortification caused from falling on your ass.

So Garrett had been pissed and maybe I had called him an "unwashed waste of space." Sue me; I don't like being yelled at.

Then there was the time I had gotten drunk at one of their shows and I walked into the girls' bathroom, only to find Garrett screwing some girl in a stall, with the door open. I mean, who does that? It's completely gross!

Drunken Riley has zero filter (well less than zero because sober Riley's filter was deficient enough) and I had kind of made a nasty comment about herpes. Well, I alluded to Garrett having herpes and maybe the girl should think before letting him stick his diseased penis in any of her orifices.

I don't know why I had said that. I was ignorant of any venereal diseases where Garrett was concerned and that was a really shitty thing to say about someone I didn't even know. All I can say in my defense is I was rendered blind by the sight and spewed out the first thing that came to mind to make it stop.

Come on! They were having sex. On top of a toilet. That is beyond nasty.

So you can see why I was not Garrett Bellows' favorite person. And my thoughts about him were anything but pleasant. I don't think I was unjustified in my feelings of overall disgust.

Looking at him standing in front of me, I couldn't see past the blood shot eyes, messy shirt, and torn jeans. And I didn't want to either. Garrett was who he was and I knew without a doubt that we were never destined to mix. Not that he would give a crap what I thought about him anyway.

So I cocked my head to the side and regarded him coldly before replying.

"Not fast enough, apparently," I quipped, turning my back on him as I headed back to my section to clock myself out.

"You really should give the poor guy a break. I think he'll need stitches from your particular brand of razor sharp bitchiness," Maysie said. She had followed me to my section and was now lounging with her feet propped up on one of the chairs.

I glanced over to the bar to where Garrett was now schmoozing it up with a couple of girls I recognized from their honorary barfly status at Barton's. "I think he's over it," I smirked, nodding his direction.

As if he could feel the weight of my stare, Garrett's eyes met mine over the shoulder of the girl straddling his lap. I should have looked away. The whole thing was horribly embarrassing. But I voyeuristically watched as Garrett gripped her hips and ground the girl onto his groin.

My cheeks felt hot and I forced myself to look away. I swallowed thickly and turned back to Maysie who was watching me with a puzzled look on her face. I smiled thinly and wiped down the last table.

"I think you should come with me to the after party. It would do you good," Maysie commented. I fell down into a chair beside my roommate. A refusal was on the tip of my tongue. I had a million and one instant excuses ready. *I'm tired. I've got a killer headache. I have an early shift tomorrow.*

But then I noticed Jaz and Damien talking in a corner. I knew body language and there was an uncomfortable amount of sexual awareness between the two. My heart hurt in my chest and I felt dangerously close to crying again.

Then I looked back at the bar and was startled to find Garrett still watching me. The girl who had been dry humping his crotch was gone and he was slowly nursing a beer. He lifted the bottle to his lips and took a drink, his eyebrow cocking as he looked at me. He lowered the drink and an annoying smirk lifted his mouth.

Damn, I wanted to punch that smirk off his obnoxious mouth.

I straightened my back and got to my feet, picking up the rag from the table and bunching it in my clenched hand. "You know what, I think I *will* come," I said firmly. Maysie blinked a few times in surprise.

"Wow, I was expecting to have to argue with you a bit more than that. What's gotten into you?" she teased. I noticed Garrett, Jordan, and the other guys were starting to get ready for their set. This would have normally been my cue to run for the hills.

But not tonight.

Tonight I felt like being unpredictable.

I turned and grinned at Maysie. "I feel like being a bit of a bad girl," I said and Maysie laughed.

"Riley Walker a bad girl? Now that I got to see."

Well, just maybe she would.

Chapter 3

An hour later I had changed into my favorite jeans and shirt that I had hand stitched myself. Yes, I, on occasion, liked to make my own clothes. And I didn't care what anyone thought about it. I was proud of my pretty, patchwork shirt, and it made me feel good to wear it. It really was all about the small stuff at this point.

So here I was once again sat beside Maysie at the bar, trying not to stare at Damien and Jaz as they laughed in a booth five feet away. Generation Rejects were three songs in and the place was packed.

I wasn't in the right frame of mind to grin and bear it. I wanted to go home but Mays insisted that I needed to make a point. Show the world that Riley Walker wasn't down for the count.

"Total assholes. She's off my Christmas card list," Maysie yelled in my ear while I purposefully looked anywhere but in the direction of my ex-boyfriend. I grit my teeth, trying really hard not to give into the almost overwhelming urge to channel my inner Incredible Hulk and start flipping tables.

"Do you even have a Christmas card list?" I asked her. Maysie snorted.

"Well, no, but bitch wouldn't be on it," she muttered, finishing off her third Long Island Iced Tea. I saw the telltale signs of inebriation overtake her. Maysie was a drinker. A partier by nature. Miss Social Butterfly. Which was perfect for the lifestyle she now found herself in, being the card carrying girlfriend of one hot-astic drummer of the crazily popular Generation Rejects. But the truth was I just couldn't keep up. When it came to boozing and doing it up crazy style, I was still on the first lap.

"I appreciate you going all vengeful she-beast, but it's unnecessary. This girl can fight her own battles," I assured her chugging my soda before slamming the glass down on the bar top. I grabbed my apron and order pad. "I think I'm going to head home. I'm exhausted," I said, wanting nothing more than a hot bath and the huge bag of Reese's Peanut Butter Cups sitting in the pantry.

Maysie grabbed my upper arm and gave me a yank. For such a scrawny girl, she had some serious upper body strength. "Excuse me? Is there a reason you're digging your nails into my flesh?" I pinched my lips together, trying not to get annoyed.

"You're not going anywhere. You promised you'd come to Garrett's with me. Don't you dare puss out on me! What happened to unleashing your inner bad girl?" she asked, though she wisely loosened her grip.

"My inner bad girl is being punched in the throat by my inner sensible girl who has had about all she can stomach of this scene for one night," I told her, handing my empty glass to Lyla.

"Heading home all ready, Riley? You are looking pretty washed out." My shoulders stiffened and I saw Maysie's lips purse together.

"And you've never been able to stop the stupid shit that comes out of your mouth, so I say we're both having a crappy evening," I snarled, giving Jaz my best *say one more word and you die* look. Jaz's answering laugh was fake and slightly nervous and was akin to nails on a chalkboard. I was really tempted to tear her hair out. But flicking my eyes over to my traitorous ex who was watching our exchange somewhat anxiously, I knew without a doubt that the douch bag wasn't worth a chick fight.

"Fuck off, Jaz," Maysie piped in. Jaz's eyes widened and I could see she was hurt by the curt tone in Maysie's voice. Jaz and Maysie had always been friends. But what Miss Sloppy Seconds didn't understand was my roommate's loyalties ran deep where I was concerned. You mess with me, you mess with Maysie Ardin. We were a rag tag duo.

"I'm only worried about her, Mays. I didn't mean anything by it," Jaz backpedaled. I snorted and shook my head, letting Maysie know she didn't need to jump into this particular fight. Because I was hanging up the gloves. Some things weren't worth the hassle.

I turned in my stool, purposefully giving Jaz and Dumbass Damien my back. "I think I will come after all. Even if I'm looking a little *washed out*," I said with a grin. Maysie smiled back.

"I guess I'll see you guys later," Jaz said but Maysie and I ignored her. She finally got the point and slinked back to the booth where Damien was watching. I didn't even bother to look in his direction.

"Can I get another soda, Lyla?" I called out to the bartender over the deafening roar of Generation Rejects' music. I sat through the remainder of the set and even made myself engage in some seat dancing. Woohoo! Riley Walker was cutting loose! Look out world!

I waited with Maysie while the guys broke down their equipment and basked in the fawning adulation of their fans. "I need to send Vivian and Gracie a text letting them know we're heading over to the party," Maysie said pulling out her phone.

"I thought Cole and Vivian broke up," I commented, nodding my head in the lead singer's direction as he squeezed a random girl's ass. Vivian Bailey was Maysie's former sorority sister. She had graduated in May and was taking a year off to "find herself," whatever the hell that meant. In my opinion if you need to look, then perhaps you shouldn't be found.

Vivian and Cole had some sort of friends with benefits situation. Except they weren't ever friends and I was pretty sure Cole shared those "benefits" with most of the girls who came out to see their shows.

Whatever they had ended a couple of weeks ago in pure Vivian Bailey fashion. Meaning there was lots of screaming. Lots of drama. Lots of piss and vinegar spewed in the most public way possible. Unfortunately (or fortunately, depending on how much of a voyeur into people's lives you are), it happened to be right after the Rejects' show downtown. Vivian had been drunk and Cole's attention was a little too focused on a girl who *wasn't* Vivien.

Apparently there had been high volume yelling, some glasses were smashed. Vivian pulled out a clump of hair from the poor girl who had the unfortunate luck of catching Cole's eye that evening. All in all, it had been a melee of epic proportions. And I had missed it. It was the one time I wished I had let Maysie talk me into joining her. Because watching Vivian lose her shit was better than any reality television show.

Maysie shook her head as she wound up a guitar cable and handed it to Mitch. "Yeah, well Gracie said Cole spent the night last weekend. So who the hell knows....ahh!" Maysie screamed as Jordan grabbed her and bent her low over his arm, kissing her soundly in front of everyone.

His bandmates whistled, Barton's staff catcalled, and there were a lot of pissed off groupies. I distinctly heard "whore" and "slut" muttered not so quietly. I glared at the group of girls behind me.

"You got a problem?" I asked them pointedly. I eyeballed each of them, giving them the ubiquitous girl once over, taking in their too tight clothes and cheap efforts to look sexy. I curled my lip in disgust and gave them my best sneer.

The girls, three of them, sneered back weakly. "No," a red head said petulantly, sounding like a child who didn't get the toy she wanted.

I flicked my fingers in their direction. "Well I think it's time you leave. Barton's is closing and this," I motioned to the group of people who had gathered around the guys as they had their after show beers. "Is a private party." I leaned in closer. "Meaning you aren't invited," I said slowly and purposefully.

The one with the overly styled blonde hair tossed her locks over her shoulder. "Bitch," she bit out.

I smiled. "You know it," I said to them as they turned and left.

Maysie had seen the whole exchange and shook her head at me. "Retract the claws she-lion. If I got upset every time one of these girls said something nasty about me, I'd never leave my room. And I've been there done that, girlfriend," she teased.

I shrugged. "What can I say, you bring out my maternal instincts." Maysie hugged me around the shoulders and I decided to let her. Like I said, she was the touchy-feely kind.

"You ready to head out, baby?" Jordan wrapped his arm around Maysie's waist and kissed the back of her neck. Her eyes drooped in that way that meant she was melting into a puddle at his feet. I had to look away.

Excessive PDA made me mildly nauseous.

"Maysie says you're coming this time, Riley. You wanna catch a ride with us?" Jordan asked, tucking his hand into Maysie's jean pocket, making her giggle.

"I'm cool. I'll follow you there. You know I like to have my own wheels. Plus, I've seen the trailer for the Jordan/Maysie porn show. I could do without the full feature," I joked. Jordan laughed and Maysie flushed in embarrassment.

I walked out of the bar, trying not to care that Damien and Jaz were noticeably missing. I hated that it hurt. That I had been brought so low by the one person I had trusted with my heart. Damien Green was a big pile of suck.

"Time to let your hair down, Riley. Fun is definitely on the agenda," Jordan said as I unlocked my car. I pumped my fist in the air and let out a whoop.

"Hell to the yeah!" I hollered. Jordan didn't miss the heavily laced sarcasm, thus warranting an affectionate smack on the back of the head for yours truly.

"Do you need me to kick his ass, Ri? I will you know. Just say the word and Damien's face will get up close and personal with Mr. I-Will-Break-Your-Nose." Jordan held up his fist and smacked it into his palm in a feigned threatening gesture.

Maysie and I laughed. Jordan was a good guy. And I was lucky to have such great friends willing to commit assault and battery on my behalf. It really did give a girl the case of the tingles.

I held up my own fist and shook it. "I think Miss I-Will-Mess-You-Up has first dibs." Jordan grinned and bumped my knuckles with his.

"Well if she needs backup, let this guy know," he told me as he pulled Maysie towards his monstrosity of a truck. Getting into my car and turning on my music, I felt just a tiny bit better.

Chapter 4

DEAR god on everything that is holy, please don't let me strangle this guy! I gnashed my teeth together, feeling the overwhelming urge to smack the crap out of Maysie for dragging me to the seventh level of hell with her.

Sure, this may be her thing. She played the part of rock star girlfriend really well. And more power to her. But she had gotten a wild hair up her ass thinking I needed to party, enjoy my youth, blah blah blah. And I had, in a moment of institutional crazies, agreed.

So here I was, surrounding myself with drunken jackasses as they tried to rub against each other (or me if I wasn't paying attention) in some sort of scary mating ritual. Sorry, I missed that episode of Wild Planet. I know I had intended to let my dormant bad girl out to play but instead this whole scene had her in permanent hiding.

"Don't you think?"

Huh?

I blinked in exaggerated slowness, making it clear that I hadn't heard a damn thing he had said. He being none other than Garrett Bellows.

Garrett wasn't put off by my blatant disinterest. I think the dude could talk to a brick wall. I was just surprised he had chosen to share his sparkling wit with me. Though it could be the fact that I was the one person in the room who couldn't give a shit about anything he had to say. It was sort of like how cats always gravitated toward the one person who hated them the most. It was some sort of passive aggressive mind fuck. *Oh you don't like me? Well now I'm going to be all up in your face.*

And like flies to garbage, Garrett had circled around me all evening until he had finally cornered me. It was as though he had been lying in wait for his chance to bore me to death. We had been engaged in a one-sided conversation for the past fifteen minutes. One-sided meaning that he was talking and I couldn't care less. I had tuned out around the time he started waxing poetic about surfing at night during some trip to Hawaii last year.

I really hated these pseudo-philosophical types. You know the ones that smoked a bowl or two and suddenly they were Plato reincarnate, talking about the meaning of life and how it had to be a government conspiracy that McDonald's only rolled out the McRib a few times a year.

"I'm sorry. You'll have to run that by me again. I was too busy trying to remember why the hell I let Maysie talk me into coming here in the first place," I said, infusing more than a little bit of jerk into my tone. Okay, so maybe the guy didn't deserve to have a firsthand encounter with Riley Walker, mega witch, but I was in a bad mood and feeling a little heartbroken; which made me rude and more than a little punchy. Plus, Mr. Lead Guitar Player was the last person I wanted to be sharing air space with.

I fully expected Garrett to call me a bitch and leave me alone to stew in my bitter juices. I was really hoping he would anyway. It would give me an excuse to be justified in my feelings of annoyance and outrage where he was concerned. But the idiot did no such thing.

Instead he laughed. He freaking laughed! Was he missing a few of those brain cells that were required to recognize when someone was being a complete and total fuck face to you? Oh god, maybe he thought my attitude was endearing! Great, I hadn't thought that maybe he was one of those crazies who got off on bitchy girls.

Retreat Riley! Retreat!

"You have one huge ass chip on your shoulder. Does it work

for you?" Garrett asked lazily and my eyes snapped up to his. He spoke in that slow drawl of his that was either meant to be dead sexy or a perfect cure for insomnia.

"Does what work for me?" I asked him warily, not sure where he was going with this. He pushed a hand through his hair and narrowed a pair of thoughtful blue eyes in my direction. I couldn't really make up my mind if I thought Garrett was good looking or not. His dirty blond hair was on the longish side, hanging down to his shoulders. I wasn't typically into guys with long hair, but for this dude, it sort of worked it. He wasn't overly tall, probably coming in around five foot eleven with a wiry frame that he seemed to like to show off by the amount of time he spent without a shirt on. Though if I had abs that defined, I'd probably be topless all the time, tits and all.

His cornflower blue eyes could have been appealing if they weren't blood shot and glazed over. He exuded that laid back couldn't give a toss demeanor that only came after inhaling a copious amount of THC into your system. And given the number of chicks who had attempted to get his attention since he had plopped down beside me to begin the most asinine conversation in history; he must have some sort of magnetism. Too bad I was wearing my armor of snark and not remotely susceptible to any of his possible charms.

I could admit that I had already dismissed him as a small-brained stoner who was smoking away the last of his brain cells. We had never carried on a meaningful conversation and I had never expected him to bother having one with me. But then his question and following statement caught me off guard.

Garrett leaned forward and rested his elbows on his knees. He waved a hand in my direction. "This. The whole 'I'm a bitch so stay away' act. I get that this probably isn't your scene. I bet you'd rather be at some eco-warrior recycling meeting or something. You seem like the idealistic save the world type." I bristled at his annoyingly astute observation.

"Wow, so you picked that all up from the complete lack of conversation we were having? Can I add deluded quasi-psychic to your resume. Right under wannabe rock star?" I said rather nastily, not wanting to give anybody the upper hand. Particularly this grunged out dope head whose eyes seemed to have cleared a bit. And I couldn't help but notice that yeah, they were pretty appealing.

How obnoxious.

"Well, you're wearing Reco jeans, which points to the fact that you think you're environmentally conscious but in reality it smacks of pretention, if you ask me." I opened my mouth to tell him he could take his bullshit preconceptions and shove them straight where the sun don't shine. But I didn't get a chance because he just kept going.

"And then there's that shirt. I'm sure you spent a long time stitching all those patches together. Does that make you feel better than everyone else? The fact that you sew your own clothes and wear pants made from plant shit? Because I bet you just feel really lonely. And sad. So you throw out this attitude and judgmental BS hoping no one calls you on it. And if they do, that only proves they aren't worth your notice or your time." Garrett delivered his stinging critique with an annoyingly blasé smile. Like he was commenting on the damn weather. When in truth, he was flaying me alive. I wanted to punch him in his stupidly attractive face. Because yes damn it, I suddenly realized he was pretty damn cute. And I hated him.

"Whatever," I hissed getting to my feet. Garrett laughed and I realized I had reacted just as he expected me to. Well, who cares, I didn't need this crap.

"Have fun dulling your senses and killing your brain cells," I bit out as he pulled a joint from his pocket and lit up.

He pulled in a lung full of smoke and slowly exhaled. "And you enjoy standing up on your soap box while you dole out your all-important criticisms. I'm sure it'll make for a fun evening," he said drolly as he turned to a pretty girl who sat down beside him, taking the seat I had just vacated. She giggled and leaned into him as he slung an arm around her shoulders. He literally turned his back to me as though I had been dismissed.

What a dick!

I stood there fuming. No one out bantered Riley Walker. Especially not a guitar playing, pot smoking, needs a haircut in the worst way, jackass.

So I stormed off. It was only much later that I realized Garrett Bellows had done something more than piss me off and incited my urge to maim and kill. He had made me forget about Damien. And for the first time in a week I hadn't been depressed and miserable.

Huh. Interesting.

I WAS on beer number four and I was teetering on the edge of full-blown drunkenness. I will admit to being a lightweight and embrace it, damn it! My liver was still intact and I didn't binge on the weekends. Drinking wasn't a recreational hobby that I indulged in often. So when I chose to imbibe, it never took me long to feel like a raging lush.

Though the alcohol did nothing to minimize my feelings of total and complete social awkwardness. When I say that the Generation Rejects after parties weren't my scene, I wasn't being hateful. Or just making excuses because I thought I was too good to hang out.

I sat on the couch in the worn and shabby living room, watching as people I either didn't know, or only recognized in passing, engage in a variety of drunken shenanigans. These were people who lived to party. Who lived and breathed for this sort of debauched free for all.

Yeah, ladies and gents, that just ain't me. And I knew I stuck out like a sore thumb. A great big, stick-in-the-mud thumb.

I could see Vivian sitting on the pool table with Cole stood between her legs. She made a show of pretending not to notice the way he continued to check out every other girl in the room while simultaneously stroking her leg. But even from my vantage point, I could see the tightening around her mouth and the cold steel in her eyes. This had the makings of an explosion of epic proportions. And while I felt bad for Vivian, my sympathy only extended so far. After all, she was the one her put herself in the same crappy situation over and over again with a guy who never intended to change his man whore ways.

Gracie was dancing in a circle across the room. I had spent all of ten minutes hanging out with her earlier before she ditched me for a guy with a buzzed head and gauges in his ears. I never took

Gracie to dig the skinhead type but seeing the way she had been pawing the dude all evening, I deduced her tastes were varied in the penis department.

I downed the rest of my beer and prayed it would be enough to enjoy myself. Maysie plopped down beside me, and nudged me with her shoulder. "Your face is gonna freeze like that, just sayin'," she warned, taking the empty bottle out of my hand and putting it on the coffee table. I plastered a smile on my face and widened my eyes dramatically.

"Better?" I asked through gritted teeth. Maysie grimaced.

"You look like an ax murderer, stop it!" My mouth relaxed and I sighed.

"Do you mind if I head out soon? I'm just not feeling this tonight," I asked as a girl with too much makeup and had somehow lost half of her clothing, stepped on my foot as she walked by.

"Oh sorry," she slurred, leaning down precariously to pat the top of my foot. I snatched it back and held up my hand.

"No big. It's fine," I said, not really meaning it. That had really hurt! The girl squinted at me as she swayed on her feet.

"Is your name Leah?" she asked suddenly. I glanced at Maysie who was looking amused.

"Can't say it is," I replied. The girl grinned and sat down beside me, leaning into my face.

"Good because if you were I'd have to kick your ass. That bitch slept with my boyfriend," she said unevenly. She stuck her face within an inch of mine forcing me to lean back.

"Have you seen her? Cause I'ma gonna kicksh her ash," the girl slurred. Jeesh, understanding her almost necessitated a translator.

I pointed over the girl's shoulder. "I saw her go in there," I said. Drunk girl fell forward, wrapping her arms around me in what I supposed was meant to be a hug.

"Thanksh so mush. I'ma gonna kicksh her ash," she mumbled, getting unsteadily to her feet and hobbling in the direction I had sent her.

"Did you know who she was talking about?" Maysie asked after the girl had left.

I shook me head. "Hell no. I just needed my personal space back," I retorted, digging my cell phone out of my pocket. "Mays, it's already one in the morning, I really think I'm gonna head out," I pleaded. Maysie patted my back.

"Okay, okay. I know when you've had your fill. Let me go find Jordan and he can give you a lift, you've had way too much to drink. He'll be ready to get out of here anyway." Maysie smiled at me and held up a finger. "Just give me one minute," she promised.

"What about my car?" I asked in a panic, not wanting to leave my baby here. Who knows what these people would do to her? Okay, I talked about my car like it was an actual person. What can I say, I was attached to it.

Maysie rolled her eyes. "It'll be fine. I'll bring you back in the morning to get it," she promised. "Now just hang tight, I'll be right back."

I narrowed my eyes. "Just make sure that one minute doesn't turn into twenty. Or I'm hunting you down," I warned. Maysie grinned and left me alone.

Well not for long.

"This seat taken?"

The cushion sagged under the weight of my new couch buddy. I looked over and had to suppress a groan. Garrett Bellows popped the top off a beer and handed it to me. Hadn't we already said enough to each other earlier this evening? What could top being labeled a pretentious stuck up? Not much I'm sure.

"You're lookin' a little thirsty, sweetheart," he said before opening his own drink and taking a swig. I held the frosty bottle in my hand, wondering what sort of horrible thing I had done in a past life to warrant these repeated forms of torture.

I wobbled a bit; feeling the full weight of alcohol hit my system. My tongue felt heavy and my lips sort of numb. I thought about saying something nasty right out of the gate, just to get the upper hand. But his following words caught my drunk girl brain off guard.

"It's all sort of ridiculous, right?" he asked, his voice soft and barely audible over the noise. I squinted at him, feeling my beer goggles slip firmly in place. Because right now, Garrett Bellows was perhaps the best looking guy I had ever seen. Even when I was a hundred percent sober, I could sort of appreciate his looks. There was nothing conventional about the guy who sat beside me.

He was the epitome of everything I chose to stay away from. But right now, with him leaning into me, my heart still feeling the after effects of a world class bludgeoning, I forgot about why he bugged the shit out of me.

"What's ridiculous?" I asked, clueless to his point, my nose filled with a scent that was at once unfamiliar but also absurdly tantalizing. Garrett smelled like musk and man and it was a total turn on.

In point two seconds the twisty thread of undeniable attraction took hold. I wasn't expecting the way my hormones took over all rational thought. This was new. And at the moment, I kind of liked it.

My eyes were drooping a bit and I was having a hard time focusing on what he was saying. Mostly because I was suddenly and inexplicably horny.

Garrett cocked his eyebrow at me; as though he were picking up on the crazy amount of pheromones I was suddenly slinging his way. He looked amused but there was a heat in his eyes that I knew was for me alone.

He leaned in further until his lips were next to my ear and the warmth of his breath teased the hair at my neck. "All of this." He gestured to the party around us. "I get tired of it all, you know? Sometimes I wish these people would just disappear."

His words surprised me. "Well, why do it then? Why continue to have these things if you don't want to?" I asked, genuinely curious.

Garrett pulled back and I was irrationally bereft at the sudden space between us.

He drank the rest of his beer and promptly opened another one. I recognized in him the same drunken looseness that I was currently feeling. The pair of us were a hot mess. Two sad drunks, feeling sorry for ourselves.

He sighed and looked at me again. His blue eyes were red

and unfocused but in my current state of inebriation, I swore that he saw me better than anyone else ever could. Yes, alcohol clearly unleashed my inner poet. The hyperbole going through my head was completely over the top.

"It's what everyone expects of me. And I guess I'd rather have people around than be by myself," Garrett replied finally. I found myself nodding, understanding all too well this need to live up to some sort of twisted expectation you had for yourself. He was making a scary sort of sense right now.

After that we sat together in silence, watching the partygoers and drinking more beer. Finally after what felt like an hour, but was most likely only a few minutes, Garrett got to his feet and held out his hand. I looked at it as though it were a snake about to bite me.

Garrett chuckled, obviously finding my response funny as hell. He inclined his head toward the staircase behind him. "Come on. Let's get away from all of this. So we can hear ourselves think." His suggestion seemed, in that moment, to be totally logical.

But I caught the underlying meaning behind his words. Garrett Bellows wanted to have sex.

With me.

Oh crap. Did I want to have sex with him?

I drank in the sight of his chest (he had lost his shirt totally by this point), which was ripped and toned. I wanted to wrap my hands around his biceps and squeeze with all my girlie might.

Oh yeah. I could imagine what the rest of him looked like. I could almost taste the anticipation of getting him naked on my tongue. The edges of a tattoo wrapped around his side, disappearing behind his back. It looked like words in a script that was impossible to read at this distance.

I wanted to read it. I wanted to lick it. I wanted to eat this man whole with a side of screw me senseless.

So yep, Riley Walker was having sex tonight.

Garrett's eyes were hot pools of lust as they regarded me steadily and I felt myself flush. My inhibitions were noticeably absent and I for one was glad to see them go. Because I wanted to get my freak on with this fine specimen of male standing in front of me.

Looking up into his pretty blue eyes I put my hand in his and got unsteadily to my feet. I almost fell as I stood and Garrett's arm was suddenly around my waist, holding me upright. I could feel his erection poking my thigh as he held me.

Time to take a ride on the Garrett Express all the way to Fuck Me town.

"Yeehaw!" I yelled a little louder than I intended to. People looked over at us and I should have been mortified by my scandalous lack of morality. But I was down with some One Night Stand action.

Garrett cocked his eyebrow and bit down on his lip as though he were trying not to laugh. He'd better not laugh at me, or I'd have to knee him in the balls. Which would be a pisser since I wanted to suck those sweet pieces of man meat into my mouth and make them my bitch.

"I think someone is ready to get ridden," I purred. At least it sounded seductive in my own ears. Most likely I sounded more like Betty White than Jenna Jamison, but who cared.

Right now, I was Riley Walker Sex Goddess! And I wanted to play a few rounds of Mr. Wobbly Hides the Helmet!

Garrett shook his head and I wondered if he'd tell me to get lost. Crap, if this guy, of all people, rejected me, I think I'd have to put myself out of commission forever. Being told no by the guy with zero standards would be the worst insult imaginable.

Maybe I could just yell "gotcha" and then run out the back door.

Yes, that was a good plan.

But instead of kicking my drunk ass to the curb, Garrett took my empty beer bottle from my hand and dropped it in the trashcan as he led me out of the room and up the stairs.

I was going to do this.

I was going to have sex.

With Garrett freaking Bellows.

And I was going to enjoy it. I was going to have orgasms and slap his tight little ass until he made walking the next morning impossible.

This all made one hundred percent perfect sense as I followed him away from the party. Away from Maysie, who would be wondering where the hell I had gone. Away from any semblance of rational decision-making.

Because I was getting laid.

Yee-Haw!

Chapter 5

I WAS being smothered! I literally could not get air in and out of my lungs. My brain was fuzzy. My head felt like it was being clenched in a vice and my eyes were having a hard time adjusting in the pitch-blackness.

Where the fuck was I?

I tried to sit up and realized that the reason I was having such a hard time drawing breath had to do with the heavy, sweaty male form lying prostrate over me.

And did I mention this male form was NAKED?

Oh God! I was NAKED!

I tried to roll from underneath the unidentified man but all I got for my efforts was to be squeezed even tighter against the hot, sweaty, NAKED guy.

I flopped back down on the bed, trying not to freak out at the feel of a very erect penis digging into my hip. Because it was quite obvious that I had engaged in drunken, monkey sex with my current bed partner.

And what was even more messed up was I had no idea who he was. My brain just couldn't compute who I would have found myself in bed with.

Sober Riley wanted to kick Drunk Riley's ass!

I couldn't make out anything about him in the darkness. But his hair was tickling the hell out of my nose and I was trying really hard not to sneeze and blow snot all over him and thus making this awkward and mortifying experience all that much better.

The guy mumbled something in his sleep and he nuzzled his face into my neck. I was a rigid block of stone. I needed an escape plan.

Like two minutes ago.

But one thing was for sure. Whoever ambiguous sex dude was, he smelled good. We're talking really, really good. Like musk and man and sort of outdoorsy. The smell twinged my memory. As though I should remember who smelled like a hot lumberjack.

But I couldn't give a shit if he smelled like chocolate and vomited up hundred dollar bills, I had made a decision last night based on too much alcohol and a bad case of rebounditis. And that made my feelings about the current situation bordering on hysteria.

I glanced over at the alarm clock on the small bedside table. It claimed to be five-thirty in the morning. Entirely too early to be up under normal circumstances. But this was anything but *normal*. Because I was living in morning after hell. And that was about as far from my *normal* as one could get.

Mr. Stiffy rolled his hips, grinding his ever-present erection into my side again. And Riley Walker Junior, who had been happily slumbering between my legs, began to stir.

Go back to sleep, you wanton slut! I screamed silently at my insolent vagina. She and I were *not* in agreement as to the best way to handle this.

Because even though my brain couldn't remember my night of lust, other parts of my body obviously had crystal clear memories of it.

Once mystery guy settled back into sleep, I started the futile process of trying to wiggle out from underneath him. My hands pressed into surprisingly smooth and hard skin and I flattened my palms against a seemingly muscular chest in an effort to budge the massive amounts of man pinning me to the bed.

Even in my moment of self-mortifying disgust, I was pleased that my bed partner appeared to have a nice body. Glad to know that even in my drunken psychosis I could still be called on to pick a guy with a nice set of abs.

Get a grip, Riley! As if his body matters when you're trying to walk of shame out of here! I scolded myself harshly.

After a few minutes, I grudgingly realized I was stuck. My ass wasn't going anywhere. And now I had to pee. My bladder was being pressed painfully by the guy's weight.

Ah, fuck it!

"Hey!" I yelled, shoving the dude's shoulder. He grunted and tightened his ironclad grip around my waist. If he didn't get off me in about ten seconds, he was going to wake up in a very wet bed.

I leaned in close and moved some hair away from his ear, making a concerted effort to *not* notice how soft and silky it felt between my fingers.

"Wake up!" I yelled and then smacked the back of his head for good measure.

Yep, that did the trick.

The guy bolted straight up in bed. "What the fuck?" he growled and leaned over to flip on the lamp. And it was then that I got my first glimpse of my one-night stand.

"You have GOT to be freaking kidding me!" I screeched, hurriedly pulling up the sheet to cover my entirely too naked breasts.

Garrett Bellows ran a hand through his shoulder length blond hair and blinked at me in confusion. "What the hell is your problem?" he asked, scrubbing his face with his hands before dropping back onto the bed. My eyes drifted down the length of his very toned and obnoxiously nice body until they stopped and honed in on a very prominent part of his anatomy that I only too recently felt pressed intimately against me. And Mr. Veined and Throbbing was at attention and on very prominent display. I swallowed thickly as images came swimming back through my hazy memory.

Garrett kissing me as though I had been the air he breathed. Garrett softly touching me an then laying me out on the bed I now found myself in. I closed my eyes and could see him over me as his weight pressed me into the mattress.

I shivered uncontrollably. Shit, shit, shit!

I opened my eyes and sneered at him, throwing a sheet over his lower half. "Cover yourself up, will you?" I snarled, leaning over the side of the bed and finding my shirt from the night before. I quickly pulled it over my head and felt better at having a barrier between Garrett and my skin.

Garrett had lowered his arm and was watching me. He didn't look angry by my attitude. He didn't appear to be hurt in any way by my obvious dismissal of him. This was both a relief and strangely disappointing.

He seemed only thoughtful. Curious even.

What the hell?

"Where are my pants?" I muttered under my breath. I got out of bed, trying not to die of total embarrassment as I flashed Garrett a pretty picture of my ass while I bent over to retrieve the rest of my discarded clothing. As I finished getting dressed, I grumbled, I cursed, and I otherwise fumed at my total idiocy.

And Garrett freaking Bellows didn't say a damned thing. He just lay there, watching me, as though he found me supremely entertaining.

"Do you know where my keys are?" I asked him, hating that I had to talk to him at all. I would rather have left with my head hung in shame, never to reveal my night as Miss Skankalicious to anyone ever.

Garrett pointed across the room. "You dropped your bag when we came in here last night. I'm guessing you'll find them in there," he remarked dryly. He stood up and I was treated to another view of his body. And my body tingled in response.

My eyes fell onto the tattoo on his side and words floated through my brain.

Blessed are the hearts that can bend; they shall never be broken.

Where the heck did that come from? My chest pitter-pattered painfully for some unknown reason.

Time to shut this crap down here and now.

"I just need to get out of here," I said more to myself than to him but he heard me loud and clear.

"Why the rush?" Garrett asked, cocking his eyebrow. His blasé nonchalance prickled my already testy nerves and reminded me of why he annoyed the shit out of me. People that laid back drove me crazy.

"No sense in wasting anymore of your time. I think we're done here," I spat out, glaring at him. I knew I was being horrible but I was mortified by my behavior.

Riley Walker does *not* get so drunk she blacks out.

Riley Walker does *not* have sex with a guy she barely knows; particularly when said guy was one she could barely stand.

And apparently Riley Walker was *now* talking about herself in the third person. Hello insanity!

Garrett pulled on a pair of sweat pants and lifted my purse. I grit my teeth as he crooked his finger in my direction. "You want it, come over here and get it." He was messing with me. Trying to make me more uncomfortable than I already was.

Well screw him!

Wait… I had already done that…Ugh!

I snatched it from him, making sure not to touch him as I did so. More flashes flooded my brain.

His lips. His hands. The way he said my name right before he kissed me.

What I wouldn't give for another bought of alcohol-induced amnesia right about now.

Garrett's eyes heated for a moment, as though he could read my mind. His gaze slid down the length of me and then came back up to meet my eyes where they cooled slowly. His mouth, entirely too pretty to be a guy's, set into a firm line and for a second, I felt a flash of regret.

Not for our night together. But for the way I was treating him. He didn't deserve to be shitted on because I was feeling like a fuck up. I opened my mouth to apologize, a Riley Walker first, when he beat me to the punch.

He walked passed me to the bedroom door and opened it wide. He gave me a cold smile. "Oh, we're done here all right." Garrett ran his fingers down the side of my neck and I couldn't help but notice the way his face softened a bit before he went in for the kill.

"It was fun, but I won't be signing up for round two. You can leave now." His grin was as brittle as broken glass and I felt my face flush red in a mixture of humiliation and gnaw-through-his-jugular rage.

To hell with the apology!

I leaned up on my tiptoes, my hands gripping his shoulders. My lips hovered near his and I smirked inwardly at the hitch in his breathing. "Well it's a good thing you were entirely forgettable then," I whispered, licking my lips slowly and chuckling as Garrett's eyes dropped to my mouth.

"Now get the fuck out of my way," I bit out, moving away from him. Garrett blinked, his eyes becoming once again glacial cool and he gestured me out into the hallway and then proceeded to slam the door behind me.

Well that went well, I thought as I made my way as stealthily as possible out of the house. There were a few people passed out on the couch in the living room, a guy snoring on top of the pool table. I could hear voices in the kitchen, recognizing Cole and Mitch. I scurried out of the house as fast as my little legs could carry me.

I remembered that Maysie had most likely came and looked for me last night. Crap! She must think I was dead in a ditch somewhere. Or worse. She could know that I spent the night at Garrett's house! How was I going to explain that one?

I was abducted by aliens and just now escaped. No. How about *I was playing a riveting game of Scrabble and lost all track of the time?*

I was done for.

Bad mistakes were Maysie Ardin's MO, not mine. I felt like a miserable failure on all fronts. I was hung-over and ashamed. Not a good combination when you felt like throwing up all over your shoes.

I practically ran to my car and got inside. I started it up and was then compelled by some masochistic urge to look one last time toward the house. Curtains moved in a second story window and I knew that I saw the unmistakable outline of Garrett against the glass.

Crap, there it was again.

Regret.

And as I drove away from Garrett's house, I wanted desperately to leave that unfortunate feeling behind but it took up quiet residence in my heart. And I feared it wouldn't let go anytime soon.

My mind was a mess of hazy recollections from the night before and the memory of Garrett's face when I essentially told him to fuck off. Man, I had been such a shrew.

I could remember talking to him on the couch last night. Being with him must have made some crazy sort of sense at some point.

I shook my head and turned on my radio, hoping the sound of angsty chick rock could drown out the remnants of my guilt.

My phone chirped from inside my purse. Digging it out, I glanced at the screen, feeling an encroaching sense of dread as I saw the number of missed calls and texts from Maysie.

Was it too late to make a run for it? Maybe I could head to Mexico and assume a secret identity. That way I could avoid the morning after explanations my roommate would be expecting.

So I took my time heading home. I stopped at McDonald's and got myself a coffee. Then I decided I needed a few magazines. And while I was at it, I needed to fill my car up with gas.

And you know what, a lovely scenic drive on the back roads of Bakersville was just what the doctor ordered.

I had successfully prolonged the inevitable for a whole hour and a half. It was almost eight when I finally pulled into the apartment complex parking lot. I cut off the engine and sat there for a while.

Why was I so scared to go in and face Maysie? It could be because I felt like such a hypocritical loser. I was notorious for dishing out advice, telling my best friend how she should be living her life. Laying into her when she makes choices I deemed irresponsible. And yes, I had judged her for it. I hated that I had, but it didn't change the fact that Judgmental was my middle name.

And here I was coming home, wearing the same gross clothes I had worn last night, still smelling like Eau de Garrett.

I finally headed toward the apartment. Just as I put my key into the lock, the door flung open and a very angry Maysie stood before me with her hands on her hips.

She grabbed me by the arm and yanked me inside, slamming the door behind me. She took in the sight of me, noticing my current state of disarray. Her eyes narrowed as she processed what my arrival this morning meant.

Then her furious expression changed and her lips split into a devious grin that was ten times more frightening.

"Oh my god! I want details!" Maysie pulled me into the kitchen where she already had the coffee maker going and cups set out on the counter as though she were waiting for me to show up.

"What the heck are you doing up at this hour?" I asked, hoping to delay the inevitable interrogation.

Maysie poured us both a cup of coffee and got out the creamer, handing to me. "I've been waiting for you, jerk face! You had me worried to death!" I took a sip and cringed. It was the worst coffee I had ever had. Maybe that was my roommate's sadistic plan of revenge for worrying her; kill me with bad coffee and endless hounding for information. It was definitely the most horrendous death *I* could think of.

"Uh, yeah, sorry about that," I said, hopping up on one of the stools by the island.

Maysie sat beside me and stirred her drink, watching me closely. "Yeah, well Jordan said he saw you go off with Garrett who told us he'd give you a ride home later. I argued that the last person in the world you'd want to drive you home was Garrett Bellows. But when I tried to find you…well let's just say I got an eye full," she said, poking my arm.

My neck and face flushed red and I felt as though I were on fire. Oh Jesus Christ. What the hell had been my problem last night? I wish I could recall exactly why sleeping with Garrett had seemed like a *good* idea.

"I'm a bit shocked, I must say. He was the last guy I would have ever guessed to hit the Riley Walker crazy sex radar. But I've heard he's a tiger in the sack. Plus, he's totally hot in that 'I couldn't give a crap about anything but making you come' sort of way. Don't you dare tell Jordan that I said that," Maysie rambled. I was having difficulty keeping up with her at this point in my morning. And honestly, the whole thing was making my already pounding head, crack open so my brains could spill out on the floor.

I was in overload. I couldn't wrap my head around the way my life had detoured in the last twelve hours. It was too much for my poor morning after brain to compute.

I hung my head, not meeting her eyes. "Can we not do this, Mays? I'm exhausted and I have to work tonight," I pleaded, hoping if I sounded pitiful enough she'd stop.

Maysie was quiet and I looked up to find her staring at me strangely. "What?" I asked her.

She shook her head and gave me a smile. "Nothing. I just don't understand you," she stated, putting her mug in the sink.

"What do you mean? Just spit it out. My head hurts, I've already dry heaved a few times on the drive home. I'm not in the mood to play who's smarter than Maysie," I said shortly.

Maysie opened her mouth but then promptly shut it again. "Mays, baby? What are you doing? I don't like waking up without you." Jordan came into the kitchen and pulled his girlfriend into his arms, holding her tightly. She leaned into him and I gave an exaggerated cough. The Maysie and Jordan version of a donkey show would need to wait until I was safely out of the room. Unless they like wearing projectile vomit as a legit style.

Jordan looked over at me and smiled. "Hey girl. You just getting home?" he asked me incredulously. Okay, now I was getting annoyed. I could barely deal with the shocked questioning from my roommate. But I didn't need a round of "I can't believe Riley made a bunch of shitty decisions" from Jordan freaking Levitt.

I could barely stomach hypocrisy on a good day. So being force-fed a hefty dose of my own was beyond what I wanted to deal with right then. I threw my hands into the air in exasperation.

"Yes, I decided to play the slut kitten last night and engaged in a round of barely conscious sex. I don't remember much about it. I don't think I *want* to remember *anything* about it. So let's just put this all in the *I will never drink that much again* category and move on," I said loudly. I blew out a breath and walked passed the pair, heading to my room.

Maysie followed me and stood in the doorway. "It's okay, you know," she said as I pulled back the blankets on my bed so I could crawl in and forget last night ever happened.

"What?" I asked with more than a little annoyance.

"That you slept with Garrett. It doesn't make you a slut. I'm just a little surprised is all. But we can talk about it later. Get some sleep before you grow your talons and claw everyone's eyes out," she said good-naturedly and with entirely too much supportive understanding for this time in the morning.

"We will not be talking about this later, Mays. There's nothing to talk about. So put that thought right out of that head of yours," I said stubbornly. I kicked off my shoes and got into bed. "Now I'm gonna try to sleep this hangover away before I have to work this evening," I said pointedly.

And thankfully Maysie left it at that. After she closed the door, I found that no matter how much I tried, I couldn't get to sleep. I tossed and turned but every time I closed my eyes all I could see was Garrett's face as I left this morning.

I had the feeling I had made a bigger mess than I realized.

Chapter 6

I'M so excited that we got chosen for this internship! Can you believe it, Riley? Out of all the seniors in the English department, we are the ones that get to work at the Bakersville Times for an entire semester! It's gonna be epic!" Gracie Cook was practically bouncing in the passenger seat as I drove toward the local newspaper's downtown office.

Even though I wasn't as effusive as Gracie when it came to showing my enthusiasm, I could admit I was pretty damn excited. Gracie and I were both English majors with concentrations in journalism. We had been in the same classes for most of our college career.

At one time that had bugged the crap out of me. Gracie and I had only ever pretended to get along. We put on the happy smiles for Maysie's sake since we were both friends of hers. However, last school year we had formed an uneasy alliance during the Maysie and Jordan Crazypalooza and had inexplicably become friends.

And once again the gods snickered in delight at throwing together the train wreck of all friendships. I seemed to have a lot of those. Gracie was the opposite of me in every way possible. She was perky and full of energy. I was…well…less perky.

But somehow, someway, over the last year, I found that I was less and less irritated by her chipmunk squealing and even found her…gasp…endearing. Sure, she looked like she stepped straight out of some deep south molly sue magazine. The girl spent way too much time on her makeup and lately was becoming entirely too acquainted with the drunk end of a bottle of vodka, but I dug her. She had a sharp edge to her that I could identify with. Even if she did hide it under layers of pastels and lip gloss.

The thing about Gracie is she played the part of the ditzy blonde but in reality she was one of the smartest people I knew. She had an almost photographic memory and I knew for a fact her GPA was almost as impressive as my own. Why she continued to act like the proverbial Scarecrow without a brain was beyond me.

We had found out a few weeks back that we had both been awarded the highly coveted Bakersville Times internship. To say it was a big deal was an understatement. Every senior in the English department vied for the chance to gain hands-on experience at the award winning newspaper. It opened doors that we all desperately wanted kicked open for us.

Sure, Bakersville was a small town, but its newspaper was one of the most respected on the east coast. It had a lot to do with Gary Findle, the editor in chief who had been a reporter for the Washington Post for almost twenty years. When he moved to Bakersville with his wife fifteen years ago, he took on the failing newspaper and turned it into what it is today.

So Rinard students wanting to break into journalism would sell their kidneys for the chance to learn from him. Three students were chosen out of hundreds and somehow, Gracie and I had earned the spots.

"Yeah, it should be pretty sweet," I said, trying to affect a nonchalance I didn't feel. Because inside I was bouncing as much as Gracie. But it would blow my too cool for school cover to scream like a banshee at the top of my lungs.

Gracie playfully punched me in the arm. "Pretty sweet? Admit it, you're ready to piss yourself," she teased. I snorted and let out a small whoop, making Gracie laugh.

"You're a lost cause, Ri," Gracie complained good-naturedly.

"Well, it's a good thing you've cornered the market on excitable energy. I'll just syphon off yours," I told her, turning left at the red light and cutting off a bright blue BMW that honked loudly at me. I waved my middle finger out the window, earning me a look from my friend.

"What? They were totally in my way," I stated innocently. Gracie only shook her head and then moved the topic into less comfortable territory.

"So where did you disappear to on Saturday?" she asked me and I had to cough around the squeak that escaped my mouth. The question was asked in obvious ignorance so I hoped like hell that Maysie hadn't opened her big mouth. And if she had, there was a lake and a pair of cement shoes with her name on it.

"Huh? What are you talking about?" I asked indifferently. I was one cool ass bitch! That's right, Samuel L. Jackson ain't got nothin' on me, mothafucker!

I had successfully dodged Maysie's not so subtle attempts at conversation around my night as a college slut bag. If I wasn't going to get into the dirty details with her, I wasn't about to spill the naughty to Gracie.

My plan was to pretend that the whole thing hadn't happened. My memories of the night in question were hazy at best. Though what I *could* remember left me feeling mortified.

I seemed to recall following Garrett into his bedroom and promptly removing my clothes. I don't think I gave the poor guy a chance to say anything before I was on him. It was then that my mind went mercifully blank. I had either experienced some sort of psychotic break or I had been possessed by the evil spirit of a dead porn star.

Because one thing was for certain, the girl who had jumped into Garrett Bellows' bed was not the Riley I worked hard to be. Knowing I had so willingly spread my legs for a guy I could barely stomach did a number on my sense of self-respect.

I wasn't a prude. I wasn't a goody goody. I didn't subscribe to the antiquated notion that I needed to wait for marriage to have sex. I had chucked my v-card out the window a long time ago. But I always prided myself on sharing that intimate experience with someone that *mattered*. Someone that was invested in me as a person.

And it was obvious Garrett barely invested in himself, let

alone anyone else. The guy was a wreck in the worst possible way.

Gracie snapped her fingers in front of my face. "Earth to Riley. What the heck girl? I've been talking for like five minutes and you just totally spaced out," Gracie harrumphed. I gave her a weak smile.

"Sorry, G. Give me a recap," I said, turning into the parking lot of the Bakersville Times. I found a spot in the very back of the lot, meaning we'd have to hoof it to get to our internship on time. I grabbed my bag off the back seat and took off toward the building with Gracie scurrying behind me.

"Wait up, Ri! My short little legs can't keep up!" she yelled. I slowed down and let her catch up to me. She gave me an annoyed look. "I was saying before you decided to check out of the conversation, that I looked for you later at Garrett's. But you disappeared. Maysie had no idea where you went. We looked forever for you. Where'd you go?" Gracie asked, her words coming in short bursts as she struggled to keep up with my long legged gait.

She must not have looked too hard; otherwise I'm sure she would have known exactly where I ended up. I let out a relieved sigh that I hoped Gracie didn't notice.

"I was tired," was all I said, hoping she'd drop it. "Plus, I figured you were busy with Mr. Shaved and Tattooed." I expertly maneuvered the conversation into more palatable terrain. Gracie giggled on cue.

"His name was Dave. And he's in the Army. And he was so freaking hot," Gracie began an overly detailed rundown of her weekend bed buddy's amazing characteristics. I nodded and made suitable comments when necessary. Thanks god for Gracie's one-track mind.

As we approached the office, any semblance of conversation was halted over the sound of drills and hammers. The front of the Times building was a veritable construction zone. We headed toward the side of the office to use another door, trying to stay out of the way of the construction workers.

Of course the whistles and catcalls ensued as soon as the

sweaty, mucky men caught sight of us. I couldn't help but notice the way Gracie put a bit more sway to her hips as we walked, throwing flirty grins at some of the guys as we passed. I rolled my eyes and grabbed her arm.

"We don't have time for you to play Bachelorette with the construction crew. We're going to be late." I gave Gracie a tug and pulled her into the building behind me, cutting off the sound of the sexually laced comments that followed us. I didn't have time to hear about how much they wanted to grab my ass.

We walked up to the receptionist and explained we were the new interns. The rather harried looking woman with a head full of frizzy grey hair and glasses entirely too big for her hawkish face pointed to the row of chairs behind us. We made ourselves comfortable as we waited until someone noticed we were there. I sat picking at my nails while Gracie scrolled through her texts. And then my day sank firmly into a big pile of suck.

"Riley," a voice I recognized all too well said from behind me. Gracie's head shot up and her eyes widened. My mouth thinned and I clenched my jaw so tightly I was worried I'd break a tooth.

Deep breaths. Deep, cleansing breaths.

I slowly turned around and stared into the green eyes that up until a month ago were my entire world. Another pair of eyes flashed through my mind. A pretty blue darkening with desire as they looked at me.

Not now, Riley! You are such a ho!

"Damien," I said in a tone reserved for sales calls and door-to-door missionaries. Of course Damien had gotten the other internship spot. Because my life needed some added crap thrown at it.

Gracie's eyes were practically bugging out of her head. She watched me as though waiting for me to go berzerker on his ass. Which wasn't a half bad idea...

Damien smiled nervously. He looked good in his perfectly pressed khakis and green polo shirt. His wavy hair was tamed into a messy style around his forehead. His signature dark framed glasses slid down his nose and he pushed them back up with his forefinger in a gesture that was at once familiar and surprisingly annoying.

"I heard you got one of the spots. Congrats. I know how much you wanted it," Damien said and then cleared his throat. He looked at Gracie as though she would save him from the dense sea of awkwardness we were drowning in. She looked back at him blankly.

"Yep," I let my lips pop around the word. He stood there, his hands shoved into his pockets, his teeth gnawing at his bottom lip anxiously. I should have been pleased that he was uncomfortable. Reveling in how off balanced I made him but all I felt was sad that two people who used to love each other were now barely speaking.

A woman who was all business saved us. She barely looked at us as she introduced herself as Diane Carleton. She was the assistant editor and would be showing us around. This was all told in the briefest way possible, with minimal interaction. She seemed irritated that she was the one tasked with intern duty. I got it. We were the peons at the bottom of the shit pile. And we were going to be treated accordingly.

That was fine. I appreciated knowing exactly where I stood in the grand scheme of things. No surprises. I could function in that sort of environment. It's what I was comfortable in.

Despite the frosty greeting, I couldn't help but get excited as we walked through the bustling newsroom full of chatter and ringing telephones. It was a hive of activity and I hummed with it. This was my scene. This is what I wanted to do with my life. This is where I belonged.

"And here are your desks. Sorry you've got such a crappy workspace but the building is undergoing major renovations. And since you're on the low rung of the ladder, you get this," Diane said, not sounding sorry at all as she indicated three desks shoved into a corner beside a large plastic sheet that separated the usable work space with a demolition zone.

It was loud. Sounds of construction and loud voices would make it virtually impossible to concentrate. But I didn't care. I would go home covered in plaster dust every day but I was here, and that's what mattered.

I dropped my purse on one of the desks. "How long are the

renovations going to last?" I asked, wincing over the ear splitting sounds of drills and nail guns.

"Longer than you three will be here," she replied with a patronizing smile. "I've put folders on your desk detailing the history of the newspaper as well as your duties and responsibilities. There is a code of ethics as well as our work policies that you will need to read and sign off on. When you're finished bring the paperwork to me. You'll be assigned your jobs for the week after you bring me everything." Diane had already started walking away, leaving us.

"Well this is a lot less glamorous than I thought it would be," Gracie pouted, sitting down in one of the office chairs with a sigh. I rubbed at my temples, feeling the beginning twinges of a headache. The noise level was painful

"Yeah, well, we just need to suck it up and remember this is the best internship at Rinard," I reminded her. Damien had already sat down and was reading the information in his folder. Following suit, I started to thumb through the material we were expected to go over. I tried not to feel deflated, particularly as I read that most of our "duties" would involve glorified gopher tasks.

The commotion behind the plastic sheet behind us was extremely distracting. I read the same sentence at least a dozen times before I closed the notebook with a decisive bang. Coffee. I needed coffee.

Gracie wasn't even reading. She was staring at the construction workers walking back and forth beyond her desk. She had that dreamy look on her face as she ogled the guys hefting their sledgehammers as they took down one of the partition walls. They weren't even that cute, but it didn't take much to get Gracie's attention.

Then her expression changed and she lit up like a Christmas tree. Her lips spread in a smile I recognized as her signature man-eater grin. She fluffed her hair and wiggled her shoulders, causing her shirt to droop suggestively low exposing an inappropriate amount of cleavage.

"Garrett!" she squealed in delight. I turned around to find

my disastrous one night stand standing behind me with some sort of power tool in his hands. He looked dirty and sweaty and obnoxiously attractive.

Well damn it all to hell.

Garrett gave Gracie a lazy smile. "Hey," he said, the low timber of his voice doing strange things to my insides. I purposefully turned back around, hoping that he hadn't noticed me.

"Hey, Riley," he said in a tone that dared me to ignore him. I lifted my hand in a wave without facing him. I resolutely opened my folder and tried to focus on the words blurring on the page in front of me. I felt the back of my neck flush and my ears burned hot.

"Do you work here?" Gracie asked in a high-pitched voice that could cut glass. Clearly Garrett's seductive charms were working on my friend.

Garrett walked around until he was stood directly in front of my desk, making ignoring him impossible. He was doing this on purpose. He looked down at me, with an amused smirk on his face. He was enjoying my discomfort. In fact, he seemed to be loving it.

"I sure do. I'm part of the crew working on the renovations," he said, still looking at me, even though he was talking to Gracie. I met his eyes directly and even though my face was most likely bright red I met his bold gaze head on. I would not let him see me sweat.

"Oh, that's great. We'll get to see you all the time then," Gracie said, trying to get his attention. Unfortunately for her, we were too busy playing *the first one who looks away is a pussy*.

"Super," Garrett responded dryly, looking as though he wanted to laugh. Oh fuck this. I got to my feet.

"Gracie, Damien, you want a coffee?" I asked. Sure I was giving him the satisfaction of seeing me run but at that moment I didn't care. I just needed some breathing space. Because seeing him again, so soon after our night together, was like dunking me in a molten fire pit. I tingled from my scalp to my toes with an awareness of the way this man had touched and kissed me, even though my mind was still hazy with the details. Clearly my body remembered all too well.

And I did *not* appreciate the reminders here of all places. This was *my* internship. *My* world. And Garrett did not belong inside my happy little bubble. Seeing him threw me in ways I couldn't explain.

"I'll come with you," Damien said quickly. I had to suppress my groan. Could this get any better? I looked at Garrett again, whose amusement had faded. Damien reached out to touch my arm but I moved away before his fingers could make contact. Something flashed in Garrett's eyes and his face darkened dangerously. He flicked his eyes from me back to Damien and he almost seemed to be working through something in that head of his. Seeing him focus on anything was more of a shock than finding him working here.

But one thing was for sure, his nonchalant demeanor was noticeably absent as he stared down my oblivious ex-boyfriend.

"Garrett, when is your next gig? I hate that I missed the last one," Gracie said excitedly and I used that as my cue to leave. With Damien on my heels, I hurried to the break room.

"Ri, wait up!" Damien called out and grudgingly waited for him to join me. "You okay?" he asked, peering at me closely. Despite how horrible our end was it didn't change the fact that Damien Green knew me better than most. He knew when I was rattled. And I was most definitely feeling rattled.

I gave him a thin smile. "Fine. Just need some coffee. You know I'm like Dawn of the Dead until I get my caffeine," I replied. Damien smiled back tentatively, looking a little antsy. His eyes darted around the room, maybe looking for any possible weapons. The boy already knew what I was capable of with a lamp at my disposal.

"I mean are you okay with us doing this together. I know it'll be.."

"Awkward? Weird? Annoying as hell?" I interjected before he could finish.

Damien lifted his shoulders in a shrug and his smile was strangely more relaxed. As though my snarkiness was something he could deal with. As opposed to the giant pile of sad I had been before.

"Exactly," he said softly, staring at me in that way of his that at one time made me weak in the knees. He stepped closer, his hand resting on my arm meaning to be comforting. Really it just made me feel icky. Like I wanted to scrub myself clean after he touched me. Who the hell did he think he was talking and touching me like this? I was torn between self-righteous anger and total dumbfoundeness.

"Ah, so this is where the coffee is," I jerked back as though doused in ice water. Garrett moved purposefully into the room. I blinked in surprise as he walked between Damien and me. Damien stumbled backwards. Did Garrett really just shoulder check Damien?

Damien frowned at Garrett and I knew he was irritated by the interruption. "Let's get back to our desks, Ri," Damien said trying to meet my eyes again.

Garrett poured his coffee into a thermos and screwed on the lid. "Actually, can I talk to you for a sec, *Ri*," Garrett sneered, turning around to look at me. His expression dared me to refuse. To ignore him and walk away.

"Yeah, sure," I said defiantly. Damien's frown deepened as he looked between Garrett and me as though trying to decipher the mysterious vibe that was most certainly humming between us.

Garrett glanced at Damien. "This isn't a group conversation." I had to cover my mouth so I wouldn't chuckle out loud. Damien's face flushed in indignation and I maliciously enjoyed my ex's discomfort. Without another word, Damien left, though he looked anything but happy about it.

"Rude much?" I asked testily, swallowing the enjoyment I felt at Garrett's posturing and intimidation of Damien. Crossing my arms over my chest, I leveled him with my best *you are wasting my time* look. Garrett took a drink of his coffee and shoved his other hand in his jean pocket. He had a smudge of dirt across his cheek and I had to stop myself from wiping it off. Not because I wanted to touch him or anything. It was just seriously messing with my OCD.

"If I thought you actually cared about me being rude to that douche bag, I might actually apologize," Garrett said, his mouth twitching in an effort not to smile. Well I'm glad I amused him so freaking much. That's me, Riley Walker, three ring circus.

I started to tap my foot to indicate my impatience. Garrett took another drink. "Now who's being rude," he commented lazily as though he had all the time in the world to taunt me.

"Don't you have a job to do? Because I sure as hell do," I bit out, feeling irrationally frustrated with the whole situation.

"You're such a prickly little pear, aren't you?" he mused, causing me to grit my teeth. I didn't respond, knowing that's exactly what he wanted. And I was feeling very oppositional. Garrett put his thermos down on the table, and mirrored my stance by folding his rather muscular arms (come on, they were practically on display in his too tight wife beater) over his chest.

"So we're playing like it didn't happen," he stated rather than asked. He looked at me with an unreadable expression. I couldn't tell whether this is how he wanted it to be or rather it bothered him. Garrett Bellows was apparently a guy with few emotions. His expression was bland and unconcerned as though we were talking about the latest football stats as opposed to our round of naked twister.

"Like what didn't happen?" I asked pointedly, narrowing my eyes, waiting for him to say something else to piss me off.

Garrett didn't say anything for a moment. He simply watched me as though trying to see something. What, I didn't know. And I refused to care either.

Finally he nodded. "Good," was all he said. He picked up his thermos and walked out of the break room without another look in my direction. I should have been relieved that our secret rendezvous would remain a secret. But relief wasn't exactly what I was feeling. And I refused to admit to myself that it was disappointment that fluttered in my stomach.

Chapter 7

"**I** CALL girls' night!" Maysie yelled coming in the front door and throwing her book bag on the couch. I sat with my feet propped up on the coffee table, dutifully highlighting and making notes while I forced myself to read through my grammatical structure textbook.

Maysie snatched my highlighter and capped it, shoving my legs as she pushed passed me. "Sorry if I'm in your way," I muttered, closing my book and deciding that giving my roommate the attention she desired was easier than ignoring her. Maysie was like a neglected cat when she was ignored. Rubbing up on you until you either smacked her away or gave up and began to rub her.

"So, girls' night. You, Gracie, Viv, and me. Bars, booze, boys. The three Bs necessary for a good time. You are not allowed to say no. You are not allowed to bitch about how you have homework. You *are* going to put a smile on that pretty face of yours and you are going to suffer through an evening of laughing and fun. Think you can handle that?" she asked, cocking an eyebrow, waiting for me to start complaining.

"Will there be drunken tattoos and really bad karaoke," I asked, sighing. Maysie grinned and it was a truly evil sight. The girl was ruthless when it came to piling on the peer pressure.

"There just might be, Ri," she laughed and rubbed her hands together like a cheesy Bond villain.

"Fine. But you are not permitted to pick out my clothes. If I choose to wear my combat boots, I will and you are not allowed to make one disparaging remark about them. In fact, since I'm being made to do something against my will, I insist on it," I warned, shaking my finger in her face.

Maysie rolled her eyes and snorted. "As if you'd let me get you within ten feet of a curling iron or a mini skirt. You are just no fun," she pouted and I let out a huff of indignation.

"I'm more fun than you can handle, girlfriend," I replied, snapping my fingers in her face and giving her my best sex face. Maysie dissolved into a fit of giggles before jumping to her feet to hurry into the kitchen.

"Vivian and Gracie are on their way over, we're cabbing it tonight, so let's pre-game!" Maysie said excitedly coming back into the living room with a bottle of Vodka and a jug of orange juice.

"Uh, sweetheart, I didn't check the *looking for liver failure* box on my college application. I'm quite happy to sail this boat sober. Someone's got to make sure we don't end up in Mexico with a guy named Bubba," I stated, pushing the make-me-puke cocktail out of my face.

I had done the drunk thing. I had played the part of Riley who makes bad decisions. I was thinking of getting the *I got drunk and sexed up a random* T-shirt just so I could advertise my shame. I had no plans of repeating that particular evening anytime soon. And when Maysie and the girls got their party on, mayhem was sure to follow.

"I'm not crying in my Wheaties anymore, Mays. There's no need to force me into a night of debauchery with the delusion of doing me a favor. I've donned my cape and am Super Riley once again," I proclaimed.

Maysie huffed. "I warned you that saying 'no' wasn't an option." She waggled her eyebrows and I threw up my hands in defeat.

At that moment, our door flew open and Vivian waltzed into the room, wearing her "ready to fuck" outfit consisting of red mini-dress and hooker heals. Her hair was over curled and over styled and her makeup would have to be scraped off in the morning but she owned it. I could admit I dug her self-confidence. There was something appealing about being that self-assured.

I had never suffered from poor self-esteem. I didn't spend endless hours wondering why people didn't like me or moaning about the way I looked. That had been Maysie's hang-up for years. I'll admit it used to drive me crazy. There was only so much backstroking a gal could stomach before you resorted to shaking the shit out of your friend and telling her to grow up.

I had performed varying degrees of tough love on my best friend in the past and wasn't shy in telling people what I thought. But even I would never feel comfortable enough to let my body hang all out like that. I wasn't sure if it was a niggling lack of confidence or a greater sense of pride. But whatever it was, Vivian didn't give a crap and for that I could appreciate her.

"What's up my bitches!" she yelled, dropping her coat on the floor and putting a grocery bag full of beer on the TV stand. Gracie came in behind her, looking much more subdued in a jean skirt and frilly top. But even she exuded a crazy energy. These girls were ready to get their party on whether I wanted to or not.

"Where are we going tonight? And please tell me you aren't wearing that, Riley," Vivian said, plopping down beside me on the couch. Her dress rode up and I could see way too much of her leopard print underwear.

"Well at least I'm not waving my vagina around like a flag," I said, giving her a pointed look.

Vivian let out a pleased cackle and did nothing to pull her skirt down. "Damn straight! This flag is saying single and ready to mingle!" she shouted. Clearly Vivian had already been at the happy sauce.

Gracie rolled her eyes. "She and Cole had a fight. They broke up *again*," Gracie explained, pulling a beer out of the bag and popping the top before sitting down on the loveseat.

"Don't you have to be doing something more than banging in order to break up?" I asked.

Vivian leaned over and grabbed the beer out of Gracie's hand. "I thought we had a meaningful relationship built on the appreciation of each other's bodies. But it came to my attention that mine is not the only body Cole has an appreciation for. So he can go to hell. These legs will never spread for him again!" Vivian declared, waving her beer in a wide circle before drinking half its contents.

I looked over at Maysie who was shaking her head. "Oh, so this is going to be a guy hating, holding Vivian's hair while she pukes kind of evening. Why didn't you say so?" I asked sarcastically.

"Shut up, Riley," Maysie volleyed back. "Vivian, Cole's an idiot. Just remember where his cock has been the next time he wants to get up your skirt," she advised, knowing as well as the rest of us that this was just the latest drama in the ongoing saga of Vivian and Cole.

"Damn straight! I need a guy who keeps his shit at home! Do you know who he's screwing?" Vivian asked, looking at us as though we knew aleady.

Each of us shrugged. "Cira, that bitch. I always knew she was a slut," Vivian muttered. Maysie and Gracie exchanged a look. Cira was their former sorority sister and anything Chi Delta related was a touchy subject where they were concerned.

I smacked my hands down on my knees and got to my feet. "Well as much as I'm enjoying this riveting discussion about the notches on Cole's bedpost, I'm going to go get changed. Gotta put my party face on, right?" I asked, smirking at Maysie who stuck her tongue out.

A half an hour later, the four of us were piled in the back of a cab and headed for downtown Bakersville. We were dropped off in front of The Boogie Lounge, the town's one and only dance club. It was a Tuesday night and the place was heaving.

I realized why when we didn't have to pay a cover and were informed by the guy at the door that it was Ladies' Night and all our drinks would be half price. "It's Ladies' Night!" Vivian yelled as we made our way to the bar. Gracie laughed and pulled me by the hand.

"Let's get you a drink so you'll do some dancing," she yelled over the bad techno music. I couldn't help but smile and let her lead me through the crowd. Maysie followed close behind. We ordered our drinks and were quickly ditched by Vivian who had instantly latched onto a Sophomore guy I knew from the English department.

"Girl's going cougar tonight, I see," I commented, watching Vivian press herself against the poor guy.

Gracie rolled her eyes. "She just needs to stop trying to make Cole her boyfriend, then she'll be a hell of a lot happier. That guy will never commit and she ends up upset and acting like a moron every time she's reminded of what a slut he is," she said, picking up her drink and turning toward the crowd.

"I don't know, they are kind of perfect when they actually have their shit together," Maysie reasoned as we made our way to the second floor so we could people watch.

"Perfect like a case of genital warts," I muttered and the girls laughed.

"Well, what about you, Ri? Have you sorted out your guy issues?" Gracie asked innocently and my stomach dropped. Crap, what did she know? I glanced at Maysie who stared back blandly. If she told anyone about Garrett, there was going to be a full on chick fight, friend or not.

"Uh, what do you mean?" I asked, sipping on my luke warm beer.

"I mean with you and Damien," she said, giving me a confused look. My chest loosened and I let out a little sigh of relief. I really had to stop freaking out every time I was asked a question about boys.

"Damien's a tool," I said shortly, not wanting my ex to soil the evening I was being forced to have.

"I've just never seen you like that, Riley. It was a little scary," Gracie stated and I grit my teeth. Gracie meant well, she was just a little oblivious at times, particularly when she was drinking. I could tell by the flush on her face and neck that she was well on her way to smashed, a state she seemed to be falling into a lot lately.

"Wow, thanks, G, I appreciate that," I remarked, leaning against the railing and watching the people on the dance floor beneath me.

"I just meant that douche isn't worth you being so upset over him. I really wish we didn't have to see him so much at the newspaper. And now that he's dating Jaz, that just sucks," Gracie rambled and I turned on her sharply.

"He's dating Jaz?" I asked, feeling my throat tighten. But what was strange was I couldn't decide if I was upset or not. My emotions were feeling oddly jumbled.

Maysie leaned across me to smack Gracie's arm. "Seriously, Gracie, enough," she said, her voice hard. Gracie grimaced.

"Oops, did you not know they went out last week? I thought you knew," she murmured and I shook my head.

"Must have missed the bulletin," I answered, turning back to stare out into the crowd. I was officially done talking about Damien Freaking Green.

"Shut up!" Maysie said less kindly.

"What? I thought she knew!" Gracie hissed to Maysie behind me. Then she squealed loudly and I looked over my shoulder.

And then promptly wished the floor would open up and swallow me whole.

"Garrett! Mitch! I didn't know you guys were coming tonight!" Gracie shrieked as Garrett, Jordan, Mitch, and Cole walked up to us, looking very much like a group of guys looking for trouble.

Jordan pulled Maysie up against his chest, kissing her soundly. "Sorry to interrupt your girls' night. We decided to come out for some drinks and I knew you were going to be here. I couldn't stay away," he said softly against her mouth and I had to look away. Their blatant affection making me feel uncomfortable.

I was normally able to stomach (with much queasiness of course) their PDA, but knowing Garrett was standing so close, I felt stiff and awkward. I'm sure it had absolutely nothing to do with the fact that he had seen me naked not so long ago. Or the fact that my friend was practically dry humping his leg as she clung to him.

"Please stay! It will be so much more fun with you here!" Gracie pleaded, hugging Garrett's arm. Garrett's face was impassive and even in the dim light, I could tell his eyes were bloodshot and puffy. His blatant drug use disgusted me. And I was even more disgusted with myself for sleeping with someone who had such a disregard for himself.

Garrett glanced at me and he smiled. It was a small grin but it magically transformed his face and made my heart pound just a little bit harder. And all thoughts of disgust and shame were drowned by a more concerning emotion known as lust.

"You girls seem like you're doing fine without us. Far be it from me to mess with your good time," Garrett stated, his eyes roaming over my body in an intimately familiar way that had me flushing in equal parts indignation and frustrating desire. Clearly my body was ready to have a repeat performance whether my head was on board or not.

"Come on, just for a little while," Gracie begged, turning to Mitch who lit up at her attention. Huh, how had I not seen that before? Mitch stepped toward Gracie but then his face fell when she turned back to Garrett, who had yet to look away from me.

I refused to acknowledge Garrett and instead noticed the way Mitch looked like a boy who had just heard that Christmas had been cancelled. He realized I was watching him and shrugged as if Gracie's rejection didn't matter.

"No, we've got to get Cole home. He's ready to pass out already," Jordan said, kissing Maysie again.

"I think Cole's found his second wind," I commented, pointing across the room to where Vivian and Cole were making out in the corner. Cole's hand was up her dress and she was pushing against him, leaving very little doubt as to what Cole was doing inside her panties.

"God, they're ridiculous," Maysie breathed out in annoyance and I nodded.

"I don't know, they look like they're having a good time," Garrett drawled, giving me a wicked grin that I resolutely, 100% ignored. Yeah, I caught the innuendo; I just refused to acknowledge it.

"I want to dance! Come on everyone!" Gracie squealed, grabbing Maysie's hand as she ran passed, heading toward the staircase. Jordan and Mitch followed them but I stayed behind. I leaned over the railing and smirked as I watched my friends bump and grind to the horrible music. Gracie draped her arms around some guy's neck while Mitch tried not to look bothered by it. Jordan and Maysie were practically screwing on the dance floor.

My eyes drifted over the dancers until they stopped on something I'd rather not see. Damien, in all of his preppy glory, standing against the wall. But he wasn't alone. Hell no. The jerk was with Jaz, who was pressed against him as if she could crawl up inside him like a gerbil.

From this distance I couldn't see his expression, but Jaz's writhing on his thigh left little to the imagination. I thought I'd feel devastated. Horrified. Wrecked.

But in truth I just felt angry. Humiliated and disappointed. And those feelings had more to do with my own pride than watching my ex clearly hooking up with a girl I couldn't stand.

"Is that your ex?"

I jumped, forgetting that Garrett still stood beside me.

I turned around and leaned against the metal railing, resting my elbows beside me. "That's him in the 'I'm a Jackass' outfit down there," I answered, sounding a little annoyed but nothing else.

Garrett leaned beside me, his shirt unbuttoned and billowed open to reveal his chest. Seriously had this guy never been taught how to wear his clothing properly?

"He's an idiot," he said shortly and with zero emotion.

I frowned at him, not understanding him at all. "Huh?" I asked, confused.

Garrett tilted his head toward me, dipping his lips toward my ear. "If he could let you go, he's a fucking moron. Not worth the mud on your shoes. You are so much more than *that*."

His words had me tingling inside, filling me with something indescribable. My mouth fell open but nothing came out. I was speechless. Garrett Bellows had rendered me completely mute.

Garrett pulled his keys out of his pocket and inclined his head towards the stairs. This guy could say more with his head movements than anyone I had ever seen. It was like a new form of stoner language; grunt and nod instead of talking.

"Are you asking me something?" I asked him snottily.

Garrett smiled at my attitude. He really did seem to get off on it. "You wanna get out of here? I get the feeling you're crawling out of your skin," he observed.

Did I want to leave with him? Would he expect me to have sex with him again? Because I was damn sure not going there. Been there, screwed that.

"We can just go and hang out. That's it," Garrett said, as though reading my mind.

Well...that *did* sound appealing. Because the last thing I wanted was to stand around and watch my friends get wasted and Damien mack on Jaz. I'd rather tear my fingernails off one at a time...slowly.

And being with Garrett right now seemed the lesser of two evils.

I looked back down at Maysie and the others. Gracie was now on top of a speaker, flashing the world her rainbow panties. I shook my head at her obliviousness.

"What about the others? Didn't you drive them here?" I asked, not wanting to leave everyone without a ride even if I wanted to take off so badly I was willing to sacrifice a night with Garrett to make it happen. This place seriously sucked balls.

"I already warned them they'd have to cab it back. This place pretty much sucks balls," Garrett stated and I let out a loud snort at his choice of words. Though it terrified me that our minds were operating on the same wavelength. That should have been a sign of the impending apocalypse.

"True that," I agreed, snickering.

Garrett gave me a lopsided grin and motioned for me to head down the stairs. "Then let's get the hell out of here," he said.

I sent a quick text to my friends letting them know I had found a ride and would be home later. Then I promptly turned off my phone, not wanting the barrage of calls that would most likely ensue once they realized I had left.

Garrett unlocked the passenger side door of his van and held it open for me. I refused to feel all girlie about him playing the part of the gentleman. No tingles in my nether regions as he closed the door behind me after I had gotten inside.

Nope, no girliness here.

"You mind coming over to my place for a while? I'd really like to chill out before the guys get back," Garrett said and I swallowed around the lump that formed in my throat at the suggestion.

He wanted to go to his house. Where we had sex. And we'd be alone. Uh...

"Sure," I found myself saying, surprising us both.

"Cool," Garrett said and turned on the radio. There was no further conversation and I found that the silence wasn't uncomfortable like I thought it would be.

Fifteen minutes later, Garrett was pulling off the main road and driving down the narrow, graveled path that led to his house. Parking in his driveway, he cut off the van. His house was set in the middle of the woods and the only light came from the moon overhead.

I looked around at the over grown trees and realized they'd be a great spot to bury my disemboweled body if Garrett turned out to be a serial killer.

"You coming?" Garrett asked from the front porch. A tree branch snapped off to my left, making me jump and I practically ran up to meet him.

Garrett looked at me as I tried to get my breathing under control. "I won't let the forest monster get you, I promise," he teased and I smacked his arm.

"Shut up, will you and open the damn door," I growled, making him laugh.

He was still laughing at me as he let me into his house, turning on the hallway light. It was strange being here without the mob of people. I had never taken the time to notice his home before. It had just been the scene of the party. Not a place where he ate and slept and lived his life.

There was a faded print on the wall just inside the door. I recognized it as a Monet reproduction. Seeing it there surprised me. I had expected beer posters and pictures of half naked girls. Definitely not Monet.

"Do you want something to drink? I've got beer and beer," Garrett offered and I smiled.

"I think I'll have a beer. Thanks," I said, taking off my coat and hanging it on the hook in the corner.

"You can head on to the living room. You know where it is, right?" Garrett asked and I pointed down the hallway to where I knew it to be.

He went into the kitchen and I walked down the hallway. It was so quiet, it was almost disconcerting. Entering the dark room, I fumbled around for the light switch, banging my shin on a table in the process.

"Mother fucking Christ!" I yelled, leaning over to rub my wounded leg. The lights came on and Garrett stared at me as though I had lost my mind.

"Your stupid table attacked me," I explained, pointing at the offending piece of furniture.

"Ah. I should have warned you about that table. It can be temperamental," he joked, handing me the beer. "You okay? Let me see what that nasty piece of wood did to you," he teased, getting down on his knees in front of me and slowly lifted the leg of my jeans.

My breath caught in my throat as his fingers slid along my skin as he rolled up the fabric to reveal the red welt on my shin.

"Ouch. That'll hurt like hell in the morning. Let me get you some ice," Garrett said, lightly rubbing the spot on my leg. It already hurt like hell, but all I could feel at that moment was the way his fingers set off butterflies in my stomach.

Those stupid butterflies needed to die now!

I jerked my leg away and quickly rolled down my pants. "That's okay. I'll live. But it's war on the rest of your furniture, fair warning," I told him, hoping I successfully hid the trembling in my voice.

Garrett got to his feet and shrugged. "It's your leg," he retorted and seemed strangely frustrated.

Not wanting to stand there like an idiot I started to wander around the room, taking in everything that I had never bothered to notice before. On one side of the room was a large fireplace. The mantle was covered with framed photographs. Looking at them, I recognized a younger and completely adorable Garrett.

There was a picture of Garrett with a fishing pole, holding up a huge trout by a river.

In another one, Garrett was flanked by a nice looking man and woman on a beach. The same man and woman appeared in several photographs. Some with the young Garrett, others by themselves. These were obviously his parents.

His dad looked like a clean-cut version of Garrett. His mom was pretty in an understated way. In every picture, they looked like a happy family. Maysie had told me his parents had passed away but I didn't know the story. And I didn't feel comfortable asking him.

I picked up a trophy and read the inscription: *First place All County Debate Tournament, 2008.*

I snickered at the thought of Garrett being on the debate team. The image didn't quite compute with what I knew of him.

"What's so funny?" he asked with amusement. I held up the trophy.

"Did you buy this as a joke?" I asked.

Garrett's eyes narrowed a bit at my ribbing. "No, I was on the debate team for three years in high school. The team went to Nationals my senior year. But that was right after I quit," he said and it seemed like a touchy subject. I wished I hadn't brought it up.

"I know I don't look like the brainy type, but I'm not a complete dumbass," he muttered, looking almost embarrassed by my perception of him. I felt shame for my snap judgment.

"No, it's just I was on the debate team back home as well," I hurried on, trying to cover my colossal jerkiness.

Garrett's eyebrows raised. "I guess we have something in common then," he said as I placed the trophy back on the mantle. I was distracted from his comment at the sight of an eight by ten photograph of Garrett. I assumed it was his senior portrait. It was one of those cheesy, overly posed photographs that we looked back a year later and cringed over.

This one wasn't too bad as far as portraits go. He was leaned against a fence wearing a plaid shirt and jeans. His blond hair was cut short and he looked surprisingly well kempt and a lot like your typical preppy guy in high school.

Looking over my shoulder I stared at the man he was now. He was pulling a guitar case out from underneath the couch and unclipping the snaps. His long hair fell across his face as he leaned down. He had ditched the shirt as soon as we stepped into his house.

The guy in the picture was leaner and less muscular. His eyes were clear and his face clean-shaven. The guy behind me affected an air of indifference to everything around him. So different from the boy in the photograph with the world in his eyes.

How did he get from A to B? How was it possible that in just a few years he went from your every day boy next door to this party loving, toke a joint on a regular basis, living life without a clue guy?

I turned away from the tantalizing glimpses of a Garrett I would never know to face the Garrett who I was currently with. He was now strumming an acoustic guitar. He played around for a bit, plucking out an unfamiliar tune.

I listened silently, not sure what to do or say. This quiet, introspective side of Garrett had me off balance.

And when he started to hum along to the strange melody I had to stop myself from sighing aloud. Hey, even I wasn't immune to a good-looking musician. I *did* possess the double X chromosome, you know.

His eyes were closed and his fingers moved along the fret board with a confidence that was definitely appealing. His face was open and unguarded and I could watch him like this forever.

I liked *this* Garrett. I *more* than liked this Garrett. He fascinated me.

Garrett opened his eyes and found me watching him. The air heated between us, the molecules practically crackling with electricity.

"God, you're beautiful," he said softly, as though more to himself than to me.

My heart was beating at a frantic pace in my chest, his words twinging something in my brain. Images flashed in my head of him kissing the inside of my thighs. I could almost feel his lips as they moved up my skin to taste between my legs.

73

The memory was so vivid that I knew it could only be from *that* night. Shit, I remembered him fucking me with his tongue before he crawled over top of me and told me how beautiful I was. And the look in his eyes had been earth shattering.

I tingled from head to toe and I desperately wanted to remember more.

Garrett continued to watch me as he strummed his guitar, humming that incredible melody. I was melting. Dear lord, I was turning into a big pile of goo.

"I bet you say that to all the gals," I said lightly, trying to hide the fact that I had morphed into a giant, throbbing vagina.

Garrett frowned and got to his feet. He moved slowly, as though he had all the time in the world. When he finally reached me, I was on high alert. Was he going to touch me? Sweet Jesus, I really wanted him to touch me.

No I didn't!

Stop it, Riley! This is not the time to let the sex beast out! Lock it away, now!

"Why do you do you that?" he asked, puzzled.

"Why do I do what?" I asked, just as puzzled.

"Blow off a compliment. Make everything a joke. When I tell you you're beautiful, I'm not just saying that. I'm saying it because you *are*. You. Are. Beautiful. And I want to kiss you more than I've ever wanted anything in my entire life," he said in a hush.

"Oh," was all I could say.

Oh? I was somehow rendered mentally deficient. Please, someone locate my brain! It was desperately needed to stop me from acting like a total dork!

Garrett's eyes dropped to my lips and I couldn't help but wet them with my tongue. Something fierce and smoldering took over his typically unemotional face and I went from pile of goo to molten lava in point three seconds.

He was going to kiss me.

He was going to touch me.

We were most likely going to have sex again.

And just like that the evil sex beast busted from her cage.

74

Hell yeah! Mama wanted to get her sex on, right now, with this hunky slacker that tells me I'm beautiful. Apparently all it took was a syrupy compliment to make me spread the legs I swore would stay resolutely closed.

See, I *was* a total hussy!

"Yo, Garrett, you in here?" a voice yelled from the front of the house, yanking me out of my trance. Garrett blinked and he stepped away from me, giving me room to breathe again. His face pinched and he looked pissed off.

He gave me an apologetic look before calling out, "Back here!"

Suddenly the room was full of people. Cole and Vivian came stumbling in, barely standing. Behind them came Gracie and Mitch as well as Jordan and Maysie. But it wasn't just our friends crashing the moment we had been having. It seemed they had brought half the town with them.

Garrett went back to put his guitar in its case, sliding it under the couch. I wanted him to look at me again the way he just had, but it was as though I were no longer there. I was apparently being ignored.

And that made me really, really mad. After being told you're beautiful, it would be nice to be treated as though you were more than another piece of furniture in the room. Excuse me for thinking I was worth a bit more than that.

"You bailed, man. Lucky for you, I scored some great shit," Cole slurred, passing Garrett a joint. The instant change in Garrett was startling. He effortlessly transformed from Mr. Look At Me I'm So Sensitive to I Couldn't Give a Shit And Acting Like a Butthole.

And there it was. The familiar disgust I was used to feeling around Garrett.

Garrett pulled a lighter out of his pocket and lit the joint and gave it a long pull. He blew out a cloud of smoke, permeating the air with the smell of burnt garbage. I coughed and waved my hand in front of my face.

"Oh, I didn't see Riley over there. What the fuck are you doing here?" Cole asked rudely, earning him an elbow to the ribs from Vivian.

"Shut up, Cole. You are such an asshole!" she yelled, pushing away from him clumsily. Cole stumbled backwards, grabbing ahold of Mitch so he wouldn't fall over.

"What the hell, Viv? Don't fucking walk away from me!" he hollered at her retreating form.

"Screw you, fucker!" she screamed back at him.

Cole took off after her and we could hear the back door slam and their yelling out in the yard. The party started to flow around me and I hated the way the Garrett I had seen a few moments before disappear the higher he became.

I had been forgotten.

Garrett lounged back on the couch and he was soon joined by a girl I vaguely recognized as one of the groupie skanks that were front and center for all of the Rejects' shows. I didn't know her name, only that I wasn't used to seeing her with so much clothing on. And that was saying something, considering her boobs were barely covered by the thin, slip of fabric she had on.

Jealousy, hot and lethal, flashed through me and I had visions of ripping her away from him by her hair and then wailing on my chest caveman style.

But I realized quickly, Garrett Bellows was not worth the effort it would take to exert such violence.

"Want a drag?" Garrett asked, holding the roach out for me to take.

I curled my lip at him, hating that I had been suckered, however briefly, into thinking he was anything but a stoned out loser. "I'd rather keep my brain cells, thanks," I responded, turning away from him. But not before I saw the cold set to his eyes. He was making a point here. To show everyone in the room that there was nothing to see here. Look away folks, it's just the same ol' shit.

And I hated that guy with as much passion as I was starting to like the other Garrett. The one who could play me a song on the guitar and tell me I was beautiful and mean it.

A few of the guys around us ooh'd at my rejection, taunting Garrett by my obvious dismissal.

"You'd better keep those, babe. Cause they're all you've got going for you," he responded hatefully, earning him a riot of laughter from his friends. Garrett looked away and I saw a tiny sliver of regret on his face as though he wished he could take his words back. Well sorry buddy, words stick but I sure as hell wasn't.

Without saying a word, I walked away. And I was left feeling oddly bereft. Maybe it was for not getting the last word in. Maybe it was for wasting a chance at insulting him back.

Or maybe it was for losing sight of the man I had glimpsed for only a few seconds. A man I could find myself actually wanting to be around.

Chapter
8

THE weeks passed and my life fell into the complacency of routine. Between school, working my shifts at Barton's, and my internship I had little time for anything else and that was good for me. I liked keeping busy. I had a clear picture of my future and I was steadfastly plodding toward it. No one could ever accuse me of being unsure.

Just call me Slow and Steady Riley. On second thought, don't you dare.

My parents had always joked that my serious focus was a result of some mutation of the genes. Because they were the most laid back people on the planet (excluding a certain doped out guitarist I knew of course). My father and mother had met at a commune in upstate New York in the early eighties. It had been love at first sight. Or it could have been the copious amount of psychedelic mushrooms they had just ingested. Whatever the cause for their instant connection, it brought about a quickie marriage after dating for less than two weeks.

And yet after all these years and three children later, they were still going strong. Hell, I hoped to be with someone I could remotely stand after that amount of time. I couldn't imagine sharing a space with anyone that long and not wanting to inflict bodily harm. Who could stand hair in the sink and the toilet seat being left up for more than a month? Not me, that's for sure.

But my parents were made of different stuff. Because I grew

up in a home filled with love and laughter and all that Hallmark crap. I was the baby of the family, born almost sixteen years after my sister. I was the "oops" child. The result of a weekend getaway to Maine for my parents' twentieth wedding anniversary. So I was raised essentially as an only child, both of my much older siblings having flown the roost while I was still a toddler.

My brother, Gavin, was a schoolteacher, my sister, Felicity, a stay at home mom to my two nieces. Gavin still lived in Maryland, ten minutes from parents. Fliss was in Pennsylvania. Then there was me.

I had never been a partier, more concerned with doing well in school and over extending myself through endless extracurricular activities and a part time job when I was a teen. My parents were proud, if not a little perplexed, as to how they had raised such a straight edged kid when they had spent their youth following The Grateful Dead. Since I wasn't into the wild and crazy, my brand of teenage rebellion took the course of L. L. Bean and the debate team.

Despite our polar differences, I knew how lucky I was to have my parents' unconditional love and support. The liberty to make my own choices and go where the wind took me, knowing that no matter where my feet landed I had two people in this world who would always be there if I needed them.

After seeing the relationship Maysie had with her parents, I had been more appreciative of my own mom and dad. Maysie's parents lived in a constant state of disapproval where their daughter was concerned. Nothing she did would ever be good enough. I hated it for her. No one deserved to feel second best by their own parents.

When my phone rang Friday after classes, I answered it, pleased to hear my mother's voice on the other end. "Riley Louise, finally! You have been incommunicado for weeks!" my mother exclaimed, scolding me in that pleasant way of hers that let me know she was upset but not enough to unleash the full weight of motherly disapproval.

"I know, Mom. Things have been crazy," I said, digging my keys out of my book bag as I headed across the parking lot toward my car.

"Such a busy bee. How is school? The internship? I want to hear about everything!" My mom was the most enthusiastic person I knew. When I was a surly teenager, she drove me nuts. Her incessant perkiness was at odds with my more morose and subtle personality. She wanted me to wear pink, I swore off all colors but black. She played Captain and Tennille at full volume; I preferred to listen to Damien Rice with my lights off.

But now that I'm older, I could appreciate her glass is half-full mentality. And I no longer felt the need to buck the system by whining endlessly about all the ways the world sucks.

"Things are good. My senior symposium is kicking my ass. We have to read three books a week. But I'm loving it. The internship is interesting. I've graduated from gopher girl, Queen of the Coffee Machine to full-on reporter lackey. I'm hoping to be able to write a piece by the end of the month," I said as I got into my car. The mundane tedium of small talk wasn't my mother's way so I waited for her to get to the grit of the phone call. But she had to go through the niceties first. Having been raised in Alabama, she was insistent on good manners.

"Wow, that's amazing, Riley Boo!" she exclaimed and I had to roll my eyes at her persistent use of my childhood nickname. Riley Boo, Gavey Love, Flutterfly. My siblings and I had to endure these little testaments of our parents love for our whole lives. It often put our teeth on edge but we'd never even think of telling mom to stop. It was easier to suck it up and not act mortally humiliated when we were referred to by said nicknames in a public setting.

"Yep, pretty amazing," I agreed dryly. I put the phone on speaker and placed it into the hands free set on my dashboard so I could start heading home.

"How are things with Damien?" she asked in a sympathetic tone. The mention of his name had lost a lot of its power over the last few weeks but it still landed an emotional punch. Seeing him almost every day didn't help. Particularly when he was making it his mission to remind me of why I had fallen in love with him in the first place. I wasn't entirely sure what happened with Jaz, but I could tell that they were most definitely *not* dating.

I had overheard Jaz making a snide comment to Dina, another

waitress at Barton's, about the fact he had never called her after going to The Boogey Lounge. Honestly, I wasn't trying to snoop, but it did give me a sense of supreme satisfaction to know that she had been handed her rejection so quickly.

She had turned around after her tirade over Damien, to find me wiping down my tables. She had given me a sugary sweet smile, followed by a fake "Hiya, Riley!" before flouncing off to her own section. But I could see her face color with mortification at having me overhear her tale of dating gone wrong.

So, whatever had happened between him and Jaz, he was now sniffing around my skirts more than he ever had while we were together. It must be my magnetic I'm-moving-on-with-my-life perfume. Apparently it made me irresistible.

"Really Mom? Is that why you called? To snoop around in my love life? Because I can assure you, it's about as interesting as watching paint dry," I commented as I pulled up to a red light.

"Oh come on. Are the two of you still not back together? I thought you were absolutely perfect together. Riley, people make mistakes. You can't hold grudges. It's not good for your karma," she lectured.

I listened as my mom started to regale me with the ways I could cleanse my energy. I typically tuned out at this inevitable point in the conversation. The loud thumping of bass caught my attention. Why do people have to listen to music at internal organ shutdown levels? Particularly when it was seriously crappy music?

I debated on blowing my horn at the jerkoff sat beside me in traffic. I could only see the back of his head because he was facing someone in the passenger seat. The windows of my car were vibrating and I could feel the thumping in my bones. I noticed the blonde hair of the passenger and realized it was Gracie. She must have felt my eyes on her because she started waving, her mouth moving as she spoke to the driver, pointing in my direction.

The driver turned back around in his seat and glanced at me and I was glad I wasn't driving because I would surely have crashed. What the hell was Gracie doing in Garrett's van? My hands gripped the steering wheel. My mouth fell open in absolute and complete shock. I felt sick at the realization that Garrett was most likely playing "tag that ass" with one of my friends. Because everyone knew it wasn't that difficult to get Gracie to agree to a naked meet a greet.

As soon as our eyes connected, I looked away and was thankful that the light turned green so I could speed away, squealing my tires in the process.

Shit.

What if Gracie slept with Garrett!? Aside from the fact that it meant Gracie and I were now intimately familiar with the same person, I couldn't help but feel supremely dejected. Okay, and maybe a tad bit jealous.

Only a tad, I swear!

"Riley!" my mom yelled and I realized I had completely forgotten she was still on the phone.

"Sorry, Mom. What were you saying?" I asked, feeling distracted and out of sorts. My mind was too busy inventing horrific scenarios of Gracie and Garrett together.

Having sex together.

Oh God!

My heart squeezed painfully and I told myself it had everything to do with the uncomfortable idea of Gracie Cook and Riley Walker sharing bed partners. It had NOTHING to do with any sort of emotional connection I had felt with our particular bed partner.

No way!

Garrett Bellows was nothing to me. Just some sad, regretful mistake I had made in the heat of some serious self-pity.

"I was asking whether any other boys have caught your fancy. You're entirely too serious and focused. You need a little fun, sweetie." My mother's question coming on the heels of seeing Garrett and Gracie together had me ready to duck and cover. Shit was about to get ugly.

"No, Mom. And I've got to go," I said hurriedly, whipping into a parking space outside my apartment building. Without waiting for a goodbye, I hung up the phone.

"Is Gracie sleeping with Garrett?" I asked as soon as I entered the apartment. Maysie and Jordan were sprawled out on the couch watching TV. Under normal circumstances I would have made a snide comment about confining their excessive PDA to behind her bedroom door but I was feeling a bit frantic.

Maysie looked at me in surprise and Jordan lifted his head from its resting spot on his girlfriend's chest with an expression of complete confusion.

"What?" Maysie asked, sitting up. I dropped my bag on the couch and realized how my question must have sounded and I wished I could take it back.

Why the hell did I care if they were sleeping together? They were consenting adults doing what consenting adults do. There was nothing wrong in that. But it didn't change the fact that the very thought of it made me want to puke.

I let out an embarrassed huff and then laughed. "Nothing. Forget it. Get back to your pre-coital cuddling," I muttered, shuffling off to the kitchen as quickly as I was able without looking as though I were running.

"Uh, uh, Riley Walker. Why would you ask that?" Maysie asked, following me like a terrier nipping at my heels. Clearly, she felt this fell within her best friend duties. Interrogation and persistent nagging would follow unless I gave her something to make her happy.

"I just saw them together. I had no idea Gracie was even interested in Garrett," I said nonchalantly.

Woohoo! Point for Riley and her super powers of indifference!

Maysie crossed her arms over her chest and leaned against the wall as I pulled a bag of Doritos out of the cabinet. "I really have no idea. I mean, Gracie has made comments about thinking Garrett was hot but I don't think they've ever hooked up," Maysie said and then crinkled her nose.

"Oh, ew. I get it now."

I leveled my roommate with a narrowed look. "She doesn't know about Garrett and me right?" I asked her. Maysie looked instantly offended.

"As if I would go around broadcasting your business. Plus it's not like it'll ever happen again, so what's there to tell?" Maysie asked.

I nodded, thinking about Garrett's starring role as asshole of the hour at his house all those weeks ago.

No, that would definitely not be happening again. He and Gracie could have each other.

And there was no way that twinge in my gut had anything to do with a seething, hateful jealousy.

Absolutely not.

"Come out with Jordan and me tonight. We're going out for a few drinks. Should be fun," Maysie suggested.

"Playing third wheel sounds like a blast, Mays," I remarked, popping a chip in my mouth. Maysie peeked out into the living room. I followed her gaze and saw that Jordan was still laid out on the sofa watching TV. I looked closely at my friend and realized there was a sadness there that was new. God, what new batch of drama was brewing between those two? I thought they were past all that.

"What's going on?" I asked, dropping my voice so Jordan couldn't hear me. Maysie's eyes turned back to me and her lips stretched into a strained smile.

"Jordan and the guys are going on tour again," she said tightly. I crunched on another chip, watching as conflicting emotions warred on her face. I could tell she *wanted* to be happy for her boyfriend. But that insecure girl still lived inside of Maysie Ardin and I knew better than anyone that it would take a long time for her to go away. Even after everything Maysie and Jordan had gone through to be together.

"Wow, when? For how long?" I asked, feeling my gut twist at the news. I told myself it had everything to do with worrying about Maysie. No other hidden reasons for feeling as though my stomach had hit the floor.

Maysie heaved a giant sigh. "They're leaving in the new year for a three month tour. They'll be driving across country, stopping in most of the major cities. Mitch's cousin hooked them up with another promoter who put it all together."

Three months. That was a long time. Maysie seemed miserable and hating herself for being miserable. I normally was the first one to give her the advice she needed, but right now I didn't know what to say. My own feelings were too convoluted to give her anything to work with.

"I'm happy for him and the guys. I really am. But damn it, I hate the thought of him leaving again. I know this is what he wants but it doesn't make it any easier when he has to go. I'm a selfish bitch, right?" she asked, looking at me for either total agreement or steadfast denial.

I lifted my shoulders in a shrug. "It's okay to be upset about it, but you need to be supportive as well. Because you know if Jordan gets wind of how you really feel he's likely to call the whole thing off. Then you'd feel like crap for holding him back," I told her, proud of myself for doling out what I deemed to be pretty damn good advice.

Maysie nodded. "You're right, as usual. Guess it's time for grinning and bearing it. But you're coming tonight. I need a swift kick in the rear if I start getting too morose about it," she said, reaching out and squeezing my arm.

Focusing on someone else's problems made it easy to forget about why I had been so upset when I got home. I could pretend that I hadn't wanted to gut Garrett alive for being with my friend. I could ignore the insatiable homicidal urges that were unfairly directed at Gracie Cook.

Being needed by my best friend was the best medicine for a conflicted heart and mind.

"Sounds good," I replied, giving her a smile.

Chapter 9

The tiny, hole in the wall dive bar in the basement of a rundown building was the last place I expected Maysie and Jordan to drag me to. This was such a far cry from the crazy club and hopping bar scene they tended to inhabit that I had to look over my shoulder as we walked in to make sure they were still with me.

There was a small stage at the front and only around fifteen or so tables scattered around the dimly lit room. A bar took up most of the back wall and was lined with stools. There wasn't a pool table or television playing sports in sight. And I for one found the atmosphere to be a nice change.

There were only about thirty or so people there. If this was the meat of their Friday night crowd then I couldn't understand how it stayed in business. But the sign reading "Benny's" over the front door had proclaimed it a local treasure since prohibition where it had started as a place to run moonshine on the down low.

Maysie and Jordan walked hand in hand toward a shadowed corner and I trailed behind them like the third wheel they swore up and down I wasn't. A night spent watching two of my closest friends play tonsil hockey, now that's what I call a fantastic time. (Cue the sarcasm.)

I was happy to see that I wouldn't be alone in playing unintentional voyeur this evening. Gracie and Vivian as well as

Mitch and Cole were seated at the only large table in the place. Three pitchers of beer had already been consumed and it seemed the party had started way before our arrival.

I glanced around the bar, looking for the one person who was noticeably absent. But I'd be damned if I would ask where Garrett was.

I sat down between Mitch and Gracie. I hadn't spent an inordinate amount of time with the other guys from Generation Rejects (well aside from the naked kind of time I had spent with Garrett but that didn't count since I could barely remember it). Cole had always come across as a crude, try too hard womanizer. Mitch was the cute teddy bear with the heart of gold.

I had never thought we'd have anything in common to warrant socializing. They lived in their townie, band dominated world and I was firmly ensconced in the land of academia. But since Maysie had jumped to the dark side, I had found the lines between the two worlds becoming more and more blurred.

Mitch poured a beer into a glass and passed it to me without a word. I inclined my head in thanks and took a sip, grimacing at the taste. Mitch smirked. "We could only afford the cheap stuff. It's hard to live off playing at Barton's every other week," he explained finding my abhorrence of their chosen beverage amusing.

"Hey, I dig a cheap beer every now and then," I told him, slugging half of the beer down my throat, making an effort not to cringe. Mitch patted me on the back in genuine affection.

"Sure you do, Ri," he teased and I had to smile at his use of a nickname. I hadn't realized until then how being a part of a group could actually feel pretty darned good. It was a shot of warm fuzzies straight to the heart.

Gracie slung her arm around my shoulders. "I'm so glad you're here, Riley!" She leaned into my arm and I could tell she was barely holding her head above water. I tried not feel annoyed by her drunken affection. Typically I took her need for a tactile interaction while she was drinking with a stiff upper lip. But tonight, after seeing her this afternoon with a certain someone, I was feeling a lot less charitable.

I glanced at Maysie, hoping she'd save me from Gracie on the drunk side, but she was entirely focused on Jordan who was cupping her face in his hands as he whispered something to her. I suppose I didn't have to worry about her channeling Coldplay this evening. She seemed to be coping with her earlier freak out quite well…for Maysie.

Gracie poked my arm, still not lifting her head from my shoulder. "I think you should look for a boy tonight, Riley-Wiley! Let's find you a fuck buddy!" Gracie singsong'd loudly and I nudged her off my arm.

"Let's talk about the rapid deterioration of your motor functioning instead," I said shortly, hoping that even through her drunken haze, Gracie could see she was touching on a very sensitive subject.

"Gracie, you need to freshen your lipstick. Here use mine," Vivian intervened, shoving her tube of lipstick into our friend's face. Gracie rubbed at her lips and took the offered makeup.

"Thanks Vivvie," Gracie slurred, pulling out a compact. I looked over at the older girl and gave her a look of gratitude. She grinned and shrugged.

"So, I've never been here before. Why the sudden change in weekend venue?" I asked the guys. Cole didn't acknowledge my question, seeing as he was much too busy shoving his hands up Vivian's shirt. Apparently they were in one of their "on again" phases.

Mitch poured me another glass of beer before refilling his own mug. "They have open mic night on the first Saturday of the month. We've been coming here for the last two years," Mitch said in way of explanation.

I looked around at the small crowd and turned back to Mitch in disbelief. "Is this place harboring the next Dave Matthews and I didn't realize it?" I asked. Mitch chuckled and gave me a strange look.

"Not exactly," was all he said.

I watched as the bartender went to the tiny stage and set up a microphone stand and a small amp. He didn't announce the beginning of any act. He simply switched on the power and went back to his post behind the bar.

Slowly, a guy from the audience came up with a beat up electric guitar. He began to play a horribly out of tune version of *All Along the Watchtower*. I felt embarrassed for the poor man as he hit the wrong chord over and over again. His voice wasn't half bad but it was hard to notice over the horrendous way he butchered his guitar.

No one clapped when he finished and I felt bad for him. Two girls came up next and sang some country song I didn't recognize. They weren't as bad as the last guy but they still sucked. Jeesh, this was becoming painful.

Nobody at our table was paying a bit of attention as the acts filed up one after another. They continued to chat amongst themselves and get more and more drunk. I was completely confused. I thought this is why they had chosen to come here.

I was about to ask what the deal was when Jordan got to his feet, put two forefingers in his mouth and let out a loud whistle. Mitch and Cole joined him in a riot of cheering. Maysie was beaming as she got to her feet to clap.

I watched as someone made their way to the stage with a guitar case in hand.

I should have freaking known.

Garrett set the case down on the stage and slowly and purposefully unhooked the latches to open the top. He pulled out the well-worn Taylor acoustic I recognized as the one he played at his house. His hand smoothed down the fret board lovingly as though this inanimate object meant more to him than anything else.

He hooked the guitar strap around his neck and under his arm before sitting on the stool and resting the instrument in his lap. He blew out a breath to move his blond hair out of his eyes. He put a pick between his teeth as he began to turn the tuning pegs.

"Playing without backup this evening?" I asked Mitch dryly, trying like crazy to disguise the uncomfortable thudding of my heart at seeing Garrett on the stage by himself and strangely vulnerable. He looked so much like that *other* Garrett from weeks ago. The one I had found so compelling.

Mitch's eyes slid to me as he tried to assess whether I was being a bitch or not. It was an understandable confusion considering most of the time I was being just that. "He's been playing here every month for years. He was doing it awhile before the rest of us figured out where he was disappearing to," Cole piped up, answering my question.

Gracie clapped her hands and looked as though she were about to swoon as she watched Garrett tune his guitar. "Isn't he amazing? Seriously Riley, he's so awesome!" she remarked, patting my arm a little harder than she probably meant to in her zealousness.

"Wow, when did you become Garrett Bellows' number one fan?" I asked sarcastically. Gracie was too drunk to notice how irritated I sounded, though my overly astute roommate picked up on it instantly and gave me a funny look.

"I just think he's so freaking sexy. I mean look at him," Gracie said breathlessly. She leaned in close and said in a loud whisper in an effort to be discreet and failing miserably. "I've been trying to get him between my legs for months. And I plan to seal the deal tonight."

Ugh. I felt sick all over again. Though I had the consolation of knowing that Gracie and Garrett hadn't slept together...yet. Though the exact reason I was pleased by that knowledge was a bit unclear in my deep pit of denial.

"I think the only thing you'll be doing tonight is passing out and hoping you don't choke on your own vomit," I bit out angrily. Gracie giggled as though I had just made the funniest joke *ever*.

The soft strains of music caught my attention as Garrett began to strum a few chords. He pushed his hair back from his face and looked out into the crowd, finding our table and giving his friends a big grin. His smile lit up his face and made my breath catch in my throat. He pointed at his bandmates and made some gesture with his hand that the other three imitated, followed by a fresh round of yelling and cheering.

Without an introduction, Garrett began to play a song. It took me awhile to recognize it. Huh, he was playing an unplugged version of Soundgarden's Black Hole Sun. And damned if his voice didn't give Chris Cornell a run for his money. Garrett's voice was melodic and pleasing to the ear with a slight rasp that gave his singing a raw edge. Why in the hell had Cole become the lead singer when Garrett had a voice like that?

After he finished that song he launched into an up tempo rendition of Pink Floyd's Comfortably Numb. It was weird but oddly catchy. I found my leg bobbing up and down in time to the music. I looked around the bar and saw that aside from our table, no one else seemed as entranced with the set as I was. Conversation carried on in spite of Garrett's supreme talent. People were so freaking rude.

Garrett ended the Pink Floyd song with a screech along the strings and then promptly jumped into a new set of chords that melded in with harmonics beautifully. I remembered the gentle melody all too well. It was the same tune he had played for me before. Back all those weeks ago when I stupidly thought there might be more to him than I had originally thought.

Then he opened his mouth and began to sing. And I forgot to be bitter. I forgot to be annoyed about seeing him with Gracie. All I could think; all I could feel was complete and total awe.

I hadn't expected it
I thought you were a joke.
Your whispered words
Wrapped around my throat.
I hated that I loved it
The way you reached inside
Clawing through the wreckage
And the pieces that have died.
You don't even know it,
You're blind to what you see
The disillusioned lies
Bleeding out of me.
Quiet slumbers before the storm
Violent eyes, passionate cries,
Resisting and tormenting wanting more.
There is no beginning without an end,

No tomorrow, no future,
losing it all again.
Our story is a nightmare,
Written in stone,
Nothing can change it,
I'll still be alone.
You want me to need you.
You'll be waiting awhile,
Piercing my world
with the ice of your smile.
Your touch is toxic
Your heart's a mess
Which is why you'll always be
My perfect regret.
My perfect regret.
Regret…

Garrett's voice faded into a soft hum as he strummed his guitar in a complicated dance along the strings. His song gave me chills. Seriously, I had goose bumps on my arms. The hair was literally standing up on the back of my neck.

When Garrett had finished, Cole let out a whistle. "Damn, that was a new one. Good shit," he said, getting to his feet with the empty pitcher. I swallowed thickly, wondering, perhaps a bit vainly, whether I had been the muse of that particular song. The words rang a little too close to home for my liking.

Garrett played a few more covers and one more original song. When he was finished, our table erupted in applause and I clapped along with them. Garrett put his guitar back in the case and walked over to our group. Jordan clapped him on the back and Maysie gave him a hug.

Gracie tried to get to her feet, finally succeeding after much effort. "Garrett!" she squealed and practically fell on him as she attempted to wrap her arms around him. He laughed and helped her back into her seat.

"A little too much to drink again, huh, G?" he said with an obvious affection that annoyed the shit out of me. G? Garrett called her G? His use of *my* nickname for her bugged me more than it should. He accepted praise from the rest of his friends and purposefully ignored me the entire time. Okay, so this is how it was going to be obviously. How quickly the two of us fell back into our comfortable pattern of loathing and disdain for one another.

Garrett sat down across from me and Cole poured him a beer, which he accepted with a thanks before finishing it in one gulp. Vivian gave him a one armed hug, which he returned easily. I was the only one with my awkward hat on, feeling all kinds of socially dysfunctional.

"Good job," I finally interjected because I couldn't stand the thick layers of discomfort a moment longer. It wasn't Garrett's discomfort. It was clear he couldn't give a shit whether I was here or not. The discomfort was mine alone and I thought I was going to gag on it.

Garrett looked at me over the rim of his mug as he took a drink of beer number two. His blond eyebrow arched as he set the glass down on the table. I gave him a weak impression of a smile. "Really, that was great. I wish you guys played that kind of music all the time. I might actually start to enjoy your shows," I said, hoping my lack of composure could be hidden by a hefty dose of sarcasm.

Garrett didn't respond, he only stared at me, his face void of all emotion. No verbal joisting. No snappy comeback. No barely laced annoyance. Just a big heap of nothing. And that bugged me...a lot.

I was starting to hate the lack of anything resembling an expression on his face.

Mitch took pity on the gaping sea of disquiet brewing between his bandmate and me and rustled my hair. "No way, Riley. We have an image as hardcore bad asses to protect," he said and I smiled at him in appreciation. A silent thank you for rescuing me from Garrett's icy attack of silence.

"Of course, can't forget about the all important bad assery," I agreed, my eyes flicking back to Garrett who had turned away from me. Like I wasn't even there.

"I really dug that Perfect Regret song, dude. Is that new?" Jordan asked Garrett, who gave him a shy smile. See, there it was again! That lovely, unguarded side of Garrett that I wanted to wrap in a blanket and cuddle to death.

"Yeah, it's new. I've been messing around with the chords for a while. But I just wrote the lyrics a few weeks ago," Garrett told Jordan, his eyes flickering to me briefly before sliding away.

Ha! I knew it! That damn song was totally about me! Wait a second. I thought back over the lyrics and started to feel more than a little pissed off. Because as far as songs go, that one wasn't the most flattering he could write. In fact, it sounded more like a great big musical kiss off.

Well, forget him!

The truth was Garrett and I had never gotten along. But at least before our disastrous tumble in the sheets and subsequent almost romantic moment we had been able to coexist. Even if that meant it was the acknowledgement of one another through a series of barbs and insults.

The frosty snubs and hateful songs weren't something I was okay with. It made me feel as though I had done something wrong. And I didn't like questioning my choices on any level. I had done enough of that recently, I sure as hell wasn't willing to start again over Garrett.

So I spoke to everyone *but* Garrett. And Garrett looked at everyone *but* me. The effort to pretend that there wasn't this gigantic elephant in the room was exhausting. I knew by around midnight that I was done. I needed to go home and regroup. Mostly I just needed to sleep and wake up feeling like Riley Walker again.

I knew Maysie wasn't ready to leave. She was most likely going back to Garrett and Jordan's. I patted my jeans pockets and realized I must have left my cellphone in Jordan's truck. "Hey Jordan, can I have the keys. I left my phone on the seat," I asked. Jordan tossed me his keys and I hurried out of the bar.

Once I had my phone, I started looking up numbers for local cab companies. The sound of footsteps crunching on gravel made me look up. Garrett was headed toward me with his guitar case in hand. He stopped several feet in front of me and dropped the case to the ground. Shoving his hands into his jeans pocket he regarded me levelly.

"Guess you're headed home," he stated.

Wow, he was talking to me. What had I done to deserve such a privilege?

I continued to scroll through the taxicab listings, ignoring Garrett just as I had been ignored all evening. Hey, maturity is over rated.

"Cat got your tongue?" Garrett asked, his words sharp enough to cut.

I looked up at him, my mouth curling in sardonic disdain. "Oh I'm sorry, you're right, ignoring someone is extremely rude."

Garrett snorted and then gave me the sort of feral grin that was more a baring of teeth than anything else. "You just have to bust my balls, don't you? Is it so hard to be pleasant?" he asked harshly. The veins on the side of his neck were bulging and I could tell he was pissed.

"And you just have to be an annoying assmunch, don't you? Why do I get the feeling I'm being punished for something? If I've upset your sad excuse for male pride, please let me know," I said just as hatefully.

Garrett took a step forward and I moved back, pressing myself into Jordan's truck door. "If I wanted to punish you, Riley, I'd put you over my knee and spank the shit out of you. A red ass is the least of what you deserve," he said, his voice dropping an octave, his eyes which had been coldly observing me, had turned hot enough to burn.

"What I deserve? I'm not the one who took advantage of drunk girl in a state of total vulnerability. The whole thing is predatory. You should be ashamed of yourself," I said fiercely. My words seemed to shock Garrett because he stopped his slow advancement, his face blanking.

"Is that what you think? That I took advantage of you?" he asked softly and I knew the idea that I actually thought that hurt him. Hurt him deeply and that softened the hard layer around my heart just a smidge.

Garrett pushed his messy hair back off his forehead in a gesture I was coming to find meant he was flustered. "Shit, Riley. I was drunk. You were drunk. It happened. I never meant to take advantage of you. I just thought" he stopped abruptly and I knew that I needed to hear what he was going to say.

"Thought what?" I demanded, my tone leaving no room for refusal.

Garrett looked at the ground and I found his sudden unsurety disconcerting. Garrett was a confident guy. This person in front of me was decidedly uncertain.

"I don't know. I thought you wanted to be with me. What a fucking joke that was. I should have fucking known better," he laughed bitterly and bent to pick up his guitar case. His shoulders were tense and he wouldn't look at me. Somehow, someway I had laid this man low and I felt an immeasurable amount of guilt about it.

"Come home with me," I said and I wanted to bite my tongue. Where the hell had that come from? What was wrong with me? This was so not what I needed. This was not good for me in any way. But right now, this is what I *wanted* and that trumped any sense I had of adhering to my status quo.

I knew that my friend wanted him. That she was making a play for the very guy I was proposing to come home and knock boots with. Where was my sense of loyalty and friends before hos or whatever? I was being a slut. But I wanted this man to make me dirty.

Garrett's head snapped up in total shock. "Excuse me?" he asked, staring at me as though I had been speaking gibberish. Oh god, I wish I had been speaking gibberish. Because I couldn't take it back now. And that sick, masochistic, seriously deluded side of me didn't want to. Because it had officially taken me over. There was no other explanation for the complete personality transplant I was experiencing.

All I knew was that he had touched a nerve. His earlier admission exposed a side of him I would never have thought existed and it struck a chord in me. He was again that boy in his living room, telling me I was beautiful.

I wanted him. Tonight. And I couldn't think beyond that. The implications of my choice would have to wait for another day. Because something else was guiding my decisions right now. And it wasn't my head.

I stepped into his personal space, not touching him, but close enough that I could if I wanted to. "Come home with me. Just one more night. I want to know if throwing away my morals was worth it," I said wishing the words had sounded a little less prudish. But whatever, I sort of was a prude.

Garrett laughed, his eyes crinkling at the corners. "Are you serious?" he asked after quieting down.

"As a heart attack," I replied. Part of me knew he could reject me outright and make me look like a complete and total ass. But staring into his blue eyes I knew he wouldn't. He wanted this, whatever it was, as much as I did.

He pulled out his keys and nodded his head in the direction of his van. "Come on then," he said. He didn't take my hand. He didn't say another word, just headed to his vehicle, leaving me the choice to follow him or not.

You bet I followed him.

Chapter 10

CLEARLY this whole no strings attached sex thing was a lot less awkward when you were falling down drunk. Or maybe it was just as awkward and I thankfully couldn't remember any of it. I didn't know what to say. Sure I had initiated this, but now that Garrett and I were heading to my apartment I felt like a tool.

I didn't do casual sex. Every time I had been intimate with someone (not counting the guy who would be jumping into my hotbox in a matter of minutes) I had been in love, or at the very least, committed to them. It wasn't in my psyche to be able to handle a quick round of wam-bam-thank-you-ma'am.

Case in point, the utter shitfest I had created after sleeping with Garrett the first time. So why, do you ask, was I allowing myself to slide vagina first back into another emotional landslide? Oh because I had somehow morphed into an absolute idiot. I was now a chick obsessesed with her own destruction apparently.

Because that was what the Garrett Bellows sexcipades promised.

My ruin.

Was I being overly dramatic? Perhaps. But there was something in the way I felt with Garrett that took me out of my comfort zone and thrust me, without preamble, into the cold, hard world of lust and want. I had *never* been ruled by my hormones.

I wasn't a girl who made life decision based on what was going on between her legs. But Garrett made all sense of logic take a flying leap out the window. Or maybe it was the person I had slowly been turning into since Damien had dumped me. I felt a change at a molecular level that was both unsettling and exciting.

Garrett parked in front of my apartment building and shut off the engine. He looked over at me and I was thankful I couldn't see his face in the dark. I was already humiliated with the way I had suggested this whole thing.

"You sure?" he asked me. This was my moment. My chance to back out and return to the place where our one time indiscretion had been a fluke. Because if we did this, it changed things. I couldn't go back to pretending I had made a choice based on alcohol and the need for a rebound.

Because tonight, I was stone cold sober. And while I still felt the aftermath of my heartache, this would be no rebound bang.

This time I would be dancing the horizontal mambo because *I* wanted to and for no other reason. Because I was attracted to my complete antithesis. The guy who up until a month ago, I wanted nothing to do with but now had slithered his way under my skin. He was like a freaking parasite, sucking away everything but the desire to get him naked.

Could I flip my world on its axis like that? Was I ready for the fallout?

I opened the passenger door. "Come on," I said shortly, getting out. I headed up the stairs, not waiting to see if he was following me. Because I knew he was. And it had nothing to do with confidence or being self-assured. Nope, it had everything to do with basic chemistry and knowing despite everything, Garrett and I had that in spades.

Stupid chemistry. It had always been my least favorite subject.

Maysie's ex-whatever, Eli Bray, was sitting outside his cousin Randall's apartment as I headed down the hallway. He raised his hand in greeting and then he looked behind me at the person who was obviously following me.

Eli looked at me again and opened his mouth to speak. "Say a word and I will staple your mouth shut," I warned, causing him to close his lips. I didn't need any of his bullshit right now. I didn't like him; I didn't want to talk to him. I just wanted to get into my apartment and get my freak on before I chickened out.

I stopped in front of my door and fumbled with my keys. Garrett's hand came into my field of vision and took them from my trembling hand and slowly put the key in the lock. He pushed against the door, opening it. His front pressed against my back and I closed my eyes, taking a deep breath.

Let's do this thing!

I turned around and grabbed Garrett by the front of his shirt and gave it a tug as I moved backwards into my dark living room. I didn't turn on any lights; I just continued to tug Garrett as I moved toward my bedroom.

I kicked open the door and pulled him inside. "What am I doing? Why am I doing this?" I said under my breath as Garrett took me in his arms and placed one solitary kiss on the underside of my jaw.

We stood there for an endless moment, breathing deeply as though readying ourselves for this step we were about to take. I wish I could explain why this felt monumental. Why it felt as though I were about to jump out of a plane without a parachute.

But everything, every look, every touch, every heartbeat felt full of purpose.

And it made me want to scream.

I didn't want purpose.

I didn't want meaningful.

I wanted this man to screw my brains out. I wanted him to pull my hair and show me who was boss.

I wanted to forget the perfect linear thoughts in my head and rush headfirst into the irrational.

But it didn't stop the way my heart thudded in my chest to an uncertain rhythm...one that only Garrett could play.

Garrett kissed the side of my mouth, his lips lingering near mine. "We've found something in each other that we want. Hell if I understand why. Out of all the fish in the sea, I had to hook you. One giant, snarly toothed piranha ready to bite my fingers off." I had to laugh at his rather poetic description of me. Even if it was mildly insulting. Garrett placed his mouth on mine and I found myself parting my lips to let him inside.

His tongue swept along the bottom curve of my lip and I shuddered with the intensity of this moment. His hands gripped the bottom hem of my shirt and swept it up and over my head. He then discarded it on the floor as he touched my now naked skin almost reverently. His fingers glided up the side of my rib cage, taking in the soft contours of my body in the barest breath of a touch.

Our lips moved together in tandem, our tongues a tangled throbbing mass of need as we struggled to breathe through the heat of our kiss. He hooked his fingers underneath the straps of my bra and brought them down my shoulders. He broke off our kiss suddenly and dropped his mouth to my shoulder, tasting my flesh as he expertly traced my collarbone. He had done this many times before. But I couldn't focus on that; I just had to reap the benefits.

Pulling away, Garrett looked down at me. I could barely see him in the shadow and that somehow made the whole thing that much more intimate. But I didn't want intimate.

Did I?

He lifted my hair and swept it over my shoulder. His lips burned my skin as he kissed the sensitive skin of my neck. I felt suddenly panicked.

"We can't do this! I can't even stand you!" I said in a thready voice as I felt the tip of his tongue glide along the outside of my ear.

Garrett's eyes smoldered as he scrutinized my heightened anxiety. He moved his hands to the button of my jeans and deftly opened them, slowly lowering the zipper. He shoved the resisting fabric down past my hips, his fingers grazing my legs as he knelt in front of me. He pulled my pants off my feet and dropped them to the side. He wrapped his hands around calves and gave them a tug, so that I was spread above him. He looked up at me as he slowly brought his lips to the inside of my thigh, less than inches away from my hot, molten center.

My legs began to shake when he turned his attention to the other leg, placing his soft lips just above my knee. He rose to his feet and cupped the side of my face in a manner that was more loving than lustful.

It confused me. It bewildered me. It left me wanting so much…
more…

"I can't stand you either," he said and I knew without a doubt he was lying.

"Your mouth just doesn't know when to stop. The shit that you say makes me want to strangle you," his voice was low and rough as he cupped my breasts. His thumbs rubbing my aching nipples.

Garrett leaned down so that his lips brushed against mine again. Our breath was coming in short, erratic bursts. "I don't particularly *like* you, Riley. But right now I want to *fuck you*," he growled. The soft lover from moments before was gone and in his place was a ferocity that unfurled a wet heat deep in my belly.

My fingers curled into his hair and I pulled with enough force to make him wince. "You're an asshole," I whispered, not trusting my voice at the moment. Garrett emitted a low groan as I yanked on his hair again. I bit his bottom lip, pulling it into my mouth.

"And I *want* you to fuck me. I want to remember it this time," I said raggedly. Garrett gripped the back of my head, holding me in place as his mouth slammed down on mine. Any pretense at gentleness was lost in the unbridled fury of our need. I *hated* him. I told myself this over and over as our mouths assaulted each other, bruising and tearing as we ate each other alive.

He made me want to rip my hair out. But goddamn it, I wanted to taste every single inch of him. And I knew by the frantic way he touched me that he felt the same way.

There was no more talking. No more excuses to stop. There was only Garrett and me and the sounds of flesh pressing together and noisy, desperate breathing. In a matter of seconds, I had Garrett's shirt joining mine on the floor, followed by his jeans. Our mouths were fused together and our hands sought to explore every part of each other.

Garrett palmed my butt cheeks and hoisted me up so that I had to wrap my legs around his waist. The barrier of his thin boxer briefs was all that separated two very important parts of our anatomy. I wiggled, just slightly and he groaned low and deep in the back of his throat.

I wiggled my hips again, grinning against his mouth, feeling powerful in the way I affected him. Damien had never made me feel like I was the one with all the power. Our lovemaking was always calm and controlled and done with the intent of one, never both, of us getting off.

I had always thought it beautiful, the way it was supposed to be. But right now, with Garrett fitted between my legs, his mouth sucking, biting, loving every bit of skin he could reach, I knew the real beauty was in the surrender. Both of us giving up control to the other. It was a perfect expression of trust. Woah, when had I decided to trust Garrett? And when had he laid his at my feet?

Garrett sat down on my bed and I straddled his lap, rocking into him, wanting to appease the ache that threatened to blow me a part. I pulled my mouth away from his swollen lips and I threaded my fingers through his hair, pulling it back away from his face. I gazed down at his heavy lidded eyes blurred this time by lust rather than drugs. The straight length of his nose, the sharpness of his jaw, the tiny freckle under his left ear. Just a few months ago I would have told you that Garrett Bellows may be attractive in his own way but most definitely not my type.

But now…well…now was another story.

I was feeling entirely too mushy. I wasn't looking for some sort of *Titanic* moment here. I was no fucking Rose and Garrett was most certainly not my Jack Dawson!

I had been excited for the change. Ready to do something reckless, something dangerous. But this was bordering on too much. And when things got hard, it was in my nature to shut them down. Decisively.

So I leaned down and bit his lip a bit more aggressively than Garrett was expecting.

"Ouch!" he yelped, pulling back with a jerk, his finger going to his mouth. Shit, I had drawn blood. That's right! I'm one mean ass chick!

"What the hell, Riley?" he asked in genuine bewilderment.

"If I wanted soft and gentle, I sure as hell wouldn't have asked you to come home with me," I said harshly. I couldn't get a handle on the conflicting emotions bubbling just under the surface. So what do I do? I pulled out the bitch card. When in doubt resort to what you're good at.

Garrett's eyes, which moments ago had been smoldering and capable of causing a level ten combustion, became so cold I thought I'd suffer from some serious frostbite.

"Are we back to this then?" he asked, his voice breaking just enough to know he was feeling a lot more than anger.

I tried to get off his lap but his hands clamped down on my hips, holding me in place. His fingers dug into my skin and I wondered whether I'd have tiny little bruises to remind me of how once again I was treating this guy like crap.

But try as I might I couldn't stop. "I thought this is what you wanted," I said icily, reaching down between us to squeeze the part of him that was still hard and ready for me. Garrett moved his hand to wrap around my wrist and yanked me away.

"No, what I wanted was a girl who could set aside her fucked up perceptions for just one night. The girl who could let go and be something she *wanted* to be rather than who she thought she *needed* to be," Garrett snarled, his jaw clenched and angry.

He lifted me off his lap and set me down on the bed. He picked his jeans up off the floor and shoved his legs through them, his rage barely suppressed. So perfect time to throw some gasoline on the fire, right?

"I would think a guy like you would be used to a girl just wanting him for a fuck," I taunted. God, what was wrong with me? Why was I saying this stuff?

Garrett's back went ramrod straight, he was still turned away as he put his shirt on. I watched in lavicious interest as it fell down and molded to his back and narrow shoulders. I was some sick kind of messed up. Here I was, stomping all over his fragile male ego yet again, but I couldn't stop ogling him like a piece of meat.

Garrett put his hands through his hair and he seemed to be getting it together. He had to be experiencing a major case of blue balls. If he felt half the ache that I did between my legs than he was in some serious discomfort.

Garrett pulled his keys out of his pocket and turned his head so I could just make out his profile. "Bye, Riley," he said and then he left my room, closing the door quietly behind him.

I sat there for a long time, staring at the door. And for once, I didn't have a way to justify my actions. Not when they had been completely and totally wrong. And wrong was not a good color on me.

Chapter 11

"So Garrett came back to the apartment last night," Vivian was saying, causing me to choke on my bagel. Maysie leaned over and thumped me on the back, dislodging the bread from my windpipe. No sense in throwing up all over the table, even if my friend's out of the blue statement had me wanting to spew chunks Exorcist style.

The name *Garrett Bellows* had given my upchuck reflex a serious workout the last few weeks. I hadn't seen him since sex disaster number two. Generation Rejects had played at Barton's a few times, but thankfully my shifts hadn't coincided with any of their gigs.

Maysie had invited me to the dozens of parties that had been thrown but I turned down each and every one. My need to walk on the wild side was definitely over.

The morning after Garrett's dramatic exit I had woken up pissed. At Garrett of course. Because it was easy to find fault in his behavior and much harder to place blame on myself. Why did he have to make it into something that it wasn't? Hadn't I made my intentions perfectly clear? What was the problem? When had we ever pretended to be good for each other? When had we decided to make sex into something more than lust?

Because I missed *that* meeting. Last I had checked, Garrett was still a boy who barely tolerated me. Who couldn't function on the same level as the rest of us. This was the guy who didn't give a toss about anything unless it was a pair of boobs or a bowl pack of weed.

So when did he become the whiny girl in this scenario? I didn't like feeling guilty. It irritated me. So I refused to feel that way.

Ah hell, I still felt guilty. Even if it was laced with a healthy dose of mortified anger at having been rejected with such finality.

Who cares about Garrett Bellows? I sure didn't. Nope, not Riley Walker.

Riley Walker had bigger and better things to worry about. Like my internship. I was finally shadowing a reporter and was being allowed my very own byline.

That was cause for celebration.

Right?

So why wasn't I happier about it?

"Really? Did you guys all hang out or something?" Maysie asked, shoving a cream puff in her mouth. My best friend had a serious addiction to the Cup and Crumb's cream puffs. I think half of the coffee shop's profit margin lay in Maysie Ardin's frequent purchase of those chocolate covered pastries.

Vivian shook her head. "No, you're missing my point here. Garrett came back to the apartment," she paused for dramatic affect, making sure we were paying attention. I rolled my eyes.

"With Gracie! Can you believe it? Miss 'I will never hook up with a townie,'" Vivian giggled and bile tickled the back of my throat.

Maysie gasped. "Did they hook up?" she asked. Vivian waggled her eyebrows.

"Well, why else would he accompany a very drunk Gracie home and then disappear into her bedroom. He was still there this morning, his van was out front when I left!" Vivian exclaimed excitedly.

Shit, it had happened. Gracie and I had now both been biblically acquainted with the same penis. The thought was utterly horrible.

"He sure has a thing for drunk girls," I mumbled under my breath.

"Huh?" Vivian asked, looking at me with confusion. Maysie's

eyes were sympathetic as she watched me hurry through my breakfast so I could get far away from this conversation.

"I've got to get to class," I said in a rush, finishing off my coffee. "I'll see you guys later."

"Wait, Riley," Maysie called out, hurrying after me. I slowed down but didn't stop. We had been tiptoeing around the Garrett shaped elephant in the room for a while now but I knew that my effective evasiveness was at an end.

"Are we ever going to talk about what happened? With you and Garrett I mean. Jordan has tried to find out but Garrett is pretty tight lipped about the whole thing. I had hoped for a bit more information from my best friend. When did we stop telling each other everything?" she asked and I knew my refusal to confide hurt her. I was doing a bang up job of making the people around me feel like crap lately.

I let out a deep sigh. "What's there to talk about? We hooked up. It was a huge mistake. I feel like an idiot about it. Let's just chalk it up to very bad decision making and leave it at that," I said tiredly. Maysie looked unconvinced.

"That's it? Really?" she asked incredulously.

"Yep, really," I said firmly, thankful to see the English building in front of me that promised my sweet escape from this discussion.

"Bullshit. If that's all there is to it than explain why that chip on your shoulder has grown into a crater. You're almost bitchier than you were post Damien. What went down between you two after Benny's? Garrett's been beyond weird and you're going apocalyptic every time I leave my shoes in the living room," she said, eyeing me closely.

"Well, shoes belong in the closet, not in the middle of the floor. It's a safety issue, Mays," I remarked dryly. Maysie made a clucking noise that was a clear indicator she was ready to throttle me.

"And it doesn't bother you that he quite possibly hooked up with our friend? Because if it were me, I'd be seeing red about now," Maysie pushed. She was being relentless and I guess I deserved it. If the tables were turned I'd chip away until I got the information I wanted. Our friendship was merciless like that.

I drew myself up and squared my shoulders. "Sex does not equal ownership, Maysie. Garrett is not a guy I want in my life. To say we are different is a massive understatement. And yes, it grosses me out that he jumped from me to her, but I can't stop him. He's free to do whatever and whomever he wants," I said harshly.

"Riley," Maysie started but closed her mouth. Her eyes grew cold as she looked over my shoulder. I felt his presence before he said a word. My body had honed into him in over a year of intimate familiarity.

"Hey girls," Damien piped up, standing beside us. I smiled at my ex-boyfriend in a manner devoid of my former bitterness. When had I forgiven the heartache? When had he become nothing more than a memory? At some point, I had let him go and it was both freeing and startling.

Because I knew there was only one reason Damien Green had lost his hold on my heart.

"Hey," I said back. I turned back to my roommate who seemed confused by my civil greeting to the boy I had vowed to never speak to again. "I'll talk to you later, okay?" I said. Maysie nodded, looking unhappy and I could understand why.

"Thank you for looking out for me," I told her and then I hugged her. Maysie blinked in surprise when I released her, astounded by my display of affection.

"Always, Ri," she said sincerely. I walked toward my class feeling just a little bit better.

"Glad to see that smile again," Damien said as we headed in the same direction. I gave him a sideways look.

"Don't, Damien. Seriously, it's not necessary," I said. Damien chuckled, as if he tickled by my coldness.

"But I think it *is* necessary. Because one day, Riley, you'll understand how sorry I am for screwing everything up. You and me, we make sense. We work. I didn't get that until it was too late. And I'm prepared to do whatever it takes to make you see I'm genuine," Damien grabbed my hand to stop me.

"And Jaz didn't make sense, I guess," I snipped, aware that I sounded like the jealous ex that I wasn't. Because I *wasn't* jealous of whatever he had done with Jaz. I just thought the whole thing a miserable waste of emotional energy.

Damien tensed up. "She was a mistake. I just thought..." he cleared his throat and tried again. "I thought she pretty, okay. I wanted to see if what I felt for her would be more than what I felt for you. Because you and I had gotten to that point where we were just coasting. It was too comfortable. Too routine. Weren't you bored, Riley?" he asked me and I wanted to yell that *no* I hadn't been bored. But I knew that would be a lie.

Because he had been right to dump me. We were boring together. Who wants a relationship based on the fact that we both liked to recycle our plastics? At one time that might have been enough, but I was starting to think that wasn't an option anymore.

When I didn't say anything, Damien rushed on. "But Jaz wasn't *you*, Riley. And I knew then that I was stupid. Because comfortable isn't a bad thing. "

Wow, someone give this guy the medal for the most un-romantic sentiment ever!

Even though he meant for his words to be sweet they just made me depressed. Not once did he say that I was beautiful and he couldn't stay away from me. No, Damien's idea of romance was to let me know that boring was *good enough*.

Well it wasn't for me.

"I have to go," I said, walking around him.

"I HAVE the hangover from hell! Shoot me now!" Gracie groaned, sinking into the seat beside me. She rubbed her temples and cringed at the noise level in the commons. I took a bite of my hamburger, ketchup squeezing out from the sides and plopping down on my plate. Gracie's face went a little green.

"God, your food is going to make me puke," she whined as I wiped my face. I shrugged, not feeling remotely sympathetic.

"Why do you keep drinking yourself into this state? You'd think you would have learned around twenty hangovers ago," I pointed out, purposefully taking a huge bite of my burger and chewing loudly.

"You're sadistic, Riley. You know that?" Gracie complained, dropping her head to the table. Maysie wasn't out of class yet so it was just me and my fellow Garrett humper. This had the makings of fabulous written all over it.

"Rough night?" I asked. Okay, I was going to dig. I couldn't help myself. I wanted to know what exactly was going on with her and Garrett. It was driving me crazy *not* knowing.

"You have no idea," she whispered. I took pity on her and fished out two ibuprophen from my bag and handed them to her with my bottle of water.

"Take these and call me in the morning, " I directed, nudging her arm with the bottle. Gracie uncapped the water and drank it all in one gulp. She gave me a weak smile in thanks.

"Seriously though, Gracie, I think it might be time to reevaluate your social life," I said, putting the empty bottle on my tray. Gracie nodded in agreement.

"I think you might be right. Because I never want to drink again," she swore and I looked at her knowingly. Because come tonight, her earlier convictions would go right out the window. My good buddy was one step away from a Lindsey Lohan level catastrophe. I had always given Maysie shit for the way she partied but she had nothing on Gracie Cook.

And Gracie was a small girl. She couldn't weigh more than a hundred pounds soaking wet. She was wreaking havoc on her poor body. She'd have liver failure by the time she was thirty at this rate.

"Enough is enough, girl. You're going to kill yourself if you keep it up. We're meant to have more blood than alcohol in our system. You get that, right?" I asked caustically.

Gracie frowned. "Ha, ha. Yes, Miss Smarty-pants, I'm aware. I'm just having fun," she said defensively.

I frowned back. "Having fun doesn't involve frequent bouts of vomiting," I replied sagely.

Gracie didn't respond and instead put her head back on the table. Maybe now wasn't the time to niggle her for details about her night with Garrett.

Whatever.

"I hear you had an overnight guest last night," I said carefully. Gracie didn't lift her head but her brow furrowed as though confused. And then her forehead smoothed and she smiled, looking a bit more alive.

"Oh, you mean the guitar god himself. Yeah, he helped me get home," she said dreamily and then she looked sheepish. "He slept on my floor because he said he was afraid I'd stop breathing or something," she admitted and I felt myself practically melt in relief.

"So no booty call?" I asked, needed the clarification.

Gracie groaned again. "No, I was too busy being a drunken idiot. I finally get the guy back to my place and I pass out. He'll never look at me twice again!" she grumbled. I had to hide the satisfied smile that threatened to spread across my face.

"That's okay, I'm sure there will be plenty more where he came from," I said.

Gracie grimaced. "True, but there's something different about Garrett, don't you think? I mean who cares if he's a townie who only plays music for a living? Look at him! Those abs make you forget that he's sort of a loser."

I felt suddenly and irrationally angry.

"*That* loser just spent the entire night making sure you didn't Jimi Hendrix. So maybe you should be more appreciative," I told her harshly.

Gracie frowned at me, obviously trying to figure out why I had put on the Garrett cheerleading uniform. I wish I had just bitten my tongue and kept quiet.

"There be my bitches!" Maysie said, sitting down in one of the free chairs. She looked over at Gracie whose face was now burrowed in her arms. "What's up with her?" she asked me.

"What do you think? Possible alcohol poisoning with a side of irresponsible choices," I laughed. Maysie laughed too, though I could tell she was just as concerned as I was about Gracie. The time was quickly approaching when laughing about it wouldn't be an option. Something more serious would have to be done.

Maysie and I ate in silence and I was pretty sure Gracie had fallen asleep. If she started snoring I was going to have to smack her. "Do you have to work tonight?" Maysie asked me as we finished up. She reached over and shook Gracie's shoulder.

Our friend jolted awake, her eyes bleary. "Time to head to class, Gracie," Maysie said kindly. Gracie wiped her mouth and rubbed her eyes.

"I'm gonna head home. I can't do class right now. See you later," she said, grabbing her purse and heading out to the quad.

"Something's got to be done, Mays. I'm actually worried about her," I said, following Maysie to dump our trash. Maysie nodded.

"Yeah, Vivian and I have been talking about this a lot actually. Vivian said she's gonna call Gracie's older sister about it," she admitted. I was glad to hear that something was being done. But I was also self-aware enough to realize that news expunged my feelings of responsibility about the situation. And that was extremely selfish.

Outside, the October air was cool but the sun was shining brightly. Midterms were just around the corner. I figured I'd ace them like I always did. Because doing well in school was one thing I still had going for me.

"So anyway, you didn't answer me. Are you working tonight?" Maysie asked, pulling out a cigarette and lighting it.

"Uh yeah, I go in at five. I thought you quit," I scolded, glaring at the offending object dangling between her fingers. Maysie rolled her eyes.

"You're as bad as Jordan," she grumped but dropped the cigarette on the ground and stomped it out.

"Just trying to do my part in reducing your risk for lung cancer. You'll thank me when you don't have to drag an oxygen tank around," I said.

"Yeah, yeah. Me and my non-existent iron lung will be eternally in your debt," she said with just a small bit of sarcasm.

"So why the interest in my work schedule?" I asked her, pulling out my phone to check the time. I had twenty minutes until senior symposium.

"Oh, because Generation Rejects are playing at Barton's tonight. Just wondered if you'd be around for it," she explained, her eyes saying more than her words. She was worried about my being in the same room as Garrett. Sheesh, when had my life become an episode of The Young and The Restless?

I was fully capable of being in the same room as the guy I almost had a romantic interlude with before being publically dissed. The same guy who had most likely seen the dimple in my butt cheek. What was troublesome about that?

"I'll be there. At least I know it'll be busy and I can make some decent tips. It's been dead lately," I said, avoiding the discussion I knew she wanted to have. Clearly our roundtable conversation about this very thing that morning hadn't been enough for her. She needed to beat it like a dead horse.

"Oh, well that's good," she said and then surprisingly didn't say anything else.

"Yeah, it is. Gotta go," I said, making a hasty retreat. My afternoon was now planned out. First class then home to prepare for a night showing Mr. Thinks He's Hot Shit On The Guitar that I really didn't give a crap about him.

The problem was I was beginning to forget who I was supposed to be convincing. Him or myself.

Chapter 12

"**A**ND this one is dedicated to all of the bitches who love us. You know who you are!" Cole screamed into the mic, pointing at the girls clamoring at his feet for a moment of his attention. I think I threw up in my mouth a little.

"He really is a cocky bastard, isn't he?" I asked Vivian, who was sipping on her rum and Coke at the bar, watching her on again, off again bed buddy thrust his pelvis seductively. At least I think it was meant to be seductive. Personally I thought he looked as though he had a bad case of crabs.

Vivian shrugged a shoulder and swirled the tiny straw around in the ice. She seemed completely unconcerned by the way the man who frequently screwed her brains out make a spectacle of rounding up the next warm body.

But I knew the whole thing bugged her. Vivian was a strong, take no bullshit kind of woman. Which is why this whole situation between her and Cole was extremely perplexing. But I wasn't one to dwell too long on someone else's problems. Not when two of mine were in the same room tonight and that made me all sorts of twitchy.

Damien had officially blown off all of Jaz's advances. I knew this because every time she had tried to approach him this evening, she had been politely but coldly rebuffed. The backstabbing skank face had looked ready to bust a gasket. And yes, I loved it. If I could have bought tickets and a tub of popcorn,

I'd have been front and center for Jaz's abject humiliation.

But while Damien had jumped off the rebound train, he was clearly trying to reboard the Riley wagon. He was sniffing so hard around my skirt that I wondered whether I'd need to have him surgically removed. And this did nothing for any semblance of a good mood.

Because with every one of my ex's overtures, I felt the cold, dispassionately watchful eyes of the lead guitarist of Generation Rejects. He bore holes in my back. While I worked, he played his gig and there was a gritty edge to his performance tonight.

I was no music connoisseur but even I could hear the frenetic energy in the way he played tonight. He had already broken two strings during the set by his angry ferocity. And I knew the reason for his super happy good mood lay entirely on my I-Swear-I-Don't-Give-A-Damn shoulders.

"I married the ketchups for you, Ri," Damien said with a hesitant smile, coming into my section to hand me several bottles of condiments to put on the tables. When we were dating we routinely helped each other finish up our closing tasks. It was as familiar as apple pie. But now, there was something desperate about it. And I really wish he'd back off. He wasn't helping the fog in my head at all. In fact, Damien Green was stirring it into a thick pea soup.

There was a screech as Garrett hit a wrong note and my head snapped to the stage. Even from this distance, I could see the scowl etched on his face as he looked down at his instrument. Jordan frowned but didn't miss a beat on the drums and Cole sang on, as though the massive screw up hadn't happened at all.

Garrett's head came up and his eyes fastened to mine. I swallowed thickly and then forced myself to look away. Damien was already sweeping under my tables.

"You don't have to do that," I said, holding my hand out so I could take the broom from him. Damien's eyes were shy as he pushed his glasses up his nose.

"It's not a problem, I like doing things for you, Riley," he said, having to yell over the commotion of the song being played on the stage behind us.

Okay, enough was enough. I made a sound of irritation and snatched the broom from his hands. "Jeesh, Damien, lay it on a little thicker, why don'tcha," I said nastily. Damien blinked at me, as though shocked by my annoyance. Which proved how little he truly knew me. After over a year together, he should have anticipated my bitter response.

"I'm just trying to help." He sounded so wounded and that just made me want to smack him.

I laughed without humor. "Give me a freaking break, Damien. You lost the right to play the helpful do-gooder when you dumped me. So stop it. I don't have the time or patience for your contrite BS," I threw at him.

Damien grabbed my hand and I tried to pull away. He gripped me tightly making escape impossible and I widened my eyes in surprise. "I've told you I made a mistake. I've made it clear I want you back. We were good together, Ri. Perfect. Stop being so stubborn and let me make it up to you."

I opened my mouth to say something. I wasn't entirely sure what would come off my tongue. My mind was a mess of barely firing synapses. But then, as though saved by the hands of fate themselves, my phone buzzed in my pocket.

I pulled it out and saw my mother's name flashing across the screen and dread instantly uncoiled in my belly. Why would she be calling me this time of night?

"I've got to take this…I've…" my words trailed off and I put the phone to my ear, hurrying toward the back of the restaurant.

"Hold on, Mom," I said breathlessly after I answered it. I rushed past the stage and my eyes inadvertently met Garrett's. They were on a break between songs, Cole was working the crowd and Garrett stood there, as he always did, his guitar around his neck, his hand rubbing up and down the fret board as he waited to play.

His face that had been pinched and closed off changed suddenly when he took in my anxious expression. I knew I looked worried. Because there was no reason for my mom to call unless there was something I *should* be worrying about. Nighttime calls past ten from your parents never heralded good news.

119

Garrett recognized something was wrong and his eyes changed just slightly enough for me to see that. I couldn't think about him, or Damien, anything else. I pushed through the swinging doors into the kitchen and practically ran to the smoking area. Thankfully most of the kitchen staff was already gone for the night so I was alone.

"Mom, you still there?" I asked, more than a little out of breath.

"Riley," my mother's broken sob on the other end had my knees buckling underneath me. Shit, this was bad.

"What is it?" I asked, my voice barely above a whisper.

"It's your dad," was all she said and it felt like my heart had frozen in my chest. My face flushed hot and my fingers went numb.

"Is Dad all right?" I asked stupidly. Of course he wasn't all right! Why else would my mother be calling me at a quarter till twelve on a Saturday night crying? Get with it, Riley!

My mom took a shuddering breath. "Dad's in the hospital. He's had a heart attack," she said haltingly and I felt my world fade to black. Spots danced in front of my eyes and I found it hard to focus.

"What? A heart attack? That makes no sense! Dad's so healthy he makes healthy people look bad!" I said, knowing I was bordering on hysterical. But this was every child's worst nightmare. My dad was an ox. My Mr. T and Arnold Schwarzenegger all mushed together in a peace loving hippie package. He was bigger than life and now my mom was telling me that the man who I had hailed as my own personal hero my entire life was in fact very, very mortal.

"Sure he is but that doesn't mean he doesn't have his vices like everyone else. I've been on him to quit eating those damn greasy hamburgers at Sal's. But he swore he exercised enough and drank his wheat germ tea so he'd be fine. Stupid ass man!" I was so taken aback by my mom's use of curse words that I didn't respond immediately. My mother never, and I mean *never* cussed. This was almost as scary as the fact that my dad was in the hospital.

"Will he…I mean, is he going to…" I couldn't force myself to finish the statement. I just couldn't ask my mother whether my dad was going to live or die. Somehow putting it into words would give it power. Making all of this way too real.

My mom took another deep breath, as though trying to collect herself. "I don't know, Ri. I just don't know. But you need to get here as soon as possible. I just don't know…" she stopped talking and I could hear the sound of her quiet sobbing.

My hands were shaking and my palms were wet. The phone slipped out of my hands and when I bent to pick it up another hand reached out to get to it first. I blinked a few times, not understanding why Garrett was outside, stood beside me, with a look on his face that was both bleak and sad.

I took the phone from him and turned my back. I couldn't deal with him right now. Definitely not right now. "I'm leaving work. I'll be there as soon as I can. Is Gavin there? What about Fliss?" I asked.

"Yes, Gavin's with me at the hospital and Felicity will be here in the morning. Sam is staying behind with the girls. He'll come… later…if he has to…oh God!" My mom started to cry again and I pressed the heel of my hand against my eye so I wouldn't join her. It would do no good to fall apart. I was the strong one. The one who held everyone else together. I could do this.

"It's okay, Mom. Dad will be just fine. I'll be there soon," I promised, guaranteeing something I wasn't sure was the truth. Did that make me a liar?

My mom seemed to pull herself together a bit. "Okay, baby girl. But drive carefully. Please," she ended tiredly. I reassured her I'd be safe and hung up.

I stood there for a long time, staring out into the darkened lot behind Barton's. I needed to get home. I had to pack. I had to make a bazillion calls letting my professors and my internship and the Barton's manager, Moore, know that I'd be gone. I didn't even know how long I'd be home. And just like that my world imploded.

I fell to my knees and smashed my fists into the cold, hard concrete. I let out a deep, guttural yell and felt my body tremble under the stress of the last few minutes. I didn't cry though. For some strange reason, my tear ducts felt empty and dry.

Arms came around me, strong hands rubbing my arms as I struggled to breathe around the pain in my chest. "Let it out, Riley," Garrett said softly into my hair as he pressed his cheek against the back of my head.

I held myself rigid in his embrace, not letting myself give into the urge to lose it. Even though he was encouraging me to let him pick up my pieces, I wouldn't do it. I just couldn't.

I got to my feet and pulled out from his arms. My hands still shook and I shoved them into my pockets. "Aren't you supposed to be playing?" I asked, cringing at the way my words wobbled.

Garrett looked at me shrewdly, not put off in the least by my attempts to change the subject. "What happened?" he asked, ignoring my question.

I was tempted to tell him it was none of his business. That he should get back to playing music and pretending like he didn't care about anything. Because that's what he was good at after all.

But I didn't. Perhaps it was the knowing sympathy on his face that was surprisingly not condescending. The dull awareness in his eyes that spoke of some understanding of pain that I didn't know he possessed. Whatever it was, I found myself telling him exactly what my mom had just told me.

"My dad had a heart attack. She doesn't know…" I tried to steady myself to say what I truly feared. But Garrett said it for me, saving me from voicing the very thing that scared me the most.

"If he's going to make it," he said steadily. Our eyes met and I nodded.

"I've got to get back to the apartment and pack. I have to head out…tonight. I need to get home," I said, feeling the surge of panic over take me.

"And where's home?" Garrett asked.

"Maryland. About four and a half hours away," I said, already calculating the time and distance in my head. At this rate, I wouldn't make it to the hospital before five in the morning. The night spread out before me, long and lonely. Crap, I started shaking even harder.

"I'll drive you," Garrett said suddenly and that made me stop shaking and look at him as though he had lost his mind.

"I have a car, I've had my license for a few years now, you know," I said, appreciating the opportunity to lob a bit of my normal snark. It made me feel normal, capable.

Garrett's mouth raised into a small smile. "Yes, I'm aware, but you're in no condition to drive right now. Not after getting that kind of news," he said firmly, as though he dared me to argue with him.

Well argue with him I would.

"You can't do that. That's just ridiculous. You're in the middle of a gig. You and me…well, we're not even friends. I can't expect you to drive me to Maryland in the middle of the night," I said stupidly, really not grasping why he would offer such a thing. It made absolutely no sense at all. And my brain was so bogged down with a million other worries that this new complication in the ever-evolving Garrett and Riley saga was the last thing I had the patience for.

Garrett rolled his eyes. Yes, he actually rolled his eyes at me. "Stop it, Riley. We may not be 'friends' but that doesn't mean I can stand here and watch you drive off knowing what you have to face when you get there. Knowing how you'll be going over every awful scenario in your head for the entire drive. Trying to prepare yourself for the worst but terrified to expect the best," his voice was strained and his eyes became glassy. He was speaking from experience. And my heart, already breaking, broke a little bit more at the pain on his face.

"So let me do this for you. Please," he said gently. And I was too tired to put up any further resistance. I only nodded and went to drop my keys in his waiting palm. Then I hesitated.

"You haven't been drinking or smoking have you? Because I promised my mom I would get there in one piece," I said seriously, narrowing my eyes.

Garrett wrapped his fingers around my hand that held the keys. His gaze was unwavering as he answered me. "I would *never* risk your life like that. I would rather die then get behind the wheel under the influence. Trust me when I say you have nothing to worry about where that is concerned." His words were flinty hard and there was more to his staunch testament than I knew. But I couldn't think about it.

Right now I needed to get to Maryland.

"And the gig?" I asked, wanting to give him one last chance to bow out of from knight in shining armor duty.

Garrett peeled my fingers apart and took my keys, nudging me through the kitchen doors so I could get my purse and jacket.

"Fuck the gig. Let's get you to your dad," he said resolutely. And if I could have, I would have smiled.

Chapter 13

THE first hour into the drive passed with minimal conversation. It was already almost one in the morning. I was tired. I was heartsick. And I was almost delusional with worry. Garrett didn't attempt to pull me into meaningless chatter and for that I was grateful. I didn't have it in me to talk about the fucking weather or what I thought of the Greenhouse Effect.

I had gone to the apartment, packed up the bare essentials, sent a text to Maysie and then climbed into my car, with Garrett behind the wheel. It was a testament to how out of whack I was that I permitted anyone, besides myself and Maysie to drive my beloved Volvo. It was almost fifteen years old; the rust colored paint chipped and was slowly disappearing. I only had a tape deck and a radio that picked up just one or two stations. But I had bought the clunker with my own money. It was completely and totally mine and because of that I was over the top possessive about it.

But Garrett treated it as smoothly as though he were driving a Mercedes and for that he gained about a thousand cool points.

Somewhere outside of Richmond, I broke the silence. Because I was going crazy with my own thoughts. "Maysie told me you guys were going on tour again," I said, glancing at him out of my peripheral.

Garrett didn't take his eyes off the road, but I saw the satisfied smile dance on his lips. "Yeah. Josh, Mitch's cousin who helped us set up the tour over the summer has us lined up to for a cross-country promotional thing. He's been slinging out our demo to a bunch of radio stations and a few of the smaller ones have started putting us into rotation. It's all for the exposure, you know," Garrett explained and despite the knots in my gut, I couldn't help but be taken aback by the excitement on his face. I couldn't recall a time he *ever* seemed pumped about anything.

Even when Garrett played music, he oozed this laid back, unconcerned vibe. As though he would do the same thing in his sleep. So seeing this side to him, a side that showed enthusiasm and…well…purpose, was startling. And even in my confused mind, I could admit it was appealing.

The truth was I was beginning to learn there was *a lot* appealing about the man sitting beside me.

"Wow, that's awesome," I said tiredly. I meant it, really, but Garrett looked at me warily, as though looking for the punch line.

"Thanks," he said and then fell silent. And this time, the quiet between us was uneasy.

"I really do appreciate you taking me tonight. You were right, I would never have been able to drive myself," I said. Garrett's eyes were once again trained on the road and I noticed the tightening of his jaw, as though he were uncomfortable with my gratitude. Yeah, I get that he hadn't seen a whole lot of the nice, genial Riley Walker. I was so accustomed to being sarcastic and cutting that genuine pleasantness was like a sucker punch to the jaw. It left you wondering where the hell the fist came from.

"Like I said, I couldn't let you drive all the way home in the state you're in," he said shortly.

"You seem to speak from some kind of experience," I hedged, not knowing how my dig for information would be greeted.

Garrett started to fiddle with my radio, trying to find some music to fill the awkward tension that took over the interior of my car. "Yeah, well, I've been there. I get it," he explained without really explaining anything at all.

I took in his sloppy disheveled appearance. His blue, button down shirt gaped open, his muscular chest on proud display. His shoulder length hair was more than a little wild and I was hit

126

with a sudden surge of memory. I remember how it felt that first night to put run my fingers through it. I saw with sudden clarity the way his face looked as he hovered above me, his hair hanging down around his face. Oh God, I finally remembered the aching tenderness in his eyes as he kissed every inch of my face.

I shook my head, ridding myself of those unwanted memories. "Can you tell me how you *get* it?" I asked carefully. Garrett gave up on trying to find anything on the radio and turned it off with a frustrated flick of his fingers.

He let out a loud and noisy sigh. The hand that came up to push his hair back off of his face shook slightly. "I lost both of my parents when I was a senior in high school. I remember the call that told me they were gone. It was like my world stopped and I couldn't understand how I could keep going without them," he said gruffly. He cleared his throat as though to dislodge the lump in his throat.

I blinked rapidly, feeling warmth flood my eyes. I had never bothered to understand how the loss of his parents had shaped the person he became.

Until now. Until I could see for myself the devastation of his loss.

"I'm so sorry," I said, my voice the barest hush of a whisper.

Garrett cleared his throat again and it seemed he had to take a moment to compose himself before saying more. "It was a drunk driver. They died on impact," he said and shot a look in my direction. "That's why I will *never* drive drunk or high. *Ever!*" he proclaimed emphatically, his eyes snapping.

Who would have thought Garrett Bellows had layers. That he was more than the stoned out guitarist with no thought to doing something more. But sitting in my darkened car, hearing him speak about losing his parents. Seeing the intensity of his misery, I forgot completely that here was a guy I had sworn I had nothing in common with. That he and I were opposites in every possible way.

But we weren't so different, Garrett and I. Because Garrett was a whole mess of layers and he had a depth that left me breathless.

"And I'm sorry about your dad," he finished and all of my

ridiculous romanticism about the man who sat beside me shooting down the darkened highway, popped like a soap bubble. The reality of why I was here, with him, in this car, came crashing down on my shoulders like a hundred ton weight.

"Thanks," I whispered so softly it was if all of my bones had dissolved.

My dad might die. Hell, he might be dead already, while I made the long, arduous trek to his bedside. What would I do if I never got to talk to him again? Never got to see his smile or hear him tell me teasingly to "buck up, Riley Boo?"

"How are things going at the newspaper?" Garrett asked me a little too loudly and I was wrenched from my depressing thoughts.

I blinked a few times and stared at him. "Huh?" I asked stupidly.

Garrett gripped the steering wheel so tightly I could see his knuckles turning white. His smile was forced but I appreciated the effort. "The newspaper. I'm not sure what you're doing there, just wanted to know how it's going," he said.

"It's good. Going good, I mean. I'm there for an internship. You know, to get my own byline so I can become the next Barbara Walters or something," I answered dryly.

"Ah, so you want to write for a newspaper. That sounds cool. I can see that. Good career choice," he remarked in a tone that was almost teasing.

"Oh, and why is that?" I asked, surprised at the subtle flirtation in my voice.

"Probably because you're the type of chick who takes the world by its balls and refuses to let go. Not saying it like it's a bad thing. It just makes me want to wear a cup when I'm around you," he stated and I had to laugh.

Yes, Garrett Bellows had made me laugh. Just when I thought my world was bottoming out, here he was, taking me toward an unknown future and he was making me freaking laugh. There was something pretty wonderful about that.

"I don't know if I should be flattered or completely insulted," I told him wryly.

Garrett's smile this time wasn't forced or strained. It didn't hold any twinge of sadness or regret. This smile was one hundred percent earthshattering. Shit, it's a good thing I hadn't seen it before or I would have locked him away and thrown away the key. Guys with smiles like that were lethal.

"Oh it's definitely a compliment," he said as his smile faded and he was once again focusing on the road. Our moment of levity drifting away into the darkness rushing past us.

"Maybe you should try to sleep. We've got another few hours and you'll need your rest," Garrett suggested. My eyes felt gritty with exhaustion and I should probably take him up on his suggestion but my mind was in chaos and I knew I would never be able to shut it off.

"Why don't you tell me about some of the places you'll be going on your tour. I think I'd rather hear about that," I said. Garrett looked surprised but then nodded.

"Sure. We're going to start off in Charlotte, North Carolina at this bar called Warner's." I listened Garrett go into detail about the upcoming Generation Rejects tour and I was able to forget, just for a moment, that I would be with my very sick father in a few short hours. I could pretend that we were just two people, getting to know each other.

And I realized then that Garrett had a way of making me forget the things that haunted me. He had done it after my break up with Damien and here he was, doing it again. There was something amazing in the way he gathered up my pieces without my ever expecting him to.

For two people whose only interactions were humiliating or drunkenly sexual, our easy candor was shocking. I had never expected that the one person I had declared to have no place in my life, to be my one great regret, to fit so perfectly into my existence that it was as though he had always been there.

"Do you want to go straight to the hospital or head to your parents house first?" Garrett asked as he pulled off the interstate at exit 26. He turned right onto Route 23 toward the small, seaside town of Port David.

I squinted as I tried to read the clock on my dashboard. My eyes were blurry from my lack of sleep. It was already five-thirty in the morning. Garrett had insisted we stop for something to eat, saying I needed to keep my energy up, thus adding another forty-five minutes onto our travel time. I had been irritated by the suggestion but was now glad to have a full stomach.

"I think we should go to my parents' first. I want to see if my brother and sister are there. Drop off my stuff," I said.

"Okay, lead the way," Garrett replied and I began to rattle off directions that took him through my sleepy hometown and out toward the coast. My parents owned a small house by the ocean. Once I had headed off to college, they had sold their larger house in town and bought the small bungalow on the beach. My parents loved getting up in the morning and drinking their tea on the sand as the sun came up.

My parents' lives completely revolved around each other. Even when I was a child I knew that despite their love for their kids, their first and greatest love was for each other. Their relationship was a reassurance. A reminder that good things happen to good people.

At least until now.

Now all I could think of was if my dad didn't make it, what would my mom do? How would she go on without the love of her life? Was it even possible to come back from losing the person you hung your moon on?

"Wow, this is awesome," Garrett said as he pulled in front of the small, yellow house with its white porch and wooden fence. The sun was just coming up and it was almost magical in the way it shimmered off the rolling waves.

"Yeah, it is," I agreed, getting my bag out of the back seat and climbing out of my car. I stretched and looked around at the tiny corner of the world my parents now called home. It was so *them*. From the multi-colored mailbox to the series of stone gnomes dotting the front garden. My mom's wind chimes hung from hooks along the porch and my dad had purchased a straw welcome mat with the Grateful Dead slogan "All in the Family."

I looked over at Garrett. He had his arms stretched out above his head and I knew he had to be as tired as I was. He had driven for the last four and a half hours without complaint. I knew he'd need to sleep before heading home to Bakersville. It was agreed he'd take my car back with him and I'd figure out getting back to school when the time came.

It was cold, particularly on the water like this. The air was crisp and clean and it helped to chase some of the cobwebs from my head.

"Come on," I said, inclining my head toward the house. Garrett took my bag from my hands and slung it over his shoulder. He followed me up to the porch.

The front door wasn't locked and I thought about chastising my mother for being so lax in security until I saw her hunched over form standing at the counter in the kitchen. Her dark head, with hair the same shade as mine, with the few wisps of grey that she refused to color was bowed down as she hastily wrote on a piece of paper. She was proud of her grey hair. Called them her victory stripes.

"Mom," I called out, holding the screen door open so Garrett could follow me in. My mother looked over her shoulder and the look of relief on her face at the sight of me hit me square in the chest.

"Riley Boo," she said and I could hear the bone deep tiredness in her voice. She crossed the small kitchen until I was wrapped in her arms, inhaling the familiar smell of her shampoo and her all-natural laundry detergent.

"Why aren't you at the hospital? How's Dad?" I asked, trying not to sound as panicked as I felt. Had something happened while I was on my way here? What if I was too late?

"Dad's the same. He's really out of it. He's had a bunch of tests and the doctors say he has a blockage. They are going to do some more tests to see if he needs surgery. I had to come home and get a few things and then I'm heading back. Gavin and Felicity are with him." My mom gave me a sad smile and touched my cheek.

"I'm coming back with you," I said, grabbing Mom's keys from her hand.

"Okay. That would be great. But aren't you going to introduce me to your friend first?" my mother asked, looking behind me to Garrett. I had almost forgotten he was still there, standing quietly off to the side while I spoke with my mom.

Garrett came forward and held out his hand to Mom, who took it in hers. She didn't shake it. She simply held it firmly between her palms. She was most likely trying to read his aura or something.

"I'm a friend of your daughter's. My name is Garrett Bellows, ma'am. I offered to drive her up here after she got your phone call. I didn't want her making the trip on her own," he said and I could tell his answer pleased my mother.

"That's very thoughtful of you, Garrett. Thank you so much for taking care of my Riley," she said genuinely. Her eyes went back and forth between us and I knew she was trying to work out exactly what our relationship was.

"It was my pleasure. But I'd best be getting back on the road. I know you both need to get to the hospital," Garrett said, already moving toward the door.

My mom stopped him. "You haven't slept tonight, have you, Garrett?" she asked. Garrett looked at me then back to my mom and shook his head.

"But that's okay. Nothing a little coffee can't cure. I'll be all right to get back to Bakersville," he assured her but my mother was shaking her head.

"Absolutely not, young man. You will stay here and get some sleep. Get something to eat and *then* you can get on the road. But I will not allow you to leave until those things are done first," she scolded him good naturedly but with a firmness that brooked no argument.

Garrett opened his mouth to protest but I cut him off. "Forget it, Garrett. Mom will shackle you to the bed if she has to. Just go take a load off. Get a few hours of sleep. Please. I know you're tired," I said.

Garrett seemed unsure but my mother took him by the arm and led him down the hallway.

Chapter 14

WALKING into the ICU, the first thing I was acutely aware of was the smell. God, hospitals reeked. The horrible scent of too much disinfectant and an overabundance of stress and grief stuck in the back of my throat. The waiting room was small, with a TV mounted to the wall playing CNN on mute. There were a few other people sat around looking as anxious as I felt. I briefly wondered what their story was.

My brother, Gavin, slept slumped over in a chair in the corner. He was going to wake up with a mean crick in his neck. My sister, Felicity, was furiously tapping away on her phone. I hadn't seen either of my siblings in months. We hadn't been particularly close growing up, primarily because they were both so much older than I was. But now, seeing the two of them, I felt nothing but relief that they were there. The thing about family is that push come to shove, they had your back. It was reassuring on such a basic level.

My mom gripped my hand as we approached Felicity. She looked up startled and then got to her feet to hug Mom. Felicity was like a mini-Mom. They were exactly the same height and build and my mother could easily pass for Felicity's older sister.

Which made sense, considering my mom and dad were kids barely out of high school when Mom first got pregnant with Gavin and then ten months later with Felicity. I didn't enter the picture until sixteen years later.

So I had essentially grown up an only child. By the time I was old enough to actually understand how nice it would be to have a sibling to share things with, they were both grown up and living their own lives.

Felicity turned and gave me her Mom-like smile and enfolded me in a hug. "They just took Dad somewhere for more tests. They wanted you to come find the head nurse on duty when you got back," Felicity told my mother.

"Why don't you take your sister to get something to eat. She hasn't eaten or slept at all," my mom directed Felicity, as though I were still a child. Felicity nodded and my mom buzzed the speaker to be let through the locked doors of the ICU.

"Come on, let's go to the cafeteria. The coffee's horrible, but you may find something worth eating," Felicity led me by the arm. I looked back at my brother who had started to snore. "Leave him. He's exhausted," Felicity said and I followed her to the elevator banks.

One burnt bagel and two very bad cups of coffee later, Felicity and I were back in the waiting room of the ICU. Mom hadn't come back out and we sat there, on pins and needles waiting for news. It was the most painful hour of my life.

The not knowing.

"How are Leslie and Julia?" I asked Felicity. Leslie was ten and Julia had just turned three. I didn't get to see my nieces nearly often enough, but I made sure never to miss a birthday or a Christmas. I was cool Auntie Riley, mostly because I lavished the two girls with gifts and ice cream. I was a ruthless child briber. But I intended to keep the title of greatest aunt ever at whatever the cost.

"They're great. Leslie has decided she wants to learn how to play the guitar. So Sam bought her an old beater from the thrift shop. We'll see how long the desire lasts. Julia will be starting a new pre-school after Christmas. She's already trying to read. We call her our little Einstein," Felicity said, beaming with pride.

"That's awesome. You have some great kids, Fliss," I said, giving her as much of a smile as I could muster.

"What about you? How's school? Mom said you were

interning at the local paper. That's pretty great, Ri," my sister commented.

"Yeah…" I trailed off as the doors to the ICU opened and my mom came into the waiting room. Both Felicity and myself got to our feet and my brother was instantly awake. He barely processed the fact that I was there; he was immediately by Mom's side.

Her face was ashen and she looked sick. "What is it, Mom?" Gavin asked her. My brother looked like he had aged ten years.

Mom griped his arm, as though she couldn't stand up on her own. "They're going to start prepping him for surgery. Your father has a total blockage of one of his coronary arteries. They need to go in and repair the damage. So now is the time to see him." My mom didn't need to say *while you can*. Because that was implied. Dad's situation was obviously very serious and I just wanted to curl into a ball and cry.

"Only one of you can go back at a time," my mom said. She was totally frazzled and I could see how tenuous her grip on things was. Gavin turned to me and motioned me toward the doors.

"You just got here, Riley. We've all seen him. Go on back," he urged with a sad smile. I squeezed my big brother's hand and buzzed to be let back.

Seeing your father hooked up to a million different tubes and wires with the constant drone of beeping and wining of monitors was like a swift kick to the head. It shatters any illusion that you may have that your parents are infallible. That they are beyond mortal trappings like sickness and death.

It reminds you that your parents are human. And I think that's the truest sign that you've passed from the innocence of adolescence to the shitfest of adulthood. I think I'd like to book my return ticket back to blissful ignorance, please.

He looked so small in the hospital bed. His skin was white and seemed completely devoid of color. Even his lips were pale and seemed to blend in with the pallor of his face. It was scary seeing him like that.

I sat down beside the bed and took his hand in mine. It seemed like such a stereotypical thing to do. To cry by his bedside and plead with him to pull through. I wasn't one for clichés in any form but right now it was the only thing I could do.

My dad's eyes fluttered open and he looked at me. "Hiya kiddo," he said, his voice hoarse and unused. He tried to smile but it was a weak imitation of what I was used to from him.

"Hiya, Dad. You sure do know how to make us worry about you. If you wanted the attention, couldn't you think of a better way to get it?" I teased even as my eyes welled up with tears.

My dad's fingers squeezed mine and I knew if he had the energy he would have laughed at my bad attempt at humor. "Give your old man a break. This was my excuse for a vacation. Otherwise your mom would have made me start painting the porch," he joked and I couldn't help but grin.

The fact that my dad's sense of humor was in tact was the biggest reassurance I could have. He seemed…well…like himself. I hadn't been sure what to expect and my head had gone instantly to every horrible scenario I could imagine. I had thought that he'd be a shell. Or that he wouldn't know who I was. That's what I get for watching way too much bad television.

"Well, we can't have that right? I think you've gotten out of the honey do list for the foreseeable future," I told him and he tried to laugh but ended up coughing, his face contorting painfully. I immediately felt horrible. Why did I have to make every serious situation a joke? My defense mechanisms majorly sucked.

"Sorry, Dad," I said, contrite. My dad looked at me, his eyes dull and starting to unfocus a bit as the exhaustion took over. Talking to me was obviously taking a lot out of him.

"Don't be. I'm just glad you're here. Things are always so much better when Riley Boo's around," he said, his words dropping to the barest whisper as his eyes drooped closed.

"Well I'm not going anywhere," I promised as my dad drifted in and out of sleep. I sat with him for almost an hour, dividing my attention between watching his chest rise and fall and staring at the numbers on the monitors wishing they made some sort of sense.

I must have drifted off because the feel of my dad's hand on the back of my head had me startling awake. I rubbed at my tired eyes as my exhausted brained struggled to remember where I was. I looked over at Dad and saw that he was awake even though his skin was sallow and there were dark circles underneath his eyes. His lips were dry and cracked and he looked horrible.

"You're tired, sweetheart. You should head back to the house and get some rest," my dad said in a strained whisper.

I shook my head. "I'm fine. Stop worrying about me," I chided. My dad tried to smile but it fell short. Instead he dropped his hand from my head back into his lap, where it lay limply.

"Riley, I just want you to know that I'm proud of the woman you've become. All your mom and I have ever wanted was for you to be successful and happy," my dad said and I could see the effort it took him to speak.

"Dad, I know. You don't need to tire yourself out by telling me stuff you've already told me a million times," I scolded teasingly, patting the back of his hand.

My dad frowned. "Humor your old man, please." I shut up and propped my elbows on the bed and watched him closely, agonizingly alert for any subtle change in him. My eyes darted to the monitors out of the corner of my eye as if I could understand what they were saying.

"Have a life that matters. A life with purpose. Find your own way but don't lose sight of the journey. Do this for me," my dad said softly and I hated the finality of his words. As though he were imparting his final goodbye. It made my heartache and my stomach knot up but I took those words inside me and swore I would live them.

I nodded, wiping the tears from my face, unable to say anything. My dad seemed satisfied and closed his eyes again. After a few minutes, his breathing evened out and I realized he had fallen back asleep.

Feeling emotionally spent, I got up and kissed my dad's cheek and went back out to the waiting room so that my brother could come back.

Each of us had our time with Dad and then it was time for him to be wheeled back for surgery. His cardiologist came out and talked with Mom and explained how the surgery would go.

I hate to admit that I barely listened. Mostly it was a bunch of medical mumbo jumbo that went right over my head.

All I could hear were my dad's words to me ringing in my ears. *Have a life that matters. A life with purpose.*

Felicity went outside to call her husband and kids. Gavin went with Mom to get a coffee. I was left in the waiting room staring at the wall. I thought about calling Garrett to see if he had gotten on the road, but I quickly realized I didn't even have his number.

I checked my texts messages and saw that I had a few from Maysie, one from Gracie and a missed call from Moore Pruitt, the general manager at Barton's. I sent a quick reply to Maysie and Gracie, letting them know what was going on with Dad. I figured Moore could wait until I knew more. I needed to send an email to my professors letting them know I'd be out for a few days. I also needed to call the newspaper to let them know about my absence. But all that could wait until later.

Until I knew how Dad's surgery went.

One hour turned into two. Two into three. I ate a horrible lunch of dried out hamburger and greasy fries. Gavin and I argued over what to watch on the TV. Felicity talked Mom into taking a walk on the nature trail behind the hospital.

But the minutes crawled by like years. It was by far the longest day of my life. And when the doctor finally came out to find us it was only four hours later.

My blood rushed through my ears and all I could hear was Dad had done well and was now in recovery. My knees buckled and I had to sit down in relief. Felicity started to cry and my mom's shoulders were shaking.

The doctor continued to talk about things they were going to be looking for and the fact that the next twenty-four hours were critical. But all I heard was my dad had gotten through his surgery all right.

The relief I felt in that statement couldn't be described in words.

Once we had time to process that Dad had pulled through, Mom insisted I head back to the house and get some rest.

"You look like you're about to fall over, Ri. We'll call you if we hear anything more," Gavin assured me.

I argued that I wanted to see Dad when he woke up but was reminded he would most likely be sleeping for a while and he wouldn't be allowed visitors until much later.

I needed to sleep, I was feeling almost slaphappy. So I took Mom's van keys and headed home.

I was surprised to find that my car was still in the driveway. I would have thought Garrett would have been headed back to Bakersville by now.

I went inside and found Garrett tying his shoes. He looked like he had just gotten out of the shower, his blond hair wet and slicked back from his face. It made him look younger somehow.

"Hey," he said softly as I came in. I dropped the keys into a bowl on the counter and practically collapsed into one of the kitchen chairs.

"Hey," I said tiredly, resting my head in my hand. Garrett finished tying his shoe and sat up.

"How's your dad?" he asked.

"He just got out of bypass surgery. He made it through but the next twenty-four hours will be critical," I parroted the doctor's words, feeling my exhaustion settle into my bones. I was about to collapse.

"You need to sleep. Come on," Garrett helped me to my feet and then did something that had I not been close to a coma, would have totally freaked me out. He reached down and swept me up in his arms. He carried me down the hallway to the spare bedroom where he had slept earlier.

He laid me down on the freshly made bed and with surprising tenderness, smoothed my hair away from my face and re-positioned the pillow under my head.

"I thought you would have left by now," I stated as Garrett started to take off my shoes and socks, placing them on the floor.

Garrett shrugged. "I didn't want to leave until I knew you were okay," he said matter a factly, as though it were an obvious answer.

I didn't know what to make of him and the way he had shown me in a hundred tiny ways that he cared. This person who had I had spent a good deal of time detesting, was in truth one of the most decent guys I had ever met. I had totally misjudged him.

"I'll let you rest. I really hope your dad is okay," Garrett said, getting to his feet.

I reached out and grabbed his hand before he could walk away. "Please don't leave. Not yet," I said with more feeling than I thought I was capable of in my exhausted state.

Garrett's brow furrowed but he sat back down on the bed. "Riley, you need to rest," he said more firmly.

I tugged his arm. "Just lie down with me for a little while," I pleaded. Yes, I was practically begging this guy who I had rejected at every turn, to cuddle with me. But I was an emotional mess right now and his company was something I craved.

Slowly, Garrett kicked off the shoes he had just put on and lay down beside me. I scootched over to make room on the double bed. Garrett stretched his arm above his head, his other arm laying awkwardly beside him as though he didn't know what to do with it.

I rolled onto my side and pressed my back into him and then he got the hint. He slid over and wrapped his arm around my waist. This spooning thing really was an uncomfortable business. You never knew what to do with your arms or legs. It took forever to find that spot where you felt like you weren't a human pretzel.

But when you found that spot, it was pure bliss. And when I found that spot with Garrett I never wanted to move again. Our bodies synched up and we sort of melted into each other. Garrett tucked my head under his chin and I felt warm and secure wrapped up in him like this.

"Will you be here when I wake up?" I asked almost fearfully. I couldn't figure out why it was so important for him to be here with me. But right now it was the most necessary thing in my world.

"I'll be here as long as you want me, Riley," he whispered, his breath stirring my hair. And that's all I needed to fall into a restful sleep.

Chapter 15

TRUE to his word, Garrett was still there when I woke up three hours later. I probably could have slept longer but my mind wouldn't let me rest that long. I sat up with a start, jolting Garrett awake with my sudden movement.

I reached over top of him to grab my phone; scared to death I had missed a call or a text from my mom or one of my siblings. I quickly checked but lay back down when I realized they hadn't tried to get a hold of me.

No news was good news, right?

I rolled onto my side and looked up at Garrett, feeling suddenly shy being in bed with him. I had seen him naked. He had been with me in the most intimate way possible (even if I still couldn't recall every detail) and here I was shy while lying in a bed together, fully clothed.

Garrett's fingers traced the line of my face until his palm came to rest against the thudding pulse at my throat. His hand was warm against my skin. "How'd you sleep?" he asked.

"Pretty good actually. At least you don't hog the bed," I said, nudging his leg over with mine.

"Yeah, I picked up pretty quickly after you fell asleep that you like your space. Doesn't leave a guy much room to work with, you know." Garrett indicated the tiny, sliver of space I had left for him and I laughed, moving over.

"Yeah, sorry about that."

Garrett pressed in close to me and pulled me against his chest. My cheek rested over the thudding of his heart, strong and loud beneath my ear. The consistency of that sound lulled me into an easy peace.

"I'm not sure why you're being so nice to me after how crappy I've been to you, but I sincerely appreciate it," I said, needing him to hear again how much him being here meant to me.

"I haven't been Mr. Sunshine and Roses. And I'm a jerk when my pride gets stomped on," he responded.

Garrett's took my chin between his fingers, pressing me to look up at him. When I did, my breath caught at the way his eyes lit up when they met mine.

"You're a challenge, Riley Walker. But I knew that the day we met. Do you remember?" he asked and I shook my head.

Garrett's fingers began to thread through my hair and I wanted to purr like a cat at his touch. "You and Maysie were hanging out at the bar after your shift and I came in with Cole to meet up with Jordan. I saw you and I had to talk to you. You were the most gorgeous girl in the room," he said, smiling at the memory and I snorted.

"Oh please. Give me a break. You've already gotten in my pants, you don't need to butter me up," I said, feeling ridiculously uncomfortable with the compliment.

Garrett shook his head, his eyes amused by my response. "Never can take a compliment, can you?" His fingers continued their lazy travel through my hair. "That day, I walked over to you, thinking I'd buy you a drink, give you some line about how hot you were and you'd come home with me. All I could think about was seeing your clothes on my bedroom floor and your beautiful legs wrapped around my waist," he said huskily and I felt a familiar warmth pooling in my belly.

Garrett leaned down and kissed the tip of my nose, a silly affectionate gesture that made my heart clench. "But when I tapped you on the shoulder you turned around and looked at me with this expression on your face that said I was wasting my time. You didn't say anything. You didn't need to. I knew you were out of my league. So I turned around and walked away with my tail between my legs," he finished and I felt my face flush in embarrassment.

"God I'm so sorry, Garrett. Rude just comes naturally. I really need to work on that," I muttered, feeling not for the first time, mortified by the way I tended to respond in unfamiliar situations. When I didn't know what to say, or how to act, I always fell back on my snarky one-liners. But what I realized I was doing was keeping everyone else away. Mostly so I wasn't forced to go outside of my small, confined bubble and see the world that lay beyond it. Scared that it would prove that my perfect life plan wasn't so perfect.

Garrett pulled me up so that we were nose to nose. His lips were a breath away from mine and his eyes never left me. "I love the way you are, Riley. It's what makes you, *you*. If I didn't want the hassle, I wouldn't be here now." My heart thudded in my chest and I knew, without a doubt that I wanted this.

Right now.

Maybe for a long time after.

Garrett's hands slid up my back until he was cupping the back of my head. "I'm here because no matter what you say, or what you do, I want *you*. I want every part of you. There is something in you that calls out to the messed up pieces inside of me. And I think that you might be the girl to make my world right again."

Emotion was thick in my throat and I couldn't say anything. I didn't know what to say that would come close to how amazing his words were.

Garrett's blue eyes were soft as they regarded me as if I were the most wonderful thing he had ever seen. Not once in the year that Damien and I had been together had I ever felt that I was *it* for him. That person that he revolved around. Hell, he wanted to get back together because comfortable was *okay* with him.

But the passion and desire and absolute totality I saw in Garrett's eyes blew me apart.

Garrett softly kissed my lips. "Because I'm a mess, Riley. I have spent so long pretending like the future doesn't matter because I was terrified to plan anything. I had all ready lost the two people that meant the most to me, so I would be damned if

I would ever depend on someone like that again. And if I didn't think too much about what comes *next* I wouldn't have to think about the million and one ways I was disappointing my parents." His breath caught and he looked away, as though shamed by the secrets he had just revealed.

It was my turn to grip his chin and turn him back to face me. "Your parents would be nothing but proud of the man you've become, Garrett. You're talented and motivated by your music. You're building a future around something you *love* to do. How many people get to do that?" I leaned up and placed my lips on his for a moment and he held me tightly as we tasted each other.

I pulled back and looked at him again. "You are the guy who took a heart broken girl and put her back together again, whether you realize it or not," I whispered, my soul close to flowing over.

And it was true. Garrett held me together and he tore me a apart. And what was left behind was complete and total annihilation.

"God, Riley," he said, making it more of a strangled cry. In one swift movement he rolled us over until he was leaning over me, his hair brushing my chest as he leaned down. This was so much like the hazy memory I had of us yesterday. A recollection of our first time together that was still so much out of reach.

But this time, we were both in the here and now. And the only thing that mattered was each other.

With shaky hands, I unbuttoned his shirt and he sat back and pulled it off, tossing it on the floor. I ran my hands up his chest, the hard ridges of muscles under my palm. I gently touched the tattooed words that wrapped around his waist.

"Blessed are the hearts that can bend; they shall never be broken," he whispered, stirring the air around us. I remembered the words. Another flash of memory startled me as I recalled reading these words branded on his flesh as I kissed the skin around them.

I brushed his long hair back and cupped his cheek. "That's beautiful. But why the need to ink it?" I asked, staring into his eyes.

Garrett leaned down and kissed me with trembling lips.

"After my parents died, I swore I'd never feel that kind of empty heartache again. That I'd strengthen my heart so it would never, ever break. I knew I wouldn't be able to survive that kind of pain again."

I closed my eyes, feeling overwhelmed by this. By *him.*

Garrett swept his mouth along the curve of my jaw. "My heart isn't strong enough to survive you, Riley. You won't just bend it, you have the power to shatter it to pieces," he said quietly and with enough feeling to bring me low.

I pulled my head to the side, not able to look at him. "I don't want to shatter your heart, Garrett. But I'm not sure I can promise that I won't. I don't know what happens from here. What all this means," I told him honestly, knowing he deserved no less.

Garrett pulled my face back around so that I looked at him again. "Handle it with care, please. Because I want to give it to you. Completely," he murmured, placing my hand on his chest.

My eyes hazed over with unshed tears and I felt way too emotional. I didn't know what to do with all of these feelings. I felt choked up and downright sick to my stomach by the implications of his testament.

I had a feeling Garrett Bellows might actually love me. And that was a huge complication that I couldn't face right now.

I started to pull away, ready to shut this down when Garrett held me firm. "Don't you dare run away from this," he said harshly. And then his mouth was on mine. Rough and unapologetically brutal. And given the emotional wreckage of my current situation, I needed this.

I threw myself into kissing him. Into touching him. Into immersing myself in him.

Garrett pulled away suddenly and looked down at me, a fierce light in his eyes. "Are you sure, Riley? We've been here before and honestly I don't think I can take you turning me away right now," Garrett's words were as close to a plea as I had ever heard from him.

I shook my head. "I won't push you away," I said emphatically.

Garrett smiled down at me, lighting up the world. "You promise?" he asked.

"Promise," I swore just as he took possession of me again. Our lips moved together in unison. His tongue, my tongue, sliding and loving each other.

His hands, almost hesitant, gripped the hem of my shirt and dragged it up over my head. Once it was on the floor with his, Garrett looked down at me in wonder. "I have never seen anything so beautiful in my entire life," he said and it was on the tip of my tongue to make some sort of sarcastic remark. But the look in his eye killed the words.

I hooked my arms around his neck and forcefully brought his mouth back to mine.

After that, any hesitation on his part was gone. We were one perfect blend of want and need as we peeled each other's clothes away until we were completely naked together. Garrett's hand came up to cup my breast, his thumb rolling over the sensitive flesh as his tongue ran up the side of my throat. He suckled and nibbled as fingers circled around the taught nipple.

His mouth took the place of his hand and as he sucked my nipple into his mouth I arched back off the bed. Garrett brought my leg to wrap around his waist, lining us up perfectly. His hand came between us and touched the throbbing folds between my thighs.

"You're so fucking wet, Riley. Fuck..." he groaned into my mouth as his finger slid through the wet warmth. My hips pumped against his hand, greedy for his touch. And when his finger finally entered me, I moaned so loudly I felt a momentary mortification.

Garrett pushed my hair back off of my face. "I want to hear you, Riley. I *need* to know you like what I'm doing to you. That you want me to touch you," he said fiercely and I realized then what my continued rejection had done to him. I had taken this confident man and made him second-guess himself. And in the heat of our lust, I hated myself for that.

I pressed into his hand, feeling him slid in and out of my body and my eyes closed. "I love it, Garrett. Don't stop. Don't ever stop," I said in a thready whisper. Garrett's mouth claimed mine again and he reached for his pants and pulled out his wallet. I barely registered the tearing of foil and the slight movement as he rolled on the condom.

All I was aware of was the moment when his body lined up with mine and I felt him hard and waiting at my entrance. Garrett pulled back slightly and looked down at me.

"I want to watch you this time. I want to see your face when I'm inside you," he said and if I wasn't already flushed and excited, I would be at his words.

And then suddenly he entered me. But my body was familiar with him and it felt…right.

Garrett gripped my hips and pulled almost all of the way out before he surged forward again, pushing us both up the length of the bed.

"Ahh!" I cried out, digging my nails into the flesh of his back.

He threw his head back and let out a deep, guttural groan as he began to pound into me. Our movements were totally in tune. He was just as desperate for me as I was for him.

"Riley, my God, Riley," Garrett said over and over again as he pushed as deep into me as he could go.

My body pulsated with each stroke and I knew the second my body exploded around him that I was lost. Somehow, someway, Garrett Bellows had gotten underneath my skin. I wasn't sure how to adjust to the new feeling of having him there.

"Look at me, please," Garrett begged, kissing my mouth, but then pulling back so he could watch me as he came inside my body. His hand came up to caress my cheek, his thumb rubbing circles across my skin. His eyes never left mine as he surged forth one final time and I could feel him let go. I could feel his release, his total possession. His shoulders tensed and then he collapsed on top of me, his breath heavy on my neck.

"Don't take this away again, Riley," he said softly into the thick of my hair and all I could do was hold him as we came down from the high.

I wanted to promise him that I wouldn't. That this was the start of something new, something great for the both of us. But I knew how easy it was to promise things before our realities changed it all. And despite how much I wanted to say those words, *I promise,* I knew I'd never be able to keep them.

So I stayed quiet and tried to ignore the disquiet that had taken root deep in my bones.

Chapter
16

We weren't even recovered from our post coital bliss when my phone started to ring. I untangled myself from Garrett to grab it. I saw that it was my mother and I instantly froze.

All of the warm, glowing fuzzies I had felt only moments earlier evaporated in an instant. "Hello?" I said after answering, cringing at how out of breath I sounded.

"Ri, hey, it's Gavin," my brother said into the phone. Why in the world was he calling me from Mom's cell?

"Where's Mom? What happened?" I asked, sitting up and covering myself with a sheet. Garrett sat upright beside me, taking my hand in his.

"She's not doing too well right now. You need to get down here right away. It's Dad," Gavin broke off and I could hear his muffled sob and that made all the blood drain from my face.

I pulled away from Garrett and swung my legs over the side of the bed. With the phone still pressed to my ear, I bent down to retrieve my discarded clothing. Working one handed, I pulled my panties and jeans back on. My hands were trembling so badly, I dropped my shirt several times and finally Garrett took it from me and had me sit back down.

"What about Dad? Gavin just tell me what the hell happened!" I demanded, feeling the rising hysteria in the back of my throat.

"He was doing fine. His doctor's were feeling confident that he would be okay. But then he had another heart attack," my

149

brother's voice wobbled and I knew what was coming. I just knew that this phone call was to tell me I'd never see my father again.

"He's gone, isn't he," I stated rather than asked.

Gavin was outright crying and I don't think I had ever heard him sound so emotional about anything. He rarely became enthused or worked up. But I could hear him losing it over the phone and it was terrifying.

"He's gone, Ri. He's gone," my brother cried.

"Where's Mom?" I asked firmly, trying to get Gavin to focus. My face hardened and I felt my heart freeze over. I should be crying. I had been an emotional wreck for the last twenty-four hours. But now, when the worst had come, I found that I was like a block of stone.

"She's back with him. She won't leave his room. Fliss tried to get her to leave but she refused. You need to get down here," Gavin said and I thought how ridiculous it was that me, the baby of the family, was always called on to make things right. That out of the three of us, I was by far the most levelheaded sibling.

Gavin, even though he had a respectable career as a teacher, still lived his life like a teenager, refusing to commit to his long-term girlfriend and still coming to mooch out of Mom and Dad's pantry several times a week.

Felicity was married with kids but she still relied so much on Mom to help her make decisions in her life. She rarely did anything without running it past our parents first as though afraid to make a move without their approval.

Then there was me. I was off at college, determined to live my life on my own terms. I was the independent woman my mom and dad had raised me to be. So when shit hit the fan, I could be called on to find the reason when there didn't seem to be any.

And that's what my mother needed now. And clearly Felicity and Gavin weren't going to give it. And as much as I loved and appreciated my siblings, in that moment I just felt irritated.

"I'm on my way. Just leave her be until I get there," I directed my brother before hanging up. My brain was now in disaster recovery mode. I quickly put on my bra and shirt. I found my bag and pulled out my brush, running it through my hair. No sense going to the hospital, right after my father died, looking like I had just had my brains fucked out.

God, what kind of person was I that while my dad was dying, I was screwing the guy who up until yesterday, I was determined had no place in my life? I was a stupid, selfish brat. And I hated myself for missing out on the chance to be with my father, one last time, and was instead getting naked in their spare bedroom.

"Stop it, Riley," Garrett said suddenly, pulling me out of my bleak thoughts. I looked up at him in a mixture of annoyance and confusion.

"Stop what?" I barked, knowing that I was once again taking my negative feelings out on him and he was absolutely the last person to deserve that. But I couldn't stop the malice that poured out of me. I glared at him with scorn.

"You're going to start blaming yourself. Hell, I can see you're about to blame me as well." I curled my lip at him in irritation.

Garrett gripped me by the arms and forced me to look at him. "But you can't do that to yourself. You could do nothing to change what happened. And you can't start regretting your choices now, it'll drive you crazy," he said firmly, giving me a little shake.

"And please, don't say you regret us and what just happened. Not after everything," his voice broke and I could only shake my head.

"I can't do this right now, Garrett. Okay? I need to get to my family," I bit out, pulling away from his grasp.

Garrett hurriedly buttoned up his shirt. "Then I'm going with you," he said, leaving no room for argument.

"You don't have to..." I started but Garrett cut me off by kissing me soundly on the mouth. I blinked up at him in surprise.

"I know I don't *have* to. But I *want* to. Let me be there for you," he said and I nodded, unable to find the words to answer him.

We walked out to the kitchen and it felt like a lifetime ago that Garrett had carried me back that same hallway. My life changed in that tiny, spare room but right now all I could see was the way everything had exploded. Just when I thought things were sorting themselves out the real world gave me the big ol' middle finger.

I gave Garrett directions to the hospital but other than that we said very little to each other. Garrett seemed to recognize that I needed my space and I was lost in my own sad, little world. Garrett took my hand as we got into the elevators to take us to the fourth floor where the ICU was. His fingers laced through mine and I even in my shock I felt a small measure of happiness at having him there with me.

And then I hated myself some more for feeling happy at all. It felt wrong to garner joy from anything right now.

I dropped Garrett's hand once we came to the ICU. Because the first thing I saw was my brother and sister huddled together, their faces red from crying. I was struck dumb for a moment. I didn't know what to do.

Garrett fell behind me, allowing me to approach them by myself but with the knowledge that he was right behind me should I need him. "Fliss, Gavin," I said quietly. They looked up at me and both got to their feet, enfolding me in their arms.

I wanted to cry so badly. I felt the burning in my eyes and the tightness in my chest but for some reason, I couldn't. It was as though my tear ducts had stopped working.

"He's gone, Ri. Dad's gone!" Felicity wailed into my shoulder as she squeezed me tighter.

"I need to go to find Mom," I murmured, pulling back slightly.

"She won't leave him. The nurses and doctors have tried to get her to let go of his hand but she just sits there, staring at him, as though he'll wake up at any minute. We told Dad's doctor we had called you and you would handle Mom. You always know what to do," Gavin said and not for the first time I wondered which of us was the older sibling.

"I'll handle it," I promised. Felicity and Gavin let me go and I looked over my shoulder at Garrett who still hung back, careful not to intrude.

"Guys, this is my friend, Garrett. He drove me up here last night," I said by way of introduction. Felicity gave him a watery smile and Gavin barely acknowledged him at all. Garrett came to sit beside my sister and reached out to touch my hand before I left to help my mother.

"I'll be here," was all he said and for me, for right now, that's exactly what I needed to hear.

MOM," I said softly into the quiet hospital room. My mom was bowed over, her forehead touching my dad's hand. I couldn't look at my father just yet. I needed to keep my shit together so I could deal with Mom.

I walked slowly around the foot of the bed and sank to my haunches beside her. I rested my hand on her shoulder and leaned in close, my cheek resting on her arm. "Mom, please look at me," I whispered.

My mom didn't turn her head; she stayed bent over my dead father's hand as though she were praying. If my mother were a religious woman, I would have assumed that was what she was doing. But Mom and Dad didn't subscribe to "orthodox religious ideals," choosing the beach and the waves as their God and church.

Nope, I knew this was a woman who had lost the most important person in her life and was now crumbling in on herself.

I shook her shoulder a bit, hoping to snap her out of it. The doctors and nurses were hovering outside the door. I knew they needed to take Dad's body away. There were things that needed to be done, decisions that had to be made. But, sympathetically they were waiting on Mom.

"Come on, let's go. You need to sleep. Get something to eat. Let Fliss, Gavin and me take care of you," I said urgently, trying to get a reaction out of her. Mom shook her head and pressed a kiss to the cold hand in her grasp.

"I can't leave him," she cried, followed by a strangled moan that made me shiver.

"Mom, please. Come with me," I begged. I put my arms around my mother, holding her. Finally, she turned into me and buried her face into my shirt. She began to sob as though she were the child and I were the parent there to comfort her.

I didn't know when I would be afforded he luxury of letting

my emotions out like that, so for now, I bottled it in and took care of the woman who needed me.

Over her shoulder, I chanced a look at my father. It's true what they say, that death looks like sleep. Aside from the white pallor of his skin, Dad looked as though he were napping. The tubes and wires were gone. The machines had been turned off. The covers on his bed were pulled up over his chest as though he were chilly.

It was creepy and a discomfort filled me, making me look away and turn my attention back to my grieving mother.

"Can we go home?" I asked her and then I waited. After what felt like forever, she got to her feet, wiped her face and then slowly lifted my dad's hand to her lips. I turned away, feeling like an intruder on this last moment she would have with her husband. The last time she would feel his skin on hers. The last look at the face that had been her constant companion for over forty years.

I went to the doorway and waited and thought long and hard about what it meant to love someone to the point of losing yourself when they were gone. I hadn't loved Damien like that. Even though I had been upset and put out when he dumped me, I could recognize now that it was more about my wounded pride and being made to feel like a fool than anything else.

Yes, I had loved him. Yes, he had been a part of my life for over a year so of course I had been attached. But I had gone on without him. I had bounced back.

What had grown between my mom and dad over the years went beyond a love I had ever experienced. And even though I knew my mother would go on with her life, she would never truly heal from losing my dad. A loss like that wasn't something you could *get* over. Not really. You just learned to live through the pain.

It scared me to think of loving someone so much that to lose them would be to only half exist.

My mother followed me out to the waiting room and the first thing my eyes were drawn to was Garrett, looking at pictures on my sister's phone. He seemed impassive as usual while Felicity prattled on about her daughters. He nodded and made comments but his face revealed nothing.

Gavin jumped to his feet and rushed over to Mom. Felicity looked up and was then right behind our brother, clamoring to get to our mother. Garrett stayed seated, his calm, mellow vibe a balm on my jangled nerves.

He didn't approach me. He simply inclined his head in my direction and gave me a small smile. I didn't return it. I didn't know how to right then. But I inclined my head back before turning back to my family.

Chapter
17

STAYED in Port David for almost two weeks. Dad's funeral had been scheduled for a week after his passing. Then I stayed around to make sure Mom was settled and doing okay.

The funeral was tough, just as I knew it would be. If I could imagine a hell, watching my father be lowered into the ground had to be it. In the first few hours after Dad died, I wasn't sure if Mom would be able to make it on her own. She had seemed so small, as though she had shrunk in on herself.

My brother and sister hadn't been much better. My brother seemed lost and all my sister did was cry. It got better when Felicity's husband, Sam, showed up with the girls. My sister pulled herself together for her kids and Sam helped shoulder the load of planning Dad's service.

But I had gone into autopilot. Just call me Robo-Riley, because my emotions had gone into hibernation. There was no room at the inn for feeling sad and sorry for myself. I had to pull up my big girl panties and help my family in the way only Riley Walker could.

Garrett had stayed for a few hours after we took my mom back to the house from the hospital. I had just gotten her to lie down and rest for a bit and had come out to find Garrett sitting on the back porch steps, looking out at the ocean. Gavin had gone home and Felicity had headed to a local hotel with her family to get settled and to try and take a nap.

Garrett looked up when the screen door slammed behind me and I gave him a shaky semblance of a smile as I joined him on the steps. It had been really cold and I tucked my hands under my legs to try and keep them warm.

Garrett's hair had fallen in his face and I thought about tucking it behind his ear but I felt strange about touching him. I didn't know what my problem was. All I knew was that everything had changed in the span of a few hours and I didn't know how to fit this man into my new world order.

"I would ask how you were doing, but I know what a fucked up question that is," Garrett had said, his hands hanging limply between his knees.

"And I would have told you it's a messed up question and to stop asking me shit that should be self-explanatory," I lobbed back, smirking.

Garrett's chuckle was soft and ended too soon. "It's going to be hard. The next few months are going to be fucking miserable. But just try and take it one day at a time."

"Seriously? That's your sage advice? Take it one day at a time? What are you a walking, talking self-help book?" I asked him, my lips quirking into a tiny grin.

Garrett shrugged. "Sure, it's cliché. But it's the truth. Loss is loss and nothing will make it better but time."

I had looked at Garrett while he spoke and had thought about his tattoo. *Blessed are the hearts that can bend; for they shall never be broken.*

I got it. I really did. Losing someone you love smashes you into smithereens. It alters you in a way that I couldn't, in the deep throes of my grief, believe I'd ever move past. I understood why Garrett had shut himself off, tucked all those messy feelings away. And why being with me, a girl with a self-professed chip on her shoulder, probably scared him silly.

"Is that how you got by after your parents died?" I asked, not knowing whether I was treading on forbidden ground or not. But I figured given everything we had been through together in the last twenty-four hours I had earned the right to some personal information.

And there was something reassuring about talking to someone who had been through something equally painful. We were both card-carrying members of the dead parents club and it was a crappy club to belong to. But having him there, understanding on some level what I was experiencing, was oddly helpful.

Garrett glanced over at me before turning look out at the ocean again. "After my parents died I lost focus. I had planned to go to college, you know. I had been accepted to the University of Virginia. I wanted to be a doctor or some shit," he revealed and I tried not to look as shocked as I was.

"Really?" I asked and cringed at how incredulous I sounded. Garrett picked up on it however and I saw his shoulders tense. Great, I had just insulted the guy who was being my biggest support right now. Way to go, Riley!

"Yeah, I wasn't always a total waste of skin, Riley. I used to have the 4.0 GPA and full ride to school. I was Mr. Extracurricular Activities. But after my parents died none of it mattered anymore. I was too old to go to foster care; I had turned eighteen at the beginning of my senior year. So in the eyes of the state I was able to take care of myself, but I was still a fucking kid. I had no idea what the hell I was doing. Sure, I had a house to live in and money from their life insurance policies to keep me fed and clothed, but I was a mess. Total and complete freedom paired with a huge dose of grief, it was no wonder I fell off the freaking planet. I was out of control. I completely lost it."

Garrett took a deep breath, his eyes never leaving the breaking waves on the beach. I felt like such an ass for judging him for so long. I had spent the last few months thinking I was too good for the likes of Garrett Bellows. But I couldn't have been more wrong. I could live a thousand years and never be the girl this amazing guy deserved. And that made me feel very, very small.

"If it hadn't been for Jordan, and Mitch and Cole and being in the band, I would have joined my parents in the ground. And even though my life went in a direction I hadn't planned, I wouldn't change a thing. I'm headed down the only road that I want to be on. And that works for me." He pressed his lips together and turned his eyes to me and I could see a flinty resolve in them.

I didn't know what to make of this. He was showing me a tiny piece of his life. Showing me something beyond the guy everyone else saw. Yet at the same time he seemed to be warning me that what you see is what you get. And it was up to me to accept it or not.

But I was in no condition to ponder that. I couldn't think beyond getting through the next minute. The next hour. The next day. The pain that lived inside me was all consuming and made it hard to breathe.

"I still make mistakes. I'm still a huge fuck up in so many ways. I changed a lot the day I lost Mom and Dad. I'll never be that guy I was before they died. Those goals, that future, it seems so insignificant now in the grand scheme of things. But it doesn't change the fact that I lost myself and I don't think I've yet to find him again," Garrett said, looking sadder than I had ever seen him.

"Is that the deal with the parties and the girls and smoking pot? You're trying to find yourself? Because to me, that seems like a poor way of going about it," I snipped, realizing I sounded mean. But I felt irritated by his life choices.

Here was a guy who had the world at his feet. He clearly had a lot going for him once upon a time. But he allowed himself to be derailed. To lose his focus. He was still drifting at sea without a clue. It was frustrating to see his potential wasted in the way it was. I would never fall prey to my grief in a way that would make me lose sight of *me*. I owed it to my dad. I owed it to myself.

Garrett's eyes flickered with anger. "Yeah, maybe it is. But it's *my* life, Riley. And they're *my* choices. And I'll never be sorry for it," he said defensively. I knew he was giving me a very strong warning.

I just wasn't in the mood to hear it.

"I think that's a coward's excuse, Garrett. Don't you want more for yourself than playing in a second rate band hoping you'll '*make it*?'" I asked using air quotes just to be obnoxious. Garrett's jaw tensed and I recognized the telltale signs of his rage.

"I don't expect you to understand. And because you just lost your dad I won't tell you what I really think of you and your *'life plan.'"* Damn it, he used air quotes back at me. "I'm sure it involves graduating from college, marrying a douche like that Damien guy, having a mid-level career, popping out your two point five kids, and convincing yourself you feel fulfilled." He was getting himself worked up and I was feeling a whole lot of anger.

How it easy it was to focus on this, being self-righteous and holier than thou, than to think about the way my life had just upended on itself. Anger was better than depression any day of the week.

"You don't know anything about my life or what I want from it! What do you know about goals and having a purpose? Huh? Am I supposed to sit here and take advice from a guy who doesn't want anything more for himself than to screw a new girl every week and hoping he never runs out of pot? Really? Give me a break!"

Wow, I was on a roll and being completely unfair. Garrett's face shattered a bit and then smoothed out.

"It's a good thing my heart can bend," he muttered under his breath.

"What's that supposed to mean?" I asked him shortly, though I knew exactly what it meant.

He shook his head and got to his feet. "I don't want to upset you when you've just experienced a major loss. Apparently all we're capable of is pissing each other off. I'm sorry for that. I didn't mean to make you mad. I really didn't. I just wanted you to know that I understand where you are right now. I really do. And if you need anything, you know where to find me."

He picked up my keys and juggled them in his hand, seeming torn. I couldn't believe, after what we had shared together and how decent he had been to me, I was taking out all of my anger and hostility on him. I wish I could take back what I said. I wish I could undo the hurt I knew I had inflicted.

But it was too late. And I felt whatever closeness we had established during the last twenty-four hours drifted away as though it had never been.

"I'll leave your car at the apartment. Take care, Riley," he had said before leaving me alone, and full of guilt.

After he was gone I was left with little time to obsess over Garrett and the state of our non-existent relationship.

The crazy whirlwind of planning the funeral and seeing to every detail was both a blessing and a curse. It helped me to focus on something. To keep my brain active. But it also left little room for my own grieving. And a part of me knew that suppressing it wasn't good.

And that when it hit it would hit hard.

I had stayed with Mom until she practically kicked me out, telling me I had to get back to school. When I had protested and said she still needed me, she had played the biggest punk card of all.

"Your dad sacrificed a lot so you kids could have a college education. Don't you dare step all over his memory like that. Now get your butt back to school and make him proud. Make us both proud," she scolded me while she held back tears. I knew how hard it was for her to let me go. I hated to think of what the house would be like for her now that she would be living in it alone. But Gavin had practically moved back in since Dad's passing. I wasn't sure how I felt about this. My brother seemed to be making my father's death all about him, but for now, my mother seemed to enjoy his presence, so I didn't say anything about it.

I went back to Rinard College, hoping to fall back into my routine. Too bad I felt like some asshole playacting through their life.

But throwing myself back into school and my internship felt like what I should be doing. I put on the impenetrable "Riley is fine" mask. I had always been focused and motivated. Now I was like Riley Walker Super Student on meth. I filled my days with homework and extra hours at work. I did whatever I had to do to feel like my life had purpose again, just as my dad wanted me to.

And that purpose left very little room for any sort of relationship drama. I didn't have the time or the inclination to worry about whether my avoiding Garrett was hurting his feelings. Maybe it was insensitive and callous of me after the way he had supported me, but I just couldn't summon the energy to care.

I knew Garrett was most likely hurt and confused. Part of me knew that he was waiting for me to recognize that the moments we had shared in Maryland hadn't been a fluke of hormones and grief. That it had been the beginnings of something real.

But the truth was I was terrified of "real." I wasn't sure what we had together could be something permanent and if I couldn't count on it I didn't want to waste my time. And even though I had seen the layers that were just below the surface of Garrett, I knew that he was still a guy without a plan and I desperately needed something concrete. Something I could depend on.

And I was convinced that Garrett Bellows wasn't that guy.

Plus, it wasn't as though we had left things in a very good place. I had unloaded a serious verbal beating on him when all he had been trying to do was help me during a difficult time. I wasn't surprised when he didn't call me. Even if I was a little bit disappointed.

I figured he was leaving the ball firmly in my court. Though if he was waiting for me to make a move and admit he was what I wanted, he'd be waiting a long time.

Crazy cat lady spinsterhood, here I come.

"Someone's hoping to make employee of the month," an overly perky voice said from behind me. I continued to wipe down my meticulously clean tables, ignoring the sudden invasion of slut in my section of the restaurant.

Jaz pulled out a chair and plopped her big ass right on down as though I had invited her. Which I sure as hell didn't. She propped her feet up on the table and she watched me with a fake sympathetic smile on her lips that had I was dangerously close to knocking off.

I had low bullshit tolerance on a good day. So Jaz my-tits-are-too-small-so-I-overcompensate-by-being-a-complete-whore was in a perfect position to piss me off. It didn't take much for her to irritate me and tonight was no exception.

Generation Rejects had been playing for the last hour and I was staunchly avoiding the guitarist who had tried to get my attention for most of the night. It was hard, particularly when said guitarist was looking entirely too yummy for his own good and the image of the two of us naked, together, was burned on my brain like an itchy sunburn.

I lifted Jaz's feet off the table and dropped them on the floor. "Go bug someone else, Jaz. Cause I'm not playing," I grumbled, giving my table one last swipe with the cloth and turned to go clock out.

"Wow, who pissed in your cornflakes? I was just making the observation that you seemed to be really into your work lately. I think it's great you have your *work* to get you through such a difficult time. We all know you don't handle your emotions well. I mean look what happened after Damien dumped you," she said, dropping her voice in a feigned show of concern.

That was it, I was so done. I turned around, ready to unleash my inner Ghangis Khan on her face when we were interrupted by an unwelcome source.

"Back off, Jaz," Damien said, getting between us. Jaz's bitch knob, which had been firmly on eleven, dialed back a notch. She turned faintly pink as she gave Damien a bright smile.

"Don't be ridiculous, Damien. I'm not doing anything to Riley. Don't make me the bad guy here just because you've decided you want back into her granny panties," Jaz sneered. I grit my teeth together so hard I could have sworn I cracked a tooth or two.

"Seriously, just go," Damien's voice was clipped and hard and I was totally shocked. Damien didn't play the confrontational card very often. Jaz looked hurt by his defense of me and walked off in a huff.

He turned back and gave me a wane smile, his black hair falling into his face.

"Thanks for running interference, D. That would have only ended in a gore fest," I said and Damien's smile grew at my unintentional use of the nickname I had given him a lifetime ago.

"Moore would have been pretty pissed if you had bloodied up his brand new carpet. So it's a good thing I was here," Damien teased and I found myself smiling back.

Damien reached out to squeeze my arm and before I could pull away there was a commotion from the stage where Generation Rejects had suddenly stopped playing.

"Take your hand off her before I fucking make you," an angry voice grumbled over the sound system. I looked up in shock to see that Garrett had taken the microphone from Cole and was glaring in my direction.

Well not at me but at Damien who stood there with his mouth hanging open like an idiot.

"Is he talking to me?" Damien asked, his eyes wide with what I could only decipher as burgeoning panic. Garrett had dropped the mic on the stage, pulled his guitar from around his neck, handing it to a flabbergasted Mitch and stormed through a crowd that parted like the Red Sea.

Was this really happening?

Jordan had gotten to his feet and was right behind his friend, trying to stop him. But Garrett wasn't having it. He was a man on a mission. And clearly his mission was to kick some Damien ass.

Garrett didn't even stop before he barreled into Damien who went down with an undignified "umph." Damien sat on his butt, looking up at the scary rocker who towered over him and he seemed to be trying to disappear into the floor.

"Don't. Touch. Her. Ever. Again," Garrett growled through gritted teeth. Jordan grabbed his arm and tried to pull him back.

"What the fuck, man. We're in the middle of a show!" Jordan looked at me as if I could solve this crazy Garrett Bellows puzzle. My eyes were like saucers and I knew I was just staring at the crazy alpha male that had erupted out of Garrett like the Incredible Hulk.

"I was just talking to her. What business is it of yours anyway? She's my girlfriend," Damien said, trying to win back some of the pride that had already gotten up and run away.

Wait…what?

Did Damien just refer to me as his girlfriend?

Oh hell no!

But before I could correct my seriously deluded ex, Garrett's face turned a molten red. He hauled Damien up by the front of his shirt and then without further ado, decked him, square in the jaw, sending him back to the floor on his ass. Poor Damien's backside was sure getting a work out.

And all I could do was stand there, staring like an idiot with my mouth hanging open. No way was this my life. I avoided drama like the plague but it seemed since hooking up with Garrett, it followed me everywhere.

"Garrett, stop it!" Jordan yelled and I could see Moore coming out of the kitchen looking mad. Garrett turned his mega watt anger on me.

"Were you going to tell me you were back with this jackass? Or did you just conveniently forget while I was fucking you?" Garrett asked and everyone around us gasped. Well I guess the cat was out of the bag now.

I felt my face flush and my heart begin to pound furiously in my ears. I understood now what it meant to see red. Because that's all I saw.

Deep, murderous, I'm-gonna-rip-his-dick-off red.

"Shut the hell up, man. You have shit to say to Riley, do it somewhere private. This is not the time or place to be hashing out your issues," Jordan reasoned, trying to cut this off at the pass. Maysie suddenly materialized beside me and had grabbed me by the hand, trying to steer me away from the scene that was about to go down.

Because she knew the look on my face. And it meant I was about to get mean.

I stepped up into Garrett's personal space and looked him dead in the eye. He was angry but I could also see he was just plain hurt. Well I was also hurting right now. I hadn't expected for my private life to become front-page news because of his jealous ego. This on top of my minimal emotional functioning and I was ready to pop.

"He is *not* my boyfriend. But I guess it took too much thought to actually ask me before you made a complete *fool* of yourself." Garrett didn't seem in the least bit embarrassed. He simply looked back at me as if daring me to refute his announcement. Waiting for me to deny we had been together.

"And I obviously wasn't thinking about much when you *fucked* me because otherwise I would have stayed the hell away from an asshole like you!" I said with a steady calm that surprised even me.

Garrett flinched, a slight movement that only I noticed. My words hit home, just as I had meant for them to. I turned on my heel and started to stalk off. We had created quite the spectacle. Everyone in the bar was watching us with avid interest and I was completely mortified.

"Riley!" Garrett called out but I just kept walking, pushing and shoving my way to the back of the restaurant.

"Okay, guys, I think it's time to wrap up your set," Moore said, trying to get some control over the situation. I didn't even check to see that Damien was okay. Fuck Damien and his stupid hands and even dumber mouth.

"Riley, god damn it, stop!" Garrett yelled at the top of his lungs. Seriously fuck all of these guys!

Garrett grabbed a hold of my arm and pulled me to him. He was sweaty and still flushed from his serious case of roid rage. "Look, I'm sorry all right. That was out of line. But fucking hell, Harry Potter over there needs to keep his hands to himself. He has no right touching you," he said furiously.

I laughed. A bitter and humorless sound.

"And you do?" I asked incredulously.

Garrett leaned in close as though he were going to kiss me and damn it, I found myself leaning into him and my eyes started to close. "You're damn right I do. If anyone is going to touch this body, it's going to be me and no one else," he swore pushing his hair back off of his face.

His eyes raked over me and I couldn't help but tingle under his scrutiny. I narrowed my eyes to cover up the fact that having him in such close proximity was doing a number on my lady parts.

"I'm trying to be understanding. I'm trying to be patient. But Riley, I can't sit back and forget about everything that happened between us. I know you're hurting and angry and going through those stages of grief but I'm here, damn it," Garrett said softly, thankfully dropping his voice to a volume that only I could hear. Because our audience was still entirely too fixated on what was happening between us.

"I never asked you to be patient. Look, I'm sorry if you thought that just because we slept together a few times that meant we were *together* or something. But I'm busy. I've got school. And you've got your..." I looked around, my lip curling. "Well you have this, don't you?" I asked with more than a bit of condescension.

Yes folks, I was being a bitch. And yes it was messed up. And maybe I was being a world-class idiot. But all I could see when I looked at Garrett right then was a guy who didn't fit. I wasn't blind to everything else that he was. But this man had the power to hurt me. He could crush my heart. And I was sure my heart wouldn't bend, it would snap in two.

I was a girl hanging on by a thread. A girl whose only lifeline was the goals she had set for herself.

I was already hurting. I was already a short jump away from falling off the edge. And Garrett Bellows stood there with his heart in his eyes, asking me to skip over it with him.

I couldn't do it. I just couldn't.

I needed safe. I needed something I could depend on. And a relationship between Garrett and I would be entirely too messy.

Riley Walker didn't do messy.

Garrett's head snapped back as though I had slapped him and the warmth in his eyes cooled. "Wow, you sure know how to cut a guy at the knees," he said sharply.

I said nothing.

Garrett watched my face, as if looking for that girl who had fallen asleep in his arms. The girl who had given him her body as though he were the only guy in the world. And certainly the only one that mattered.

Well that girl had been locked away and I wasn't planning to let her out again anytime soon.

"I had planned on fighting for this, Riley. Because I thought it was something we both wanted. I know you're feeling lost. You're hurting. I wanted to be that guy to help hold you together. I thought, maybe we could start healing each other." There was a catch in Garrett's voice and he had to look away.

I swallowed around the lump in my throat and felt my resolve waver. "Garrett..." I began, not knowing exactly what I was going to say.

Garrett turned back at me and smiled. A smile that was lackadaisical and said *I-couldn't-give-a-shit*. Clearly, he knew how he was going to play this. After all, our roles had been defined early on. We had simply gotten lost in the temporary insanity brought on by lust and vulnerability.

"My bad," Garrett stated, walking past me and back toward the stage.

I turned toward the crowd and wanted to scream. Everyone stared at me. Maysie's eyes were wide, her mouth a perfect 'o.' Jaz stood off to the side, her arms crossed and a self-satisfied smirk on her face. Jordan looked concerned but annoyed as well.

And Damien, well, he was looking at me as though I had crushed all of his dreams.

Screw this.

I pushed through the press of people to get to the kitchen. I grabbed my stuff and left through the side door, ignoring the expected catcalls from Paco and Fed. I didn't even bother giving them the finger, as I normally did.

I felt like I had been run over by a bus. All I could think of was the look on Garrett's face as I cut him down.

No. I had done the right thing. We didn't belong together and pretending otherwise would only be prolonging the inevitable heartbreak. *That* was not the life I wanted for myself.

"Riley!" I rubbed at my temples, trying to stop the impending headache. I caught sight of Gracie hurrying toward me.

Gracie stopped as she reached my car, out of breath and looking at me strangely. "You're leaving?" she asked and I gave her a funny look. I waved my hand toward my car.

"That would be why I'm holding my keys and standing in front of my car," I answered, trying to keep a reign on the sarcasm.

Gracie looked at me uncomfortably. "You and Garret, huh?" she asked in a tiny voice and I wanted to shut my eyes in shame.

"I'm sorry, G. I know you like him…" I began but she held up her hand.

"Don't, Riley. Seriously, just don't. It's not like I planned for him to be the father of my kids or anything." Gracie's mouth twisted and I knew that she was more hurt than she let on. How could I, in all of the Garrett mess, had forgotten that my good friend liked him? Where was my sense of loyalty?

What happened to the girl credo *Chicks before dicks?* I felt like a heel. A total and complete jackass.

"I know, but I shouldn't have...you know. I wasn't thinking. The first time I was drunk. And then he was there after Dad and it just sort of happened. I really am sorry," I said quietly.

Gracie shook her head and her smile was as fake as her knockoff Coach purse. "You're my friend, Riley. I'm not mad at you. You're going through a rough time. I'm just disappointed you didn't tell me yourself."

I sighed, wishing I could say something to break through the unbearable tension between us. I was a shit. I had hurt Garrett and I had hurt my friend. And for what? A couple of rolls in the hay? No sex was worth that.

"I'm an ass," I muttered. Gracie lifted her shoulders but didn't say anything.

We stood there for a moment, not making eye contact.

"I guess I'll talk to you later," Gracie said, her words clipped.

"Later," I agreed and watched my friend turn and walk back into the bar.

Chapter
18

"I'll be at Jordan and Garrett's this weekend. They're finalizing the tour dates and I need to be there to help them get stuff sorted. Will you be okay by yourself?" Maysie asked, standing in the doorway of my room, as I got ready to go to my internship.

I looked at her in the mirror and arched my eyebrow. "Did I forget how to take care of myself or something? Do you need to be here to make sure I eat my vegetables and drink my milk?" I joked and Maysie shook her head.

"Such a smartass. I just wanted to make sure you were okay. We haven't really talked about how you're holding up after your dad and well, you hide things so it's hard to know if you need me here or not," Maysie said awkwardly and I gave her an appreciative smile.

"I'm okay, Mays. I swear," I said, putting my brush down and standing up to face her. My best friend came into my room and gave me a hug. And I let her; because there *were* times I needed them as much as the next person.

"How's your mom?" she asked me softly and I lifted my hands.

"She's surviving. I think that's all I can expect of her right now," I said.

"Yeah, I get that," Maysie remarked and I could tell she was uncomfortable. Knowing what to say to someone who had so recently lost a loved one was tricky. There was a fine line between being supportive and patronizing. Not many people understood that.

I may be swimming in some pretty deep denial but honestly I felt like I was doing fine. Sure, I hurt. I grieved. But for the most part I was throwing myself into school and work and making sure I did the things I had always planned. And for right now that was helping.

After my epic confrontation with Garrett at Barton's, things had gone thankfully quiet on that end. I hadn't heard from Garrett and Maysie had been wisely tightlipped, recognizing it was a topic best left alone.

And while Jordan seemed at times on the verge of saying something, he had yet to give me a reason to unleash a verbal lashing. The less people poking their well meaning noses into my personal life the better.

As for the other loose ends in my life, they were still dangling. Damien was wary and despite his black and blue ass, was still tentatively nice.

And then there was Gracie. We were so immersed in each other's lives that there was no avoiding one another. I wasn't one to run from conflict, but even I had a hard time handling the iceberg that had taken up residence between us.

Gracie wasn't the type of person to be outright nasty. She was still civil and polite. We still talked about classes and rode together to our internship, but the subject of a certain guitar playing cutie was left completely alone.

Part of me wanted to address it and get it out there in the open. I hated subtext and that's what Gracie and I had become. A huge, heaping pile of insinuation. Every conversation held the hint of something else below the surface. There were a million unspoken things between us.

But every time I thought to bring it up, Gracie intuitively shut it down.

So we continued to exist in this world where we didn't talk about the one thing that was interfering with our friendship. My recent trip into slut town chauffeured by Garrett Bellows.

Aside from that, I had school. I had my internship. I had my straight As. And most importantly I had my total and complete control over where my life was headed. I had recently sent off my grad school applications and started to make plans for what I was going to do after graduation.

Everything was just as it was supposed to be. And in my head I could hear my dad's sage words, *live a life that matters*. Well I would do that, at whatever the cost.

"The guys are supposed to head out after the holidays. They'll be gone for almost six months," Maysie was saying, snapping me out of my internal monologue.

"Wow, six months. That's a long time. I thought it was only for three?" I asked her.

"Yeah, well some of the bigger clubs out west got a hold of their demo and wanted to book them for some shows. They're even opening for Flytrap in May! How amazing is that?" Maysie said excitedly, mentioning a rock band with a hard core following on the college scene.

"That's pretty cool," I admitted but then I looked at my friend pointedly. "What are you going to do?" I asked. Hell, what was *I* going to do? Garrett would be gone for six months.

But then again, six months away from the constant tug and pull of my emotions where he was concerned sounded kind of great actually. At least that's what I told myself.

But Maysie and Jordan were a unit. I couldn't imagine Jordan being okay with leaving her behind. Even if he was doing something he loved. Because his love for Maysie trumped everything else.

Maysie's eyes were downcast and she chewed on her bottom lip. "Well, that's the thing I wanted to talk to you about," she said nervously. I watched her warily as she started to twist the rings on her fingers. She was about to tell me something she knew I wouldn't like. Or at the very least something I would give her a stern lecture about.

"I've decided to graduate early. I'm going to get my diploma at the end of the semester," she said quickly. I blinked in shock, not sure I heard her correctly.

"What?" I asked incredulously.

"I already have enough credits so I figured why not. And then...well...I'm going on the road with the guys," she announced and I sat down heavily on my bed.

Maysie was leaving. At the end of the semester. To go on tour with Jordan and the band.

Well crap.

"Are you serious?" I asked, trying not to sound as judgmental as I was feeling.

"I want to be with him, Ri. More than anything. And this is his chance to make music and change his life," she argued.

"What about your life? Your plans?" I asked, not understanding how she could give up everything to follow her boyfriend around the country. I didn't want to tell her how disappointed I was in her decision. Though I should have expected this. She and Jordan were a force unto themselves. They had always been and an all-encompassing whirlwind that teetered on the edge of disaster. And for me, the always sensible, reliable one, this had disaster written all over it.

Maysie sat down beside me and nudged me with her shoulder. "He *is* my plan, Riley. Jordan is my life. My future and his future are wrapped up in doing this together. I'm not you. I don't have these fantastic goals that I'm determined to meet. I don't have things written down and planned out. All I know is that this is what I want to do. And I've spent way too long worried about what other people think I *should* be doing. This time, I'm doing what *I* want to do," she said defensively.

"I know I should be telling you why this is a stupid idea. Because I know that's what you expect me to do. But maybe this time, I'll just say good luck," I said, putting my arm around her shoulders. She sagged in relief that it hadn't become an argument.

"I'm just gonna miss you is all," I said gruffly, feeling emotional at the thought of going through my last few months of college without my best friend.

Maysie wrapped her arm around my waist. "I'll miss you too, Ri. But who knows, maybe you could come with us or something. You know, when you're done with school. Before you head off to grad school, it might be good for you," Maysie teased and I shoved her away.

"Yeah, I don't think that's gonna happen, Maysie," I said tersely.

"Okay, I get it...it doesn't fit into your grand vision right," Maysie's dig was more than a little harsh and I realized that perhaps she was just as critical of my choices as I was of hers.

"I've got to get to the newspaper," I said getting to my feet.

"Are you picking up Gracie?" Maysie asked, not realizing how such an innocent question put me on edge.

"Uh, no, I'm not. I was just planning on driving myself. I have to work later so I figured I wouldn't have time to drop her off," I lied.

"Are things cool with you two? I know you're feeling bad about Garrett because of her, but I don't think you should let that eat you up. Gracie goes through crushes like you or I go through underwear. She's never been serious about Garrett. She just thought he was cute. So if you're beating yourself up because you thought you were being disloyal to Gracie, let it go," Maysie said firmly.

I appreciated her words. They were spoken like a true friend.

"Yeah, well it was still a dick move. But things are fine, I guess. We haven't talked much beyond what's going on in class," I replied dismissively. I really didn't want to talk about this stuff. My head was already too full with Maysie's unexpected news.

"Gracie has become a train wreck. I don't think she really cares about any of that stuff, Ri. She's too busy self-destructing. She was so messed up last night, Garrett had to give her a ride home from his house," Maysie stated and my heart sunk.

"Shit, that's awful. I knew she was partying a lot but I guess I haven't been paying that much attention. See, shitty friend award right here," I pointed at my chest.

"She's teetering on the edge, you know. She says she's just blowing off steam, but it seems excessive to me. And I know Garrett feels the same way," Maysie remarked offhandedly.

"You've talked to Garrett about Gracie?" I asked nonchalantly. Yeah, nonchalant my ass.

"Yeah, well he's had to take her home the last few times. And we were all hanging out at his house after their gig last night and Gracie got wasted…again…I know Garrett's worried," Maysie said, not picking up on the way I had tensed.

I had no right to be jealous. I should feel relieved that the world had righted itself and Gracie was spending time with Garrett, just as she had wanted to. It would go a long way to alleviate my feelings of guilt. And it sounded as though he was doing her a solid by looking out for her.

So why did I feel like there was a three ton weight in my chest?

"I'm glad to hear that he's worried for her. They really are good together. Now, I've got to get going. We'll talk more about you leaving me later," I said with a smile so she knew I was joking. Maysie looked at me in confusion.

"Uh, okay. Well, I guess I'll see you this evening," she called out as I gathered my stuff and headed to the living room.

"Oh you're actually staying here tonight?" I asked.

Maysie rolled her eyes. "Yes, Jordan and the guys are doing some guy thing that involved drinking beer and blowing stuff up. I think I'll sit that one out," she remarked.

"Smart choice," I replied, mustering up a grin even as my face felt as though it were encased in cement.

Enough of this feelings crap. I had an internship to get to.

Chapter 19

Of course the first thing I see when I pulled up at the newspaper was Garrett. Garrett sweaty and looking way too hot for his own good.

And Garrett was not alone.

Oh no.

Garrett was talking, quite intensely to my good ol' buddy Gracie.

I sat in my car for a bit, trying to inconspicuously watch them. I was trying to decipher the hidden meaning in their body language. Okay, Garrett was standing with his hands in his pocket, so he wasn't touching her. That had to mean he wasn't interested, right?

But Gracie's body was angled toward his which I seem to recall reading in one of those crap women's magazines Maysie kept by the couch meant she was sending clear signals that she wanted him.

Their heads were bowed down and close as though they were trying not to be overheard. I squinted into the sun, trying to see them better. A knock on my window had me screaming like a ninny.

I spilled my cup of coffee all over my center console and let loose a string of curse words that would make a sailor blush. My car door swung open and the scowl on my face should have made the person responsible run screaming.

Of course that wouldn't happen because not even my look of death could discourage Damien Green and his mission to whittle down my resolve to have nothing to do with him.

"Shoot, sorry Ri," he said with a grimace as he took in the giant wet spot on my pants.

"It's cool, I like walking around looking like I pissed myself," I grumbled, finding some used napkins on the dash and tried to mop up the mess. I looked up and saw that the objects of my stalking were no longer talking and Gracie was making her way towards me with a huge grin on her face.

Wonder what put that shit eating smile on her face? Maybe I should smack it off just to make me feel better.

What the hell was wrong with me?

Gracie was my friend, not my competition in a non-existent race to get inside Garrett's pants. Besides I would have already won that one. Booyah!

And yes, I did a mental fist pump. Because I'm mature like that.

Garrett was looking in my direction and I stared back, daring him to approach. Come on Guitar Boy, make my day.

God, someone rip out my inner Dirty Harry and beat the shit out of him please.

Garrett turned and went inside the building without so much as a wave. Okay then…

"Riley, what happened?" Gracie exclaimed, taking in my soaked pants.

I jerked my thumb in Damien's direction. "Ask Mr. Scared Me Shitless over here," I said with more than a little rancor.

"Well, let's hit the bathroom before heading upstairs and get you cleaned up," Gracie said, looping her arm with mine and pulling me toward the Bakersville Times building. Damien followed closely behind us.

This was the friendliest Gracie had been towards me in weeks and it made me instantly suspicious.

"I'll get you another coffee," Damien said eagerly as Gracie and I headed to the restroom in the reception area.

"Don't bother," I told him grumpily. I was annoyed. Annoyed

that I had ruined my favorite pair of dress pants. Annoyed that Maysie dropped her moving out bomb on me first thing this morning. Annoyed that I had caught Gracie yucking it up with Garrett like they were BFFs.

And most of all annoyed that Garrett hadn't acknowledged me. Not a wave or a nod of his head. Just big fat nothin', like I didn't exist.

It hurt.

It shouldn't hurt.

I had made myself pretty freaking clear on how I felt about him. But still…

Great, I had morphed into one of *those* girls. The wishy-washy kind. I hated *those* girls. I think I needed a time out. Either that or a swift kick up the butt.

Gracie pulled out a grip full of paper towels from the dispenser and handed them to me. I dabbed my pants but figured I'd just have to deal with smelling like stale coffee for the rest of the day.

I tossed the towels into the trash and was about to head out of the bathroom when Gracie touched my hand. "Can we talk for a minute before going up?" she asked me.

Gracie looked like a vulnerable little girl but she was one of the fiercest bitches I knew. I knew she could be maliciously cruel or have your back in a cage fight. It was hard to tell which Gracie I'd have the pleasure of conversing with.

"Sure, what's up?" I asked, figuring feigning ignorance my best solution at this point.

"First thing, how are you holding up? You know with your dad and all that?" Gracie asked and I relaxed a bit. Maybe we wouldn't be having a chick fight in the bathroom.

"Eh, I have my days. Thanks for asking," I said sincerely. I hoped this was a sign that our weirdness was at an end.

"I know things have been weird between us," Gracie stated, reading my mind.

I laughed uncomfortably. "Weird like wearing different color of socks or weird like hanging out with your grandma at prom?" I asked.

"Uh, definitely grandma weird," Gracie giggled and I felt

myself relax a little bit more. This was good. We were being almost normal. Maybe our relationship wasn't completely messed up.

Gracie's eyes twinkled strangely and she had me off balance again. This was not the friend I was used to. This girl reminded me of the person I loathed before we had formed a friendship. The evil sorority girl that I wanted to eradicate from the planet Godzilla style.

"But it shouldn't be, Riley. Garrett explained everything. He said it was a mistake. That the two of you would never be together. That he didn't even like you enough to be friends," she giggled even as she ripped me a new one.

"So that's the plan? For you and I to snark out over a dude? Really? Because I'm not in the mood," I said tiredly.

The bizarre gleam in Gracie's eye disappeared and her face softened. She looked ashamed. "No, Riley. That's ridiculous. You are one of my best friends. I just don't want things to be uncomfortable. Garrett is just a friend. And you guys don't even talk. So there's no reason for us to tiptoe around him like he's a stick of dynamite about to go off. Just promise me you won't keep stuff from me in the future," Gracie said, giving me a more genuine smile.

"Of course," I placated, wanting the conversation over with. We stood there in awkward silence for a few more seconds until I started to develop a serious case of claustrophobia.

"We'd better get upstairs," I said, making my way to the door.

"Yeah, we should. But let's grab a drink after this. It's been too long since we've done anything together," Gracie suggested.

"Sure, sounds good," I said distractedly, ready to put this strange discussion behind me.

Coming out of the bathroom, I found Damien waiting with another Styrofoam cup of coffee. I tried to be irritated with him. His need to make me happy was desperate and left a bad taste in my mouth. We had been there done that and I had the battle wounds to prove it.

"I've got to catch Garrett before I head up. Just tell Diane I'll be right there," Gracie said, heading off to another wing of the building.

My teeth clenched together painfully but I refused to comment.

So what? Gracie had to talk to Garrett. She had just said they were friends. Friends talk. Plus I didn't care. Garrett could talk to whomever he wanted to.

And if I silently debated this out any longer, I'd look certifiably crazy.

I took the cup from Damien and gave him a smile. "You wanna come have a few drinks with Gracie and me after work?" I asked him. His face lit up and I felt the stirrings of warning in my gut. But I ignored it. I was through letting my gut do the talking around here.

"I'd love to," he said, giving me that warm smile of his that used to make me melt. I was impervious to it now, but it still felt good to be in a place where I could accept that smile without bitterness.

I needed to focus on something, somebody that wasn't Garrett freaking Bellows and the ambiguous status of his bed partner.

"Great," I said with more conviction than I felt. We walked to the elevator together and I refused to question the sanity of my decisions.

"You invited Damien? Why?" Gracie asked as we drove to Hillbilly Tom's, another local bar in Bakersville after our internship was over for the day. It was already six-thirty and I was ready for a drink or five.

I had been forced to cover a local flower show. Rioting good time it was not. Coming up with a hundred different ways to describe floral arrangements was not what I wanted out of my journalism career.

Damien had gotten to cover a fifteen-car pile up on the highway while Gracie had been invited to sit in on a court case involving a local dog-fighting ring.

And I had been handed the flower assignment. The gods were flipping me the bird that's for sure.

I pulled in beside Damien at Hillbilly's and cut off my car.

"I don't know. I just offered. I thought it would be the nice thing to do," I said, not feeling the need to explain myself. Actually I knew the reason I had extended the invitation and it had nothing to do with Damien.

"I just hope you know what you're doing. He's hanging onto some serious hope that you two will work things out. You'll just be leading him on," Gracie warned, pulling her lip gloss out of her purse and smearing some on her mouth.

"Who says I'll be leading him on?" I asked irritably.

What?

I didn't mean that. Why did I say that?

Gracie's eyes widened. "Seriously?" she asked in disbelief, no doubt remembering my state of utter despondency after our epic breakup and my subsequent vows to never breath in Damien Green's direction again.

"I don't know. Just come on. I need a drink," I said, getting out of the car. Gracie's phone chirped and she started furiously tapping away.

"Girl, put the phone away and let's get inside," I said, though I was trying to sneak a peek at the screen.

"Sorry," Gracie mumbled, finishing up her text. I looked over her shoulder and saw Garrett's name and then made myself look away. Something was definitely going on between those two.

"Garrett's gonna be coming by in a bit after he gets off work," Gracie informed me almost defensively. She drew herself upright as though waiting for an attack.

"You sure are spending a lot of time together," I commented, refusing to take the bait that Gracie seemed to be putting out there.

Gracie shrugged. "We like being together. I hope that's not a problem," she said, blinking at me innocently. What in the hell was she playing at? All day I felt as though I were being tested and I didn't appreciate it one bit.

"Why would that be a problem?" I asked defiantly. Gracie opened her mouth but was interrupted.

"What's taking you guys so long?" Damien called out from the front door. Suddenly spending time with my ex seemed almost bearable. Anything to avoid whatever was brewing with Gracie.

"Sorry, apparently Garrett Bellows is going to be joining us," I said dryly and watched as Damien's face paled.

"Is it all right that I'm here?" Damien asked looking at me

pointedly. I sighed wishing everyone could just forget about that stupid show of testosterone at Barton's.

"This is most definitely *not* a problem," I said firmly and then flashed Damien my brightest smile. He seemed to relax then and the three of us found a table near the back.

"G and T?" Damien asked, making it a point to show that he remembered my usual drink.

"Sure, why not," I answered, reaching into my purse to dig out some cash.

Damien held up his hand. "I've got this one. You buy the next round," he said and I felt better knowing he was treating this as a casual get together rather than something more significant. He turned to Gracie.

"What about you Gracie? What's your poison?" he asked. Gracie gnawed on her bottom lip and seemed conflicted, which was strange for her. I watched her closely trying to get a read on her mood. She had been trying to be cool up until she revealed Garrett would be joining us. Something told me he was the source of her sudden tension. I just couldn't figure out why, considering the way she had thrown the information in my face.

"Uh, a beer. Yeah, just a beer. Something light. Like a Miller," she finally said after an exorbant amount of time dilerbating over it.

Damien clearly didn't pick up on Gracie's strange attitude. He gave her a quick nod and headed for the bar to put in our order. Once out of sight, Gracie pounced. "What is up, Ri? Why in the world are you hanging out with Damien? On purpose no less?" she asked, eyeing me questioningly.

I shrugged. "Don't you ever get tired of being mad at someone? Holding a grudge is exhausting," I explained, hoping she would take my double meaning.

I had grown tired of being angry with Damien, particularly after it became obvious I wasn't really mad at Damien as much as I was mad at myself. Mad that I had been caught off guard and that something I had depended on had dissolved under my feet without my realizing it.

But I was also speaking to Gracie and her apparent grudge

against me. Even if she wouldn't admit it existed. I saw it. I knew it was there.

Gracie's eyes narrowed, apparently not agreeing with my reasoning. "Uh, when Mila borrowed my green dress last year without asking and then spilled red wine all over the front, I did *not* ask the bitch to come out drinking the next night. No way! She had ruined something that was mine. She had violated my trust. And that was just over a dress, Riley. Damien violated your heart. That is way worse. I think you're letting him off way too lightly," she scolded, frowning at me as though I were disappointing her.

Yeah, the girl obviously missed my point completely.

"Well it's a good thing Damien didn't stain my dress then. Just drop it already," I said, feeling tired.

"Here you go, girls," Damien said, appearing with our drinks. I shot Gracie a pointed look before thanking him and taking my cocktail. Gracie took her beer from him with a forced smile.

We drank our respective beverages in relative silence. The bar was pretty busy with the after work crowd but even in our noisy surroundings, the lack of talking at our table was almost deafening.

Damien cleared his throat. "So, how was the flower show, Ri?" he asked.

"Probably not as cool as covering the interstate crash. Plus I had an allergic reaction to a huge display of hydrangeas and spent the last half hour sneezing my head off," I complained. Gracie and Damien each laughed at my misfortune and I grinned, taking one for the team. Hey, if my snot filled afternoon alleviated the weirdness, then I would share away.

"Yeah, well Kim, who was I shadowing, was about to kick my ass. Personally I thought the mucus made that hideous arrangement look better," I chuckled.

"It seems like you guys are having a good time," a voice said from behind me. Gracie looked over my shoulder and waved, her face lighting up in a smile. Damien went a pale and gripped his beer tighter as though expecting to have it hurled in his face.

I, on the other hand, felt chills run down my spine at the sound of the voice I had heard not so long ago, as he begged me to watch him as he made me come. I definitely shivered that time. The memory was too much for my poor brain to handle.

But my desire was quickly replaced with irrational rejection as Garrett walked around me, his arm brushing against my back as he went to Gracie's side. He pulled out a bar stool and sat down. I couldn't take my eyes off him.

He didn't acknowledge me, however. He didn't bother to look my way once. He glanced down at Gracie's beer and leaned forward to whisper something softly in her ear. She looked up at him, her eyes seeming to plead with him. They spoke quietly, only to each other, and I wished like crazy that I could hear what they were saying.

"You want to go play a game of darts?" Damien asked, pulling me out of my masochistic voyeurism. I tore my eyes away from the pair across the table and looked over at him, giving him, or at least what I hoped to be, my sincerest smile.

"Sure, that sounds good," I said overly loud. Okay, so I was hoping to get Garrett's attention. Sure it was childish and pathetic. But I hoped he would remember it was just a week ago that he had shown an entire bar how much he wanted *me*.

The problem was I couldn't decide if this need was about my feelings for him, or once again about a misplaced sense of pride. Because Garrett *had* wanted me. And now he seemed to want nothing to do with me. And nothing hurt an ego more than being cast aside for one of your friends.

I scraped my chair back, making a big production of leaving the table.

Look at me, damn it!

And then he did. Garrett looked away from Gracie and finally met my eyes. He glanced from me to Damien and something unidentifiable flickered in their depths. And then whatever I thought I saw there closed off and then there was nothing.

He turned back to Gracie and spoke quietly to her again, picking up her half empty beer and setting it aside. He held out his hand and she nodded, placing her smaller palm into his much larger one.

Gracie looked up at me and there was no self-satisfaction on her face at having Garrett there beside her. In fact she seemed upset. I wish I understood what was going on between them. Were they dating? Or were they just friends as Gracie claimed. And why oh why didn't I have the guts to come out and ask like I normally would have?

"Garrett's going to give me a ride home. I'll see you on Wednesday," Gracie said and I couldn't read the tone in her voice.

"Are you sure you don't want to hang out longer?" I asked, glancing at Garrett who seemed to be looking at everyone but me.

"Garrett, you don't feel like staying?" I asked him, taking the leap to address him directly.

"No, I think Gracie and I are going to head out," he said giving me a hard look. "Besides, you seem to be in good hands," he stated matter a factly before turning around and walking out the door.

Gracie looked at me and cocked her eyebrow, but only said a quick "goodbye" before following Garrett out of the bar.

I pushed my chair into the table hard enough for it to fall on the floor.

"What is going on between you two?" Damien asked.

"Me and Gracie?" I asked, purposefully obtuse. Damien frowned.

"No, you and that Garrett guy," he clarified and I could only shake my head.

"We were a huge mistake," I said sadly, feeling the truth of the words deep in my bones.

Damien's jaw set as he picked up on what exactly I was telling him. "So you guys really did sleep together." He pushed his hair off his forehead and grimaced. "I was really hoping that stuff you were yelling at each other last week was more about being angry than based on something that actually happened."

I sighed and scrubbed my face with my hands before dropping them back to my side. "What do you want me to say, Damien? You broke up with *me*. I was upset. I thought you and me were forever and then suddenly we weren't. I was in a really messed up place," I shot out and Damien flinched.

"And Garrett was there. He and I hooked up and I thought for a stupid second it might mean something. But that was before I remembered who he was and who I'm supposed to be."

I hated how incredibly egotistical those words sounded but it felt like honesty. Garrett and I weren't meant to be. It didn't matter that we had existed in a moment in time where we made perfect sense.

Each time we had been together had been abnormal circumstances. First when I was so drunk, sleeping with him hadn't felt like a lapse in judgment. And the second time when I was so out of my mind with misery that it seemed he was the only one to hold me together.

If I had learned anything it was that I didn't trust my heart to lead me down the right path. My emotions were too conflicted and messy where Garrett Bellows was concerned and I knew that following them would be a disaster.

I wasn't a person to allow my head to overrule my heart. Even now, in the early stages of my grieving, I clung to my reason like a lifeline. Garrett and I were too different. Even though he had shown me a side of himself that revealed a man who at one time had wanted more for his life, it didn't change the fact of where he was now.

And whom he was currently with.

And that *who* was my good friend.

"And who are *you*, Riley?" Damien asked with a hopeful expression on his face. He took my hand in his, cautiously at first but when I didn't pull immediately away, he squeezed and moved closer.

I looked into the brown eyes that at one time had signified everything I wanted in my life. Damien was my ideal match in everyway. We had the same goals, the same ambitions. Damien and I were driven in similar ways, propelled by a passionate need to succeed and thrive.

And if those likenesses felt a little empty now, I was determined to overlook that and forget about the boy with the long blond hair who made me question everything I thought I had wanted in my life.

Because how could a guy like Garrett give me my happily

ever after when we spent most our time cataloging the million and one ways we didn't work? We couldn't. End of story.

"I'm Riley Walker and I have an amazing future ahead of me. I know exactly what I want out of life and I *will* make my dad proud of me," I said with desperation. I needed those words to be true. Otherwise I didn't know what I would do.

Damien, emboldened by my seeming acceptance of his touch, put his arm around me. "And you will, Riley. If anyone can be something great, it's you," he said emphatically. His words, whether they were genuine or not, were exactly what I needed to hear.

Without thinking about what I was doing, I leaned in and kissed his mouth. Damien froze, as though worried that should he react in any way, I would bolt.

"Kiss me," I whispered against his mouth, forcing down the sudden self-loathing that tasted like bile in the back of my throat.

What was I doing? I thought furiously to myself as Damien wrapped his arms around me, his fingers curling into the back of my hair the way he had done a thousand times before.

But his lips felt foreign against mine. As if they didn't belong there anymore. It felt like kissing a stranger. Or someone I used to know but had long since outgrown.

I put those thoughts out of my mind and threw myself into kissing the boy who had so recently broken my heart. The boy I thought I would never get over until another boy came along and proved that perhaps I had never really given away my heart at all. Until him.

STOP! I screamed silently and pressed my lips so hard against Damien's that I cut the sensitive tissue against my teeth.

Damien pulled back and looked at me questioningly. He had to know there was more to this kiss than me wanting him. That desire and love had absolutely nothing to do with it. That this was a kiss born out of guilt and confusion and a staunch denial of a part of me that needed to die a quick and silent death.

Damien rubbed his thumb along my bottom lip, which had started to bleed. "What was that about?" he asked quietly, his eyes troubled.

I jerked my head away and moved out of his grip, giving

myself and my continued poor decision making some distance. "Why does it have to be about anything?" I asked with hostility, already feeling foolish.

Damien's lips quirked into a sad smile. "Because with you, Ri, it's *always* about something. I just hoped it would be about me," he said and I knew I wasn't being fair to him right now. Mostly because even as I tried not to, I couldn't stop thinking of Garrett walking out of the bar with Gracie behind him.

I couldn't stop imagining what they were doing. What they meant to each other. What *I* had meant to Garrett. I hated how much I cared. I didn't want to care. I was sick of feeling! Emotions got me nowhere but up to my chin in hurt and pain.

I gripped the front of Damien's shirt and pulled him angrily toward me. "Let's not think about it okay," I demanded him, wondering briefly if I was setting myself up for more rejection. But I knew by the way his eyes heated as he looked at me that there would be no refusal.

Damien Green wanted me in whatever way he could have me. And I was taking advantage of that. Willing to use his body to forget. To forget my life that had somehow careened off track.

"Okay," Damien said huskily, his glasses sliding down his nose as he leaned in to kiss me again.

"Can I come home with you tonight?" I asked, trying not to feel like a piece of shit for what I was propositioning.

Damien licked his lips. "There's nothing I want more," he murmured, pulling his keys out of his pocket and taking my hand in his.

You'd think I would have learned something about ill-advised hookups from jumping into Garrett's bed. They only lead to complete upheaval.

But I wanted to go back to a time when my world was what I wanted it to be. A time where my dad was still alive, my heart still in one piece and the boy who shared my life was safe and predictable.

"Let's go," I said, trying not hate myself as I followed Damien to his car.

Chapter 20

"**H**ey, Riley. Hey *Damien,*" Maysie said with a tone that reeked of disapproval. Normally that was my mode of communication and it didn't feel good hearing it come from Maysie Ardin of all people.

It was three weeks before the end of the semester. I had fallen into some form of a quasi relationship with Damien that wasn't quite dating but not just friendship. I absolutely *refused* to give him the title of boyfriend, however.

After leaving the bar with Damien that night all those weeks ago, I had gone home with him.

And no, perv, I didn't sleep with him.

Yes, I had planned to originally but once I had gotten there I couldn't do it.

Yay for self-respect!

Instead we had stayed up talking like we used to. And I was able to remember that aside from being my boyfriend, Damien had at one time been one of my closest friends.

After that, it became easier and easier to spend time with him. A drink after work. Studying at the library in the evenings. A lecture on environmental responsibility in the student hall. Small things that morphed into something else entirely.

Being around Damien again was like putting on a pair of well-worn shoes that had started to pinch my toes. He was still the liberal minded, environmentally aware, poetry writing, save the whales kind of guy. He still looked down his nose at people who didn't recycle and easily judged anyone that didn't share his single-minded vision of the world. At one time our vision had been one and the same. We were unified in our sneering, derisive judgments.

But I had come to realize it wasn't so easy to sit on your soapbox when you scratched below the surface of what you were railing against. Because what you might find there could blow your mind

But now, even as I allowed myself to be pulled back into the way things *were,* it didn't feel quite *right.* Even as I fought tooth and nail to make it all fit. Because I wanted something that was just as I remembered it. Before my life had changed too much for me to get a handle on. I craved the lack of emotional chaos and Damien provided that on some level.

Because lord knew, the rest of my universe was in a tailspin. First on the fast train to emo territory was the sad destruction of my family.

I had gone home for Thanksgiving break and it had been miserable. I had visions of creating new traditions; that somehow Mom, Gavin, Fliss and I would carve out a new niche after Dad's death. What a deluded moron I had been.

While Mom had tried to put on a brave face, it had lasted only as long as it took me to unpack. Mom broke down and cried through most of my visit. There was no large family dinner this year. Instead, my mother, brother and myself ate a crappy meal at Denny's before coming home and going to our separate bedrooms. My sister and her family didn't even bother to come, claiming the girls were sick. I knew that they just hoped to avoid exactly what I had experienced, a get together meant to induce heavy drinking.

My brother was a mess. He had moved back in with Mom and it disgusted me how she was having to take care of him even though he was almost forty years old. And I was furious that she was enabling it.

When I asked her about it, she told me, politely and gently of course, to mind my own business and that everyone dealt with grief in their own way. This was Gavin's way and I should respect that.

It had been hard, but I let it go. Hoping my mother knew the best way to handle the situation.

So after that depressing excuse for a holiday, I had latched onto school and classes as though it was all I had. And maybe in some ways it was. It was the only thing I had a hundred percent complete control over anyway.

And thankfully my desperation paid off. My midterm grades had buoyed my spirits. Straight A's. I was hoping to be on the Dean's List again this semester. And I could almost hear my dad telling me how proud he was of me. I felt obsessed with the need to prove myself.

It was no longer just about me but about showing that my dad's faith in me was founded. Part of me realized that I wasn't handling my grief in a healthy way. That I was shoving it aside in favor of a dogged determination to succeed.

My social life was non-existent. Maysie was so immersed in all things Jordan and Generation Rejects that I rarely saw her. Gracie and I had developed a relationship built on wary mistrust. Our one time friendship deteriorating under the strain of her silent bitterness. Because she would never acknowledge how she felt about me. To everyone else, we appeared friendly. Two girls who got along.

But I felt the rift and it sucked. I didn't know what to do about it. And the more time that passed, the larger the division between us became.

And with Gracie came Vivian, so there went fifty percent of my social interactions. So maybe it was more out of loneliness that I allowed Damien back into my world.

Whatever it was, he was there, like he had never left. I wish I could say it felt like finding something that I had been missing, but then I would be lying. It was more like stepping into a bath that was luke warm. Not really relaxing or comfortable, but it didn't make you jump out and take a shower instead.

Crap, my metaphors were as bad as my reasoning.

"You coming to the Rejects' gig tonight? It should be fun. This will be their last one before heading out on tour after Christmas," Maysie asked me, deliberately ignoring Damien.

Damien squeezed in closer to me, at the mention of the band. Yep, he was still feeling very insecure about Garrett and it manifested rather noticeably whenever anything Generation Rejects related was mentioned.

I tried not to feel suffocated by the way he pressed against me. "Uh, I don't think so. I'm off tonight and Damien and I were heading out to a poetry reading later," I answered, trying to inch away from an overly clingy Damien.

Maysie caught my movement and eyed me knowingly. "Poetry reading? Come on, you can do boring shit any night. Jordan asked if you'd come," Maysie needled.

"Don't get your hopes up," I said, getting to my feet. I headed into the kitchen, knowing Maysie was hot on my heels.

"Come on, Ri. I'm not sure what you're playing at right now, but the Riley Walker I know wouldn't even breathe the same air as Damien after everything he put you through. If this is about Garrett"

I held my hand up, interrupting that line of thought before it could go any further.

"Don't go there. Just don't," I warned, grabbing a bottle of water from the fridge.

Maysie sighed. "Riley, don't make the same mistakes that I did. I almost lost the most important thing in my life because I had unrealistic expectations about my life and what a relationship *should* look like," Maysie warned, pulling a bag of popcorn from the cabinet and putting it in the microwave. I didn't say anything. Mostly because I was too busy processing the fact that at some point in all of this mess I called a life, our roles had reversed. Maysie had, unbeknownst to me, become the no nonsense voice of reason and I had become the screwed up head case with a bad case of I-can't-make-up-my-mind.

I started to chew on the skin around my thumb. "I know I'm being a hypocrite. I know I'm not making any sense, but..." I let my words trail off. No reason to cut myself open completely. This conversation had me feeling way too vulnerable and touchy. I hated that my world had turned upside down because of a guy.

Somehow, someway, Garrett Bellows had gotten inside me. He was like a parasite, slowly sucking me dry. Whether I ignored his existence or not, he was still there, embedded in my intestinal track, draining me of all good sense.

"He scares you," Maysie piped up, grinning at me as she shoved a handful of popcorn into her mouth. She needed to keep that mouth full because I wasn't appreciating her on the nose analysis of my internal conflict.

I made a noise that sounded like I was choking. "Scared? Give me a break, Mays. Annoyed? Yes. Frustrated? You betcha. Ready to take off someone's head? Looking more and more like a definite," I said in warning. "But never, ever scared," I said with more conviction than I felt.

Maysie chuckled. "Oh yes he does. He gives you butterflies. He makes you sweat. He calls you on your bullshit and keeps you on your toes. You both love and hate how he does that. He has you tied up in knots and you can't get out. And Miss I-Have-My-Whole-World-Figured-Out is going crazy because of it. So you've gone into shut down. You're forcing Damien down your throat in an effort to deny what you know is there." Maysie seemed entirely too pleased with herself.

I opened my mouth to say something but she cut me off... *again!* "I'm not saying this to be mean, but Riley, you've become your own worst enemy. I know you think Garrett has nothing to offer. That you're embarrassed by the fact that you actually *like* him. But he's a good guy. He's a smart guy. And there is no one else in this world that would lay everything at your feet the way that he would. Remember that when you're sitting at that poetry reading later, trying to convince yourself that being there with Damien is the right thing. Because Damien wasn't the guy who drove you over a hundred miles in the middle of the night to see your dad. Damien wasn't the guy who stayed with you at the hospital while you tried to keep your family together."

My throat felt uncomfortably tight and I blinked rapidly to try and hold off the tears. I will not cry!

"And remember he's the guy who has made you feel like

you're worth all the hassle. That no matter what you dish out, he is there to take it. To volley it right back and is there to go toe to toe anytime you're ready." Maysie squeezed my hands. "Damien wasn't that guy for you. Garrett is," she said softly and I closed my eyes and tried to take a deep breath around the huge, crushing weight in my chest.

"Enough, Maysie. Seriously, just enough already," I begged. I didn't want to hear any of this. I couldn't.

Maysie looked disappointed by my refusal to hear her. "I just would like you there tonight. Jordan would like you there. *Garrett* would like you there. I know that matters to you, whether you want to admit it or not," she said confidentially.

I didn't bother to say anything else. I gave my best friend a final look of frustration before going back into the living room to join Damien on the couch again. I tried not to cringe as he put his arm around me.

Maysie's punch in the gut small talk had done a number on me. I could barely sit in the same room with Damien with her words ricocheting around in my head.

"You're not really thinking of going to that concert, are you?" Damien asked, flipping through the TV channels like he lived there. Another of the many Damien personality quirks that drove me nuts.

TV domination was definitely at the top of the list.

Reaching over, I grabbed the remote from his hand and purposefully turned it to an over the top reality show that we both abhorred. Damien made a face. "Since when do you watch this mind rot?" he asked dismissively.

"Since you and I stopped spending every waking hour together," I shot back, turning up the volume.

Damien rolled his eyes but didn't comment. "So we're going to the poetry reading, right?" he asked, moving the conversation back to our evening plans and Maysie's arm twisting suggestion of going to see Generation Rejects play.

Damien seemed so hopeful and eager that I couldn't say no. It would be like throwing a puppy into oncoming traffic. "Sure, poetry reading. Sounds groovy," I replied, knowing that it was by far the safer option.

Being in the same room as Garrett left way too much potential for explosion.

After Damien left, I filled the hours with every distraction I could think of. My mind too often sought to slip in a dangerous direction.

Why is it when you make up your mind about something, your heart was there to call you on your bullshit? I hated my heart; I wish it would shut the hell up. It didn't help that Maysie was there to cheer my heart on.

I had never been so thankful for the sound my ringing phone in my life. I was spending too much time in my own head and I was looking for a jailbreak.

Seeing my mom's name on the screen I tried not to feel the twinge of apprehension. I hated that I was hesitant to answer it. I used to love talking to my mother. I had enjoyed our conversations and her quirky advice.

Now I never knew what to expect. When she was good, I could pretend things were just like they were before.

But when she was bad I couldn't live in my shiny world of denial. And I liked living there, thank you very much.

"Hey, Mom," I said after answering it.

"Hey, baby girl. How are you?" Mom asked and I relaxed in relief. Mom sounded good.

"Eh, can't complain," I said, sticking with the bare bones of the truth. At one time I would have unloaded all of my drama on her very capable shoulders. Now, that ship had sailed and I worried about giving her more than she could handle.

I could hear my mother letting out a noisy breath on the other end. "Stop walking on egg shells around me, Riley. I promise I won't crack. Now talk to me. There's more to that statement then you're saying," my mother scolded and I couldn't stop myself from smiling.

"First, how are you, Mom? I know you had your support group meeting today. I was going to call you later to see how it went," I asked before she could badger me for more details about my life.

My mom had started attending a support group for people

who have lost loved ones. She had only been to three meetings and the first two times she had been such an emotional wreck afterwards that I wasn't sure she should go back.

But she was insistent that she continue going and from the sound of her, I had hope it might actually help.

"It was hard. Every second of every day is a struggle. It's hard for me to keep going in this life without your dad. I expected many more years together. I feel...cheated," she admitted quietly and I felt the familiar tightness grip my chest.

"I know, Mom. I do too," I said just as quietly.

We were silent after that for a while, neither of us willing to talk until emotions were in check.

"But everyone says time heals all wounds and I can only hold onto the hope that one day I will be able to remember you father without feeling the excruciating pain of his loss," my mom finally said and I was reminded of Garrett's words before leaving Maryland.

"Just try to take it one day at a time," I told her. My mom's chuckle eased some of the suffocating grief.

"Such a wise daughter I've raised," she teased and I laughed in return.

"I just listen to people way smarter than me," I acknowledged, surprised to find myself putting Garrett in that category.

"Very true. Now moving on to you. Tell me what's going on in your life. What's going on with that handsome boy your brought with you to Maryland? I really liked him, Ri," Mom said, and I desperately wanted to shut down this conversation as quickly as possible.

"I got approved for an independent study next semester. Professor Cartwright is going to supervise it. Now I just have to decide on a topic. I was thinking of comparing Stuart era feminism through the plays of Aphra Behn with modern poet Adrienne Riche. Professor Cartwright says he's never heard of anyone comparing those two before, so it would be something brand new," I was rambled, hoping that if I talked long enough, Mom would forget about her well intentioned intrusive line of questioning.

No such luck.

"That sounds great, Riley. But why are you avoiding us talking about your fellow? What was his name again? I'm sorry I don't remember it," my mom broke in and I knew she wouldn't let it go.

"Garrett. His name is Garrett Bellows," I admitted, knowing avoidance efforts would be defeated by my mother's information seeking militia.

"Garrett. I like that name. How did you meet him? Does he go to Rinard?" she asked and I snorted.

"Not exactly," I said, knowing I sounded judgmental.

My mom picked up on my snotty tone instantly. "What's that for? Does he go to a rival school or something? Is this like some sort of co-ed Romeo and Juliet?" she joked and I rolled my eyes even though she couldn't see me.

"No, he doesn't go to another school. He doesn't go to school at all," I said.

"Did he already graduate?" she asked.

"No, he never went," I told her.

"Oh," my mother said shortly. "And this is obviously a problem for you," she surmised.

"Well of course it's a problem! He has no goals! Well nothing that goes beyond playing guitar in his silly rock band. How could I ever fit with someone who doesn't want what I want? We have absolutely *nothing* in common, Mom!" I let out in a huff. I had gotten loud and I knew I was getting way too worked up.

Mom didn't say anything for at least thirty seconds. "Well, it sounds like your mind's made up," she said succinctly and to the point.

"Yes, yes it is," I said, feeling myself become irrationally defensive.

"But this guy with no future and no plans that you clearly have no respect for, drove you all the way to Maryland in the middle of the night so you could see your father. Huh," she said and then went silent again.

Even through my frustration with this direction of our conversation, her words hit me like a ton of bricks.

"I respect him. That's a little harsh," I bit out.

"You respect him? Then why spend all this time telling me why he is such a bad fit for you? It sounds like you're trying to convince yourself rather than me," my mother informed me, sounding entirely too smug.

"I'm going to have a life that matters, Mom. I promised Dad I would have a life that *means* something. How can I do that with someone whose life doesn't mean anything?" I asked, feeling like such a jerk for stating the thoughts that so often floated around my head. But it was the crux of my decisions where Garrett was concerned and I needed to vocalize them to the one person who wouldn't judge me for them.

"How can you say his life doesn't mean something? That's very callous of you, Riley and your father and I raised you to be tolerant, compassionate and understanding. Your father said those words to you knowing you would continue to be that amazing and loving girl that we raised. But to make your mind up about someone without giving them the opportunity to show you who they really are, well that's very *Republican* of you," my mom said firmly and I almost gasped.

She had called me a Republican. And to my granola eating, tree-hugging mother, that was the height of insult.

"Mom, how could you say that to me?" I asked, feeling like a little kid being scolded for taking the last cookie. Parents were way too good at making you feel bad.

"Riley, I'm not trying to hurt your feelings. I'm just disappointed in you. I don't know this Garrett. And from the sounds of it, you don't really either. Whose to say his life of meaning isn't just as beautiful as the one you want to have? Whose to say you can't make those lives matter *together*? Because the way that boy looked at you was something special. Your father would want you to do what makes your heart happy. Forget your head," she advised and I had no words to refute her.

Because she was right.

Damn it, Moms were always right.

Chapter 21

"**T**HAT girl's poem was so infantile. I mean who tries to compare the destruction of western civilization with rotting fruit and say it with a straight face? Talk about trying too hard. Blech," a girl named Karly said, sipping her Mocha Latte.

I was stuck at a table with four people who at one time I had considered friends. They had been acquaintances by way of my relationship with Damien. So in truth, they were *his* friends. *His* crowd. But not too long ago, I had sat around in this same kitschy coffee shop mocking everyone in order to make myself feel superior.

Wow, self-realization was a bitter pill to swallow sometimes.

Damien nodded as though Karly's comments were the smartest thing he had ever heard.

"Word," an overly skinny dude in a beret named Lou said from beside her. Had this douche really just said *word?* Had I blissfully ignored how these people reeked of pretention or had I been just as bad?

"I don't know, I thought she was pretty good," I spoke up, never one to sit by while other people were being dicks. From the way Karly looked at me in surprise, I had obviously never thought she was of the dick persuasion before.

"Are you serious, Riley? That drivel? Don't make me laugh," Karly snickered as though I couldn't possibly be serious. The rest of the group laughed, including Damien who seemed to think I had knowingly made a big funny.

"Oh god, now it's this dumbass's turn. Who wants to be the first to boo him off the stage? Because if I have to hear one more poem about Star Trek I call riot," Damien muttered, stirring his herbal tea after pouring an excessive amount of sugar in it. What was the point of herbal tea when you covered up the taste with insulin shock?

"Oh me!" Karly volunteered, going so far as to raise her hand like we were in class. Damien reached across the table to give her a high five and the peanut gallery yucked it up in anticipation of some poor guy's epic downfall.

Damien gave me an excited smile as he grabbed the hand that lay in my lap. Lacing our fingers together like we had done a million times before in this very coffee shop, I could almost delude myself into thinking this was normal. That this is what I wanted.

And I used to believe in the Tooth Fairy too.

"You know what guys, I've had enough of screaming pretentious bullshit for one night, thanks," I announced getting to my feet. Karly, Lou, and another guy named Colby stared at me with their mouths hanging open. I suppose I had somehow kept snarky Riley away from this group.

Damien looked at me frowning. "What are you talking about? I thought we were having a good time," he said, pulling that hurt look he did so well.

"Yeah, well that was before I remembered what a bunch of assholes you guys are. I've got better things to do." I pulled on my coat and wrapped my scarf around my neck. Karly and the beret twins were whispering to each other while giving me evil looks. I wanted to laugh at how ridiculous they looked sneering at me over the top of their ten dollar suburban housewife coffees. Sorry, *lattes*.

Damien got to his feet and reached out as though to stop me. "I can come with you. Just wait and let me grab another coffee." He was already reaching into his pocket for his wallet when I stopped him.

"No, Damien. There's no point. I'm going to Barton's," I told him and the look Damien gave me said *that* explained everything.

He slowly sat back down and then lifted his hand in a halfhearted wave.

"Well I guess I'll see you later then," he said, turning away from me. Huh. How easy it was to end something that should never have started back up in the first place. If only everything in life were that easy.

The guy with the Star Trek poem took the stage and I cupped my hands around my mouth and gave him a loud whoop. He looked at me startled, the group I had just left, watching me in disgust. I pumped my fist in the air.

"Rock it, dude! Star Trek rules!" I yelled, wanting to laugh at the look on Damien's face.

Without another word, I hurried out of the coffee shop, laughing hysterically the whole way. Thankfully I had driven that night. Perhaps I should have asked Damien if he was cool getting another ride, but I'm sure one of his dickhead friends could give him a ride. You know, after they eviscerated everyone's poetry and declared they were the coolest kids in the room.

I had realized while I sat at that horrible reading that the person I was striving so hard to be again, wasn't someone I necessarily liked. I knew I could be rude. I knew I could be overly obsessive when it came to following through on things. But damn it, I never thought I was outright cruel.

But I knew that was exactly what I had been one too many times before. How often had I cut someone down without a second thought? Poor Maysie had been on the receiving in of my vicious tongue more times than I could count and I considered her my best friend! What was wrong with me? I used sarcasm like a shield. Because god forbid anyone see that I was vulnerable under all this bitch.

And how I had behaved toward Garrett was perhaps my worst crime. In that moment, I needed to make it right. I needed to tell him I was sorry. We had been down this road before, when he came with me to Maryland. I had apologized, he had accepted, we had come to a place that felt fresh and right.

And what had I done? Gone and shit all over him again.

I knew to expect him to forgive me was perhaps reaching

too high. I was pretty sure that ship had sailed. I knew he and Gracie were spending time together and I had already stomped over enough hearts to get in the way of whatever was developing between them.

But I needed him to know that I realized I sucked and that I was truly sorry.

Because I'd rather he be a guitarist without a plan than a jerk with his life laid out ahead of them.

I broke several traffic laws in getting to Barton's. The place was packed so I had to park on the street. Walking into the bar, I knew that I stuck out like a sore thumb. My going out gear consisted of patchwork jeans and peasant top, paired with my Doc Martins. I had missed the dress like a hoochie memo.

I strained up on my tiptoes, trying to find Maysie's dark head in the melee. Finally, I spotted her over by the bar. She was sat with Vivian and Gracie and for a second I considered turning around and hightailing it out of there. But then I glanced at the stage and at the boy who played his guitar as though possessed and I felt the steel in my spine.

Pushing through the craziness, my ears were already ringing from the music. Cole's screaming vocals were always grating, but tonight, when I felt more than a little raw, they threatened to undo me.

But over it all I could make out Garrett's guitar and that somehow made it all better.

"Hiya, ladies," I yelled, once I had reached them. Maysie turned around and gave me a big smile.

"You made it!" she squealed, hugging me. She looked behind me. "And without the ass stain, I see," she commented, making a face.

"Nice one," Gracie piped up, giving me an almost genuine grin. "Hey, Ri!" she said, teetering on her stool and I realized why she seemed so relaxed with me. She was three sheets to the wind.

"Hey, G. Feeling good, I see," I remarked dryly, knowing she wouldn't pick up on the sarcasm. Gracie tipped her drink in my direction, dumping half of it on the floor in the process.

"You know it!" she hollered. Maysie grimaced and gave me a knowing look. Vivian was decked to the nines and gave me a preoccupied wave as she focused on the front of the stage and no doubt the hordes of barely clothed women jiggling their goods for the charismatic lead singer.

"How long have they been playing?" I asked, wanting to get my reason for being there over with. I had been so full of resolve on my drive, now I had an icky case of the dreads. I wasn't one to lack in confidence, but when you're in the wrong, it did a number on your nerves.

Maysie looked at the clock before turning back to me. "I don't know, around forty-five minutes or so. They should be having a break in the next fifteen," she informed me, pulling up a barstool so I could sit down.

My best friend leaned into me, knocking my shoulder with hers. "Seriously though, where's Damien? I thought you two were hanging out tonight," Maysie asked.

"I realized I had better things to do," was all I said and Maysie snickered.

"Told you so," she said with a smirk.

"Oh girl, you're asking for a slap. Don't you dare play the *I Told You So* card with me. Or we can start reaching into Maysie Ardin's bag of mistakes for a good time," I threatened good-naturedly. Maysie stuck her tongue out at me and I laughed over my nerves.

Now that I was here, I was seriously questioning my sanity. Why in the world was I opening a can of worms I had successfully closed shut? But the look on Garrett's face each and every time I rejected him was flashing across my brain like a neon sign.

Why had it taken a bunch of uptight jerk wads to make me realize how unfair I was being toward him? I hated how capable I was of tearing someone down. Me, the queen of the fair chance. The crusader of the lost cause could also be voted most likely to be an insensitive asshat.

I needed to say my piece and even if Garrett rightly told me to get lost, I would know that I had attempted to make things right.

I looked over at Gracie, the girl who I had considered a good friend, and knew that I needed to make peace with more than just Garrett. I hated the rift between us and wanted to get things back to the way they were. Even if some subconscious part of me knew that there was more to the freeze out than me having a party in Garrett's pants.

"Woohoo!" Gracie yelled drunkenly once the guys had concluded the song. Maysie's eyebrows pinched together and she gave me a concerned look. I hooked my arm around Gracie's waist and held her up so she wouldn't topple off the barstool.

She pushed me back and gave me a nasty look. "I don't need your help, *Riley,*" she muttered and I stood there stunned. Somewhere along the way, Gracie Cook had lost her ditzy, I-love-everybody- demeanor.

"Sorry. I was just trying to help," I said but Gracie waved me off. She seemed to pull herself together a bit and gave me a forced smile.

"I'm fine. But thanks," she then turned her back to me and waved Lyla, the bartender down for another drink.

Maysie put her hand over Gracie's. "I think you've had enough for one night, G," she said softly. Gracie frowned and looked between Maysie and me.

"I think I'll be the judge of that," she replied, pulling her hand out from underneath Maysie's. "Lyla!" she yelled, making everyone within a ten-foot radius turn to look at her.

Maysie and I both crowded in behind her as though to contain the embarrassment factor. "Where did Viv go?" I asked under my breath.

Maysie's eyes cut to me sideways. "I have no idea," she hissed back, trying to communicate with Lyla, using a complicated mixture of facial expressions and hand gestures, to stop serving an over the limit Gracie.

Lyla caught the hint and was suddenly very busy on the other side of the bar.

"Lyla! I need another!" Gracie yelled again. Maysie put her hand on her shoulder.

"Stop it, Gracie. I think you need to take it down a notch," she said placating.

Gracie reeled back, away from her touch and fell off the chair. Thank god the band was playing, so it masked the Gracie Cook detonation that was taking place.

"Just leave me alone! Both of you! I'm going outside to get some air," Gracie slurred, getting to her feet, slapping at our hands as we tried to help her.

"I'm coming with you," Maysie said, causing Gracie to glare at her.

Maysie turned to me. "I'll be back. Tell Jordan, when they take their break where I've gone," she said and I nodded, my gut twisting into knots as I watched her trail after a barely standing Gracie. I wanted to go after them, but I knew that I was currently the last person Gracie wanted to see. And I didn't want to set her off any more.

I picked up Gracie's overturned barstool and sat down. I couldn't focus on the show. I barely heard the songs. My mind working through what I would say to Garrett. Then it would flip to Gracie and how I knew without a doubt that something had to be done for her, and soon.

I was so lost in the suck fest quagmire of my depressing thoughts that I almost jumped out of my skin when someone put their hand on my shoulder.

"Ahh!" I yelled and karate chopped the unsuspecting owner of the hand in the gut.

"Ugh! What the hell, Ri!" Jordan doubled over.

Oops.

"That's what you get for creeping up on me. Next time it's a knee to the nuts, don't say I didn't warn you," I grumbled.

Jordan rubbed his stomach and gave me a pained smile. "Heard loud and clear."

The other guys in the band were milling around and I tried to make Garrett out in the crowd. I couldn't find him and I was beginning to feel like my chance was slipping through my fingers.

"Where's Mays?" Jordan asked, looking like a lost puppy. It was both incredibly sweet and incredibly nauseating how devoted he was to my friend.

"She's outside with Gracie," I said and Jordan made a face.

"That girl is getting to be a handful. Did you hear about what happened at our last show?" Jordan asked taking the beer that Lyla handed him and popping the top with a lighter.

"No, Maysie didn't mention anything," I said with surprise. I looked over Jordan's shoulder, finally catching sight of Garrett. He was talking to some chick with a shirt that looked as though it would fit a toddler. She was pressing her boobs into his chest and he was smiling his infuriatingly lazy smile down into her face.

Jealousy was an ugly emotion. One that turned me into some sort of Viking berzerker. My hands clenched into fists, my nails cutting into my palms. I had bloodthirsty visions of ripping Miss Blondie's hair out by the roots and keeping it as a battle trophy.

"She stripped down to her bra and panties and jumped on stage. I thought she was going to cause a riot," Jordan was saying and I snapped back to the conversation.

"Wait, what?" I asked, wondering if I heard him correctly. Gracie was a fun loving girl, but I could not for the life of me envision her becoming an exhibitionist. She still clung to a shred of her "good girl" image.

Jordan looked over his shoulder and then back to me with an amused smirk on his face. "Yeah, just ask Maysie. I think you've got other things to take care of right now," he said, tipping his beer back and taking a long drink.

I gave Jordan an annoyed click of my tongue as I hopped off the stool. "No one likes a know-it-all, Jordan," I lectured, walking past him.

"And no one likes someone in denial, Riley," he called over his shoulder.

Chapter 22

GARRETT was still smiling down at ho bag in the tight shirt when I finally made my way over to him. I had to shove my hands into my pants pockets so they wouldn't turn into hardcore weapons and poke the girl's eyes out.

"Garrett," I said through gritted teeth. Okay, Riley, you need to tone down the implied death threat. I took a deep breath as Garrett turned to me. His face was impassive and I couldn't read anything from his expression. *What else was new?* His eyes were clear though, so that was a plus. In fact I could see that he was totally sober.

"Hey, Riley," he said, already dismissing me. The girl, with her boobs *still* pressed into his chest, glared daggers at me. I barely gave her a look.

"Can I talk to you for a minute?" I asked, refusing to sound pleading or desperate, even if inside I was all of those things.

Garrett's eyes flickered with something I didn't recognize before he became blandly neutral again. "Well, I'm talking to…" he looked down at big boobs, clearly struggling to remember her name.

"Randa," she chirped, looking annoyed.

"Right, Randa. So Randa and I were having a conversation. I'm a little busy. Maybe later," Garrett said, clearly trying to get rid of me.

I grabbed his arm before he could walk away. "I promise I

won't keep you from *Randa* for more than a few minutes. I'm sure this scintillating interaction is too awesome to miss out on." My smile could cut glass.

Garrett looked at me as if he wished I would disappear. It hurt, knowing he didn't want me around. Particularly when there was a time I thought his attention was nothing more than an unwanted distraction. I hadn't appreciated his heart when I had it. I was a stupid. I was cruel. And worse than all that, I had lost something I hadn't realized I even wanted.

"Just a minute," I said and then added, "please" for good measure. I even batted my eyelashes. I was laying it on pretty thick.

Garrett squinted at me as though I had sprouted a set of wings but then shrugged. Turning back to *Randa* he gave her a half smile. "Catch up with you later?" he asked and I wanted to snarl. Seriously, I wanted to go jungle cat on both of them. What was wrong with me?

Randa looked from Garrett to me, then back again. I knew her bleach-fried brain was trying to make sense out of Garrett ditching *her* for the likes of *me*.

"Okay," she said in a voice that sounded as though she had spent a good deal of time huffing Helium gas.

"Lead the way," Garrett said, seeming bored as he gestured for me to walk in front of him.

I wanted to snap at him. I wanted to hurl a thousand insults at his head. But I didn't. Call it a growing maturity. Or maybe I was just losing my touch. Whatever it was, I held my tongue and moved toward the back of the restaurant.

Pushing through the swinging doors into the kitchen, I was hit with a face full of water. Looking down at my drenched white shirt I felt my fingers curve into claws and I was ready to do some serious damage.

"I told you I'd see those tits one day!" Paco hollered from his station at the dishwasher. This time I snarled. I didn't hold back the feral feline ready to come out.

"You. Are. Dead!" I yelled, before trying to run over and stick my foot down his throat.

"Woah, just chill, Riley. I have to get back on stage in ten minutes. So save the murder and mayhem for later, please," Garrett said, stopping me from wiping the floor with the pervy dishwasher.

I pointed at Paco, who wasn't laughing anymore and had a satisfying look of fear on his fleshy face. "You, later. Don't go anywhere," I threatened, before stomping toward the back doors leading to the smoking area.

I was thankful it was dark out but instantly regretted not grabbing my jacket, particularly since it was freezing and I was now in a wet shirt. Stupid jerks. I shivered but refused to be waylaid by my impending hypothermia.

"Maybe we should head inside. Your lips are turning blue," Garrett commented, eyeing me warily.

"No, just let me say something first," I insisted. Garrett shrugged as if to say, "It's your appendages."

"I've been an ass," I started and Garrett snorted. I tried really hard not to glare at him.

Garrett gave me a pointed look. "What? I'm not going to argue with you," he said matter a factly.

"I suppose I deserved that," I said, trying to unclench my jaw. Garrett snorted again, but this time I staunchly ignored it.

"I've had it in my head that we weren't right for each other. That we were going in two different directions. That you had nothing going for you. That I was *better* than you." I hated the harshness of my truth. I saw Garrett's eyes harden and I knew my words hurt.

"But I was so wrong, Garrett. I'm not better than you. I think you're entirely too good for *me*. You don't judge people, or make them feel bad. You accept everyone. You were there for me during a really difficult time. And I've since realized that those days with you, had been the most at peace I'd felt since my dad died. I'd thank you again, if those words hadn't become completely inadequate."

I couldn't tell if my confession meant anything to him. Per usual, Garrett's face gave nothing away.

"I know this is most likely too little too late. I know I've spent a lot of time making you feel like a loser and I can't erase that by saying *I'm sorry*. But I am. I am, Garrett. I'm so very sorry for ever making you feel less than what you are." I ended in a rush, wanting to get it all out before I froze to death.

Garrett didn't say anything. He was looking at me in an unreadable way. I didn't push him to respond, knowing that it would ruin whatever this moment was.

"I'm not sure what you want me to say," he broke the silence, his voice rough. Pushing his shaggy hair out of his eyes, he watched me with a hesitance that was both understandable and heartbreaking.

"I don't know that I want you to say anything. I just needed you to hear me," I said softly making Garrett laugh bitterly.

"Of course. Because it's what Riley Walker wants. So we all have to bow down to her wishes and demands. To hell with what the rest of us want or need," Garrett said angrily. I was taken aback by the hostility in his eyes. I had expected dismissal or frustration or a million other responses than his cold rage.

"I..." I started, not sure exactly what I was going to say. Garrett punched the wall beside him, making me go silent.

Well...shit.

"Do you even know how many times I wanted you to look at me, not as a loser with no future. Not as a guy in a band with no idea of what he wants in his life. I just wanted you, to just once, look at me as the guy who would give you the world. And for that to be enough," he said with a passion that was so uncharacteristic for him that I had nothing to say. Not a single, goddamn thing.

"But it wasn't enough. That first time, I get it, I was the rebound. I was the guy to help you forget. Even if *you* ended up forgetting all of it."

"Not *all* of it," I interrupted.

"No, maybe not, but you forgot the part where I told you how long I've wanted you. How I held you in my arms and knew for certain that I would never hold anyone else again. That for a single moment in time we were *everything* to each other," Garrett's voice broke and he looked away from me, as though he couldn't bear it.

I opened my mouth and then closed it. Then tried again.

"I had no idea," I said, wishing I could touch him. But I knew that wouldn't be okay right now.

"No, because you were so quick to label it a mistake. And I agreed. Mostly because I was pissed that the girl who I had been ready to lay down my world for, dismissed me like yesterday's trash. I get it. I'm a townie. I don't go to Rinard College like the rest of those douche holes that you run around with. But fucking hell, Riley, I want to think that I matter. That I have merit." He was yelling at this point and I worried someone would come outside to see what was going on. And that was the last thing I wanted.

"That's what I'm trying to tell you, Garrett. That I know that! That I was wrong! I feel like shit for thinking that. Even for one second!" I cried out as Garrett turned away from me as though to go back inside.

Garrett's shoulders slouched and his hair hung limply to his shoulders. He looked like a man defeated. "But I *am* a loser, Riley. I've wasted what my parents gave me. I never thought my life was lacking until you made me question all of it. You *shouldn't* waste your time on me. Damien is much better for you than I could ever be."

I shocked us both by smacking him. Yep, I smacked him across his pretty little face. His head flew to the side and my palm started stinging before I realized what I had done. Slowly, Garrett turned back to me, his brow furrowed, his eyes hooded. He brought his hand up to cup his cheek.

"What. In. The. Fucking. Hell?" he asked in a deadly quiet.

I cradled my stinging hand against my chest as I breathed heavily from the adrenaline rush. "Don't you *ever* say that about yourself again. You are *not* a loser. If you say anything like that again, I'll punch you," I swore emphatically.

Garrett took a step toward me, his eyes heated and furious. "Who the hell do you think you are? You spend the past year making me feel like something on the bottom of your shoe. Now you physically assault me when I'm in agreement? You're nuts, Riley. Certifiably insane," he spit out.

I moved forward, until our chests were almost touching. I looked up into his face; his right cheek splotched an angry red.

I reached up and ran my fingers along the length of the mark. "You are not a loser, Garrett. You're everything…*everything* that I want. I'm *sorry* that I ever made you question what I felt for you or what you should feel about yourself. I never want to make you feel that way again," I promised, meaning every single world.

Garrett flinched against my hand, as though afraid for me to touch him. "I wish I could believe you. But I've heard this before. I'm not a guy that likes to put myself out there over and over again just to be stomped on. Riley, I can admit that you didn't just hurt me. You shredded me. My heart that could only bend has definitely been broken. I thought to myself, here is this girl who can get me. Who, even though I'm nowhere good enough for her, might take a chance on a guy like me. And that maybe finally, I could have a future that means something. I can't do this if you're going to break me, Ri," his voice dropped into a whisper and I was having a hard time breathing around the gigantic lump that had firmly lodged itself into my throat.

"I didn't want to talk to you thinking I could persuade you to forgive me. To get you to take a chance on me after the way I've been. I just wanted you to hear, from me, that I'm sorry. You have an amazing heart and one day, you'll give it away to a girl who deserves it," I choked on my words and dropped my hand from his face.

Turning away, I planned to make my grand exit. You know, try to keep some shred of dignity.

"I've already given it away to the most beautiful girl I could ever meet. I just hope like hell she doesn't give it back," he said, his hand pressing into my back, just between my shoulder blades. I could feel the warmth of his skin through my shirt and I closed my eyes as the sensation became overwhelming.

I forgot about our crappy timing. I forgot about the thousands of ways I had sabotaged this moment. I forgot about Gracie, who was barely talking to me.

All I could think…all I could feel…was *this*. His hand on me in such an innocent yet extremely intimate way. His words rang in my ears and I knew I couldn't fight them.

Not anymore.

Turning to face him, our eyes met and in one seamless movement, we fell together. His arms going around my waist, my hands tangling in his hair. And his mouth pressed against mine like a song. Look here folks, Riley Walker the freaking poet.

But Garrett Bellows brought out my inner Byron. I wanted to blather on idiotically about the softness of his lips and the taste of his tongue. I wanted to profess ridiculous amounts of hyperboles over the color of his eyes and the smell of his skin.

Garrett Bellows short-circuited the more reasonable parts of my brain. And I now knew that wasn't such a bad thing.

I needed less concrete and more what ifs in my life. Reason will only get you so far.

The heart needed to believe in things that didn't necessarily make sense.

And Garrett Bellows and Riley Walker most certainly *did not* make sense.

But that didn't mean it wasn't *right*.

I opened my mouth under his and felt his tongue slip between my lips. I sighed like a lovesick fool as he devoured me. His hands came up to cup my face as he kissed me an intensity that both frightened and melted me.

"What about that jackass sniffing around your skirt? Your ex?" Garrett asked pulling away slightly to look down at me, his hands still holding my face. His lips were swollen and leaned up to run my tongue along the crease. Garrett's eyes closed and he groaned deep in his throat.

"He's such a non issue. Don't even mention him," I replied tersely, pulling his mouth back down to mine with enough force to bang our teeth together. We both laughed at my exuberance but continued to kiss each other like two kids exploring each other for the first time.

My eyes popped open. What about Gracie? How could I have forgotten about Gracie?

"Garrett, hang on a sec," I put my finger to his lips, stilling him. His eyes were clouded with desire and I had to resist the overwhelming urge to dissolve into him again.

"What about Gracie? She may not like this," I said, indicating the space between us.

Garrett looked legitimately confused, which in turn confused me even more.

"Why would Gracie care?" he asked. God, men were so clueless sometimes.

"Probably because she's been wanting to get in your pants for months now. She's already angry with me. I don't want to hurt her," I said, feeling a sudden wash of misery. So much for finally letting my heart do the talking. What was the point when I would never willingly hurt Gracie like that again?

Garrett's fingers combed through my hair until they laced at the nape of my neck. He touched his forehead to mine our noses brushing against each other. "Gracie is a confused, bitter and extremely sick girl. She doesn't want me anymore than I want her," he said with conviction.

His words bewildered me. "What do you mean? She's always talking about wanting to hook up with you," I said, backing away slightly.

Garrett shook his head, looking suddenly irritated. "It's not like that between Gracie and me. I'm just...helping her out. Or at least trying to. Trust me, she does not feel that way about me. She's just very confused right now. She's all over the place." He pulled me back against him and kissed me soundly.

"Your loyalty is one of the things I love about you. But in this case it's not needed. Though she will need you. More than she realizes," he said cryptically.

"What are you talking about? You act as though Gracie has cancer. Is something wrong with her?" I asked, feeling the twinges of worry overtake the lust that had so recently flooded my brain.

Garrett wrapped my hands between his and cradled them to his chest. "Gracie has a serious substance abuse problem. Maysie, Vivian, and I have been trying to get her to go get help for a while now. She's spiraling fast. I've been there, I know what it looks like to fall off the edge and Gracie is really close, Ri," he said and I felt like even more of an ass.

"I knew she was drinking and partying too much. I thought Vivian had contacted her sister and they were handling it," I said stupidly, realizing that so much was going on while I was completely oblivious.

"Yeah, that didn't go so well. And she's been getting steadily worse. After you and I fought before I left Maryland, I realized you were right about my partying. Sure I wasn't where I used to be, but it wouldn't take much for me to find myself right back on the edge. And then I saw Gracie and I saw in her the person I used to be. The person I was afraid I would become again. So I stopped. All of it. The smoking, the drinking. I haven't had a joint or a beer since Maryland. I started going to AA meetings. I tried taking Gracie with me a few times but it didn't pan out. She's in serious denial right now. It sucks watching someone you care about lose it like that," Garrett's tone implied he felt his own guilt.

I was in a state of shock. Garrett had quit smoking. Quit drinking. He was on the straight and narrow. Because of what I said.

And during his own struggles with sobriety he had been looking after my friend. He had been doing something, I should have been. I really was a shitty friend and overall human being.

"Stop it, Riley. I know you're hating on yourself right now. But you were dealing with your own shit. Just stop, please," he pleaded softly and then I stopped thinking again.

"Riley!" Maysie's panicked call pulled me out of my Garrett induced haze and out of his arms. Maysie pushed through the kitchen door and I knew instantly something was very, very wrong. Her face was a scary shade of white and she looked... stricken. That was the only word that came to mind when I saw her.

She didn't even register that I was standing with Garrett, our mouths bruised and red, and my eyes glassy from desire. Maysie grabbed me and I felt her terror.

"It's Gracie! She stopped breathing!" she cried, pulling me after her into the restaurant. Garrett immediately moved into action and pushed past us to run through the kitchen and into the front of the bar. Maysie and I ran after him and the place was in complete chaos.

Moore was trying to corral people off to the side but it was still bedlam. Maysie's grip on my hand was painful as she dragged me to the front doors. There was a ring of people around a spot on the sidewalk. I recognized Vivian sobbing into Cole's chest. There was Jaz and Dina as well as a few people from the kitchen crew.

I pushed through them and thought I was going to throw up. Jordan had his phone out and was obviously talking to a dispatcher. Mitch was knelt beside Gracie, his fingers pinching her nose as he breathed into her mouth.

My friend looked like a broken doll lying there on the sidewalk. Her blonde hair fanned around her as though she had purposefully arranged it like that. Her face was ashen and her lips blue. She looked dead.

My god, Gracie looked dead.

Garrett fell to his knees on the other side of her body and he looked ready to fall apart. He watched helplessly as Mitch breathed five times into her mouth and then listened at her mouth. Then he would take her pulse and start chest compressions.

I stood there, helpless, struck dumb by the utter tragedy that unfolded in front of me. Garrett pulled at his hair and let out a strangled howl that made my skin prickle.

I had never felt so useless in my entire life as I watched my friend's life drain from her on the cold sidewalk. I barely registered when the paramedics arrived and wheeled her into an ambulance. I saw Garrett jump into the back with Gracie, holding her hand and talking to her the entire time.

Maysie pulled on my hand, saying something about meeting them at the hospital. I didn't move. I could only stand there and watch as the flashing lights disappeared around the corner.

"Riley! Come on!" Maysie said, near hysterics. Vivian was freaking out and Cole was trying to get her to his car. Jordan had his arm around Maysie but she wouldn't let go of my hand.

And I just continued to stand there, staring into the distance where Gracie and Garrett disappeared.

"No," I said finally, after Maysie screamed in my face to snap me out of it.

"What do you mean *no?* Riley, Gracie needs us!" Maysie yelled, tears streaming down her face. Jordan was making soothing noises, trying to calm her down.

I pulled my hand back and shook my head. I couldn't go. I couldn't be in a hospital. Not again. Not so soon. I was shutting down. That was the only way I could function right now.

"Go on. Call me when you know something," I said, my voice deadened by the turmoil of the last twenty minutes. I couldn't wrap my head around it. This upheaval threatened to snap me in two.

I pulled my keys out of my pocket and walked to my car.

"Riley!" Maysie yelled after me and I heard Jordan tell her to let me go.

Chapter
23

"**A**RE you going to go by to see her?" Maysie asked me and I could hear all too clear the vaguely thinned criticism tinged with sympathy.

Maysie had just come back from visiting Gracie, who was now staying with her parents in town. Gracie had spent forty-eight hours in the hospital after being diagnosed with acute alcohol poisoning. According to Maysie, she had suffered from depressed respiratory functioning and was hooked up to an oxygen machine while the alcohol worked through her system.

And I hadn't gone to see her.

I know that made me an even shittier friend than I already was. I was painfully aware that I would not be winning friend of the year. But the thought of going to another hospital to watch someone I cared about lying in a bed, waiting for them to get better…or worse…was more than I could handle.

So I had shut down. Gone home and proceeded to hate myself for the new coward colored clothing I was wearing.

I hated that I couldn't call on the part of me that had always dominated everything. The part that would look the world in the eye and tell it to fuck off. The Riley Walker that didn't let a thing like discomfort or fear to rule her decisions.

But now I felt guilty for the way I had screwed up everything. I had screwed up my relationship with Gracie. I had screwed up my relationship with Damien. And I knew, that after everything, I had screwed up thing with Garrett.

221

Because while I had been holed up in my apartment too chicken shit to visit my friend, Garrett had proven he was everything I *should* be. He hadn't left Gracie's side, proving he was hands down a better person than I was.

"How's she doing?" I asked, not answering the question.

Maysie blew out a breath, her bangs puffing up before falling back down on her forehead. She looked tired. Her skin stretched tight and the black circles that shadowed her eyes could have had their own zip code. Maysie had taken Gracie's crash into rock bottom particularly hard.

She, just like the rest of Gracie's friends, felt responsible for where Gracie ended up. We knew she was spiraling fast. She was partying too hard. Drinking too much. Yet what had we done to stop it from happening?

Not nearly enough.

"She's not quite *Gracie,* if that makes sense. She's getting better physically. But mentally, she's still struggling. She's trying to be normal, but I can tell how difficult it is for her," Maysie answered, tucking her feet underneath her as she sat beside me on the couch.

I closed the book I had been reading for Senior Symposium and gave her my full attention.

"I get it." I could only imagine how hard it was for Gracie. Trying desperately to show everyone she was okay, but feeling anything but. "What's she going to do?" I asked. We were a week away from the end of the semester, all of us ass deep in finals. Gracie understandably, hadn't returned to school.

Maysie lifted her shoulders in a tired shrug. "I don't know. I haven't wanted to ask her. None of us want to stress her out or anything, so I have no idea…" she said, letting the words trail off.

I had to ask the other question that was eating me alive. "Have you seen Garrett?" I queried, ashamed that I was bothering to know this particular piece of information after our friend almost died. But I hated not knowing how he was doing.

I knew he was taking Gracie's situation particularly hard. It had come out after the fact that all these weeks, when I thought the two of them were possibly hooking up, Garrett had been in fact trying to keep Gracie together. He was making it his mission to keep her sober.

I figured this had more to do with his feelings regarding his parents' death at the hands of a too-drunk driver. But it didn't change the fact that he had stepped up and helped Gracie when the rest of us had failed miserably.

Maysie gave me a look that I refused to interpret. "Yeah. He was at Gracie's parents' place this afternoon. They were hanging out when I got there."

The pain that sucked my breath from my lungs was a combination of regret and guilt.

"He's been really great to her," I commented, not knowing what else to say but the truth.

"Yeah, he has been. Better than the rest of us," Maysie said, sounding miserable and sad and all the other crappy emotions that I was currently feeling.

"He asked about you," she said after a moment. I wanted to jump all over that tiny statement like white on rice. I wanted to hound out of her every infinitesimal shred of information.

But I didn't.

"Really?" I asked without a hint to the wave of something resembling hope that threatened to leap out of me with a gigantic whoop.

"Really. He wanted to know why you haven't been by to see Gracie. He just wanted to make sure you were okay." Well, that little bit of hope went straight down the toilet.

Because I knew what he was thinking because I hadn't been to see my friend. It confirmed every horrible thing he had ever thought about me. And he was right.

"Oh," I said shortly, feeling like a fool. I had bungled up so much of my life recently and all I could think was that my father would be really disappointed in me.

Maysie put her hand on my arm. "You should go and see her though. It would be good…for both of you." My roommate had become unnaturally astute in her old age.

"I'm most likely the last person she'd want to see. Or have you forgotten how I was crowned Gracie's least favorite person in the last month?" I asked bitterly.

Maysie shook her head as though I were an idiot. "You're an idiot," she muttered, confirming my thought. "Gracie hasn't been herself in a long time. I think the Gracie, who we know and love was being sucked under by all the other shit going on. She was a jerk to everyone, not just you," she stated.

"After Garrett, I don't blame her," I said.

And then Maysie slapped me. Yep, the bitch slapped me.

"What the hell?" I growled, putting my hand up to my flaming cheek.

Maysie shook out her hand. I hope it stung like hell.

"You gave me a good slap once when I needed it. So I'm now returning the favor. Stop this woe is me stuff. This is not the Riley Walker I know and adore. You made some crappy decisions. Just stand up and make the right ones now," she said firmly and I couldn't help but grin.

"Good advice. I see the grasshopper has finally learned from the master," I told her. Maysie rolled her eyes.

"Well the grasshopper is going to smack you again if you don't pull yourself out of this funk. I know you're hurting about your dad. You haven't really allowed yourself to grieve. I'm not telling you how to handle things, but I think it might be time to try something else. Because *this*," she waved her hand in my direction, "is clearly not working."

"Wow, who made you Maysie Ardin, PH.D?" I asked sarcastically.

Maysie smiled. "You know I'm right. I understand that abrasive form of sarcasm well."

"Whatever," I replied, channeling some grade school maturity.

Maysie got to her feet. "I'm going to jump in the shower. Jordan and I are going out to dinner. You wanna come?" she asked.

"And watch you eat each other's faces instead of the food? Huh. Let me think about that for a minute," I mused.

Maysie gave me a stern look and started toward the bathroom. "Seriously though. You need to go see Gracie. She needs you," she said before disappearing behind the door.

I pulled my phone out of my pocket and looked at the time. It was a little after four. I grabbed my car keys and headed out.

Maysie was right. It was time I was the friend I should have been all along.

I stopped at the store and picked up a bag of Gracie's favorite mixed chocolates as well as two incredibly horrible chick flicks. If I was going to grovel, I should probably do it baring gifts.

I knew that Gracie's parents lived in a subdivision just outside of town but I realized I didn't know the exact house number. I pulled down a road with a line of similar looking brick houses and was about to call Maysie to ask for the exact directions when I saw a familiar white van.

I pulled in behind Garrett's vehicle and turned off my car. He was just closing the front door as I walked up the path. He was digging in his pocket for his keys and hadn't noticed me yet. He was dressed in his typical slacker grunge attire that at one time I found to be horrific. His dirty blond hair brushed his shoulders and hung in his face. His beat up Vans were untied, the laces trailing to the ground. His green button shirt was only buttoned halfway, which was I assumed was him trying to be respectful of Gracie's parents. I found that I hated not being able to see the taught muscles of his stomach. God, why didn't I just go and lick his chest while I was at it?

I slowed down my walk, giving him time to see me. And when he did, I froze. Because the look on his face wasn't the one I expected to see. I had anticipated disgust or disapproval. I was so sure he was done with me after my crappy display of friendship to the girl who lived in the house behind him.

But what I saw reflected in those beautiful blue eyes was a tenderness that made me weak in the knees.

"Riley," he said in his husky voice. I had to take a deep breath to calm my rapidly beating heart. It was either that or pass out cold on the Cooks' front lawn.

"Hi, Garrett," I said, trying to smile but knowing it most likely looked like a spasm of the lips.

Garrett met me halfway and we stood there like the Two Maxs in that Dr. Seuss story. Neither of us moving, both stuck in our tracks.

"I'm here to see Gracie," I announced stupidly.

Garrett's eyebrows rose. "Yeah, I figured that, with you being at her parents' house and all."

"I know I haven't been to see her yet, I just wasn't sure…"

"Whether you could see another person you loved sick and suffering?" Garrett asked and I felt the giant knot in my stomach loosen with the realization that he got it. Just like he always did.

"Yeah," I answered.

"I'm sorry I haven't called. Especially after the way we left things," Garrett said, surprising the hell out of me.

"You've been a little busy. Frankly, I didn't expect to hear from you," I said honestly. No sense in denying the big hole of suck I had been wallowing in for the past few days.

Garrett frowned and then shocked me even further by reaching out and wrapping his hand around my wrist, tugging me forward. I stumbled toward him until the tips of our shoes were touching and were breathing in each other's air. I looked up into his eyes and almost recoiled at the depth of emotion I saw there.

I didn't spend a lot of time embracing the touchy feely. I tended to feel awkward and weird when forced to deal with it. Even when Damien had said I love you, I never felt entirely comfortable with it, so it was my natural reaction to pull away.

But there was something about the way Garrett Bellows looked at me that made running the last thing I wanted to do.

"I *should* have called you, Ri. Because after what we said to each other, you deserved to hear every second of every day that I feel the same way. That you're my girl. That we'll be together until you decide you can do better and kick me to the curb." He tugged on my arm again before moving his arms around me.

"I'm sorry," he whispered before kissing the side of my mouth softly. He let his lips linger there, not deepening the kiss but with an aching tenderness that made my knees buckle.

"Stop saying you're sorry. It's annoying," I said huskily after he moved away.

"It annoys you, huh? What else is new?" he teased before his face darkened. "I *am* sorry. But Gracie,"

"Gracie needed you. I get it," I finished for him.

"We weren't hooking up, Riley. We were never together like

226

that. I just saw in her something that reminded me way too much of myself. I just wanted to help I guess," he said, sounding like the boy who had lost his world and didn't know what to do about it. It made me sad and angry and scared. All for him.

"I get that now. You're a good guy, Garrett," I said with a small smile.

Garrett gave me a crooked grin. "Just don't tell anyone," he quipped.

I stood there in the circle of his arms, knowing this is where I wanted to be. That even in the worst of circumstances he was always there. He was steadfast and loyal and never, ever wavered.

How many people could say they'd do the same?

Because this man had proved time and time again that he could handle the ugly that life threw at him and that was the kind of person I wanted in my life.

"I'd better get in there," I told him, not wanting to move away from him, but knowing that I should. That there was someone else I needed to make things right with.

"Yeah, you should." He didn't move in to kiss me. In fact, he backed up and dropped his arms from around me. But I didn't feel like I was being rejected. In fact, it felt almost like a promise of something more. Of something that we would build on…soon.

"Can I see you later?" he asked me, sounding hesitant, as though bracing himself for my rebuff.

"Yeah, I'd like that," I said.

"Okay then. I'll call you tonight. You'll answer, right?" he asked is light tone but he meant what he asked. He needed the validation that I wouldn't turn him down again.

"Damn straight," I said fiercely, earning me a laugh.

"Cool," Garrett nodded, flipping his keys around on his finger. "Talk to you then." He gave me a salute and I headed to the front door finding Gracie standing there, her hands shoved into the pockets of an oversized sweater.

Her long, blonde hair was lank and lifeless and her face was pale but her eyes were anything but remote.

"Hey, G," I said not turning to watch Garrett drive away even as she lifted her hand to wave him off.

Once the sound of Garrett's van disappeared, Gracie held open the door and let me inside. The house was just as I pictured the place where Gracie grew up. It was prim and proper. Everything tidy and in its place. There were framed family portraits on the shelves, Christmas cards made into a wreathe on the wall.

Gracie led me into the living room where a fire burned in a huge fireplace and a magnificent Christmas tree stood in the corner. *It's a very WASPy Christmas!* I thought and then mentally scolded myself for being unkind. I didn't know her parents; maybe they were very nice people despite the Keeping Up with the Joneses air that their home gave off.

"My parents are out to dinner. Thank freaking god! They're driving me nuts!" Gracie said on a sigh, indicating for me to take a seat. Her easy naturalness threw me after months of fake civility.

"Stop looking at me like I'm an alien, Ri. I swear, I *am* Gracie Cook and not a pod person," she giggled as I sat down on the couch.

"Well I'm glad there are no pod people present. That would make for some awkward conversation," I remarked dryly. Gracie held out a bowl of walnuts, offering them to me. I shook my head and she started digging in with zeal.

"So how've you been?" she asked me after a few minutes of me listening to her crunching.

I couldn't help but laugh. Gracie looked at me questioningly.

"It's just funny that here we are, all super normal like and you're asking me how I'm doing. Shouldn't I be asking you that question?" I asked her.

Gracie made a face. "I spend all day telling people how I'm doing. It would be nice to talk about someone else. Just to shake things up a bit," she joked and I didn't know what to say. I wanted to address the reasons for my neglectful friendship. I wanted to figure out how to fix all the ways our relationship had soured. I wanted to take the bull by the horns after months of skirting issues instead of facing them head on.

And it seemed in some ways, Gracie was taking a leaf out of the Riley Walker book of confrontation. Get it out of the way as succinctly as possible.

"So I see you and Garrett are working things out," she stated matter of factly.

It's a good thing I wasn't eating any of those freaking nuts, or I would have required the Heimlich maneuver.

"Um…yeah. I guess we should talk about that," I said slowly.

Gracie blew out an exasperated breath. "Should we talk about the fact that you've been crazy in love with him for months now?" she asked me pointedly and this time I did choke.

"Excuse me?" I practically shouted.

Gracie giggled again. "I am *so* right! I knew it! You love Garrett Bellows! Riley and Garrett sitting in a tree…" she couldn't continue over her hysterical laughter.

My face flamed red. "Well, I'm glad you find this so amusing," I said, trying not to be irritated by the girl who had nearly died just days ago and was now laughing her ass off at the state of my love life.

Gracie made an effort to calm down. "I just never thought I'd see the day you would fall for a guy like Garrett." She dropped her voice into a conspiratorial whisper. "I mean, he's a townie and in a *band*. I couldn't imagine someone so *not* your type." And then she was giggling again.

Well, I didn't know what to do. This was *not* how I envisioned this conversation going. I had pictured me cataloging the thousands of ways I had failed her as a friend. Gracie giving me the understandable cold shoulder. We'd hash out our issues. Gracie would cry. I'd give her some tissues. End of scene.

I was definitely not prepared for Gracie laughing her ass off over my reality defying relationship with Garrett. Not after the months of barely polite interactions I had endured with her.

"Yeah, funny stuff," I bit out. *I will not strangle the girl who almost died of alcohol poisoning. I will not strangle the girl who almost died of alcohol poisoning. I will not…*

Gracie pinched her lips together, most likely to control her bout of hysterics. "I'm sorry. That was rude. I'm happy for your, Ri. Honest and truly. You deserve a guy like Garrett. He's pretty amazing," she said a little wistfully.

Now I could get to the root of our issues.

"You're happy for me? Because from the way things have been between us, I was expecting a dart in the neck at the very least," I said wryly and Gracie looked sheepish.

"Okay, I was pissed." Gracie grimaced. "I was jealous and angry and bitter. All I could see was perfect princess Riley getting something I wanted. I've been a mess of fucked up feelings for a while now. And I've unfairly made you a focal point for a lot of my shit," Gracie confessed.

"Two weeks sober and getting into some heavy duty therapy can make things a lot clearer. I liked Garrett. But I didn't want anything more than a new toy to play with. And when he offered only friendship I tried to manipulate it into something else. I'm a screwed up chick, Riley. Garrett says I've got Daddy issues." Gracie looked away and I realized I knew very little about Gracie's home life. I didn't know much beyond the fact that her parents lived in this perfect Suburban house and she had a close relationship with her sister.

"Who knows? I guess my therapist will dig into all that psychological stuff. My point is I've been overdosing on the crazy for too long now. I don't have those feelings for Garrett. I never did. So if that is standing in your way at all, get over it. I won't be your excuse for missing out on a relationship with a great guy," Gracie scolded me good-naturedly.

I swear I must have touched down in the Twilight Zone. I must have looked as shocked as I felt because Gracie tossed a nut at my face, which I barely swatted out of the way before it hit my nose.

"Not how you pictured this talk going? Do you want me to cry so you can give me some tissues? And then we can talk about our heavy flow or something?" Gracie teased, proving she knew me entirely too well.

I chuckled. "I'm quite okay with leaving the period discussion for another day. You know if you're feeling tired or something."

We had a moment of total normalcy. It felt unbelievably good. After months of topsy-turvy, this felt amazing.

Reaching over and grabbing a handful of M&Ms from another dish on the coffee table I finally asked one of the questions that needed to be asked. "When are you coming back to school?"

Gracie's lips thinned out and she looked down. "I'm going to take a semester off. For now. I need to get myself together. I've been going out of control for a while now. I can't go back until I know I can handle it," she said with a surety that was good to hear.

Her words weren't surprising but they made me sad all the same. Maysie would be graduating early and Gracie wouldn't be coming back next semester. It seemed as though my last semester at Rinard was going to be a lonely one. Not exactly how I pictured my senior year of college.

"You do what you need to do," I said, making sure I sounded supportive. Because Gracie was right. She needed a breather. College and parties and the stress of graduating were the last thing she needed.

"Thanks. I plan on it. And you'll be so busy being awesome you'll breeze through your last few months. Then you'll be off to some fantastic grad school so you can become a kick ass journalist and give Barbara Walters a run for her money. BW pre-View, of course," Gracie added before I could say it.

I grinned. "You know me too well, G." I tossed some more chocolate in my mouth.

"And just maybe you could spend your summer going across country with a certain hot ass guitarist and his superlicious band," Gracie suggested, wiggling her eyebrows.

Shit! I had forgotten about the tour. Garrett would be leaving. For a long time.

Gracie made a dismissive hand gesture, pulling me out of my black thoughts. "But you'll figure it all out. Because that's what you do. You figure stuff out and make the rest of us look like complete slackers for not having the slightest clue," Gracie said affectionately though I felt a sting at her words.

I reached over and grabbed her hand, surprising her. "If I've ever made you feel like that, I'm sorry. I'm no better or more together than anyone else. I'm just as screwed up and clueless and the next girl. I just hide it better," I admitted.

Gracie didn't say anything for a minute but then covered my hand with hers. "No, you've got it wrong, Ri. You could never be clueless or screwed up. You are smart and dedicated and everything I want to be. You can't be the same as the rest of us. I need something to aspire to, girlfriend," she said in a mixture of teasing lightness and absolute sincerity.

I squeezed her hand. "You give me way too much credit, Gracie and you don't give yourself enough."

She squeezed back and that piece that had been broken started to slowly mend.

Chapter 24

I WAS a nervous wreck. It was downright comical.

I was pacing back and forth in my room. I had changed my clothes three times before settling on a very un-Riley like black skirt and deep blue shirt. I had pulled my long, brown hair back into a low ponytail and even put on some makeup.

Because Garrett was coming over.

You heard that right. I had pulled out the thermoneculuer girl crazies over Garrett I Can Barely Get Myself Dressed Bellows.

As I was leaving Gracie's house, my phone had started to ring. I glanced at the number that I had never bothered to program into my phone and recognized it instantly. I would never forget those digits even if I had at one time desperately wanted to.

"You answered," Garrett said by way of greeting.

I laughed. "Well, I figured since I had nothing better to do."

Garrett laughed as well. "At least your honest," he said.

"It's a character flaw. Sorry," I teased, enjoying the easy banter that we had always been able to enjoy together.

"Definitely not a character flaw, Riley," he said gently and I was once again taken aback by this soft and tender side of Garrett. I knew it was a side very few got to see. And I was thankful to be one of those individuals.

"So can I come over later?" he asked.

"To my apartment?" I asked, wishing like hell I would stop asking such moronic questions with such obvious answers.

Garrett made a snorting nose and I couldn't stop grinning. "Well that is where you're living these days, right?"

"Your wit is astounding, Garrett," I replied. "You don't want to go out? Get something to eat?" I suggested, hoping he took me up on the offer. For some reason the thought of sitting around my apartment with him made my nerves kick into overdrive.

I had been naked with this guy on two occasions. He had kissed and touched every single inch of me, but the thought of sitting beside him on my couch making small talk had me quivering like a preacher's daughter in the backseat of her boyfriend's car.

"I'd really like to spend time with you...alone. If that's okay, I mean," he sounded unsure and I knew my hesitance was the reason.

"No, that' fine. I'd love for you to come over," I said hurriedly, not wanting him to ever think I didn't want to spend time with him. If I needed to spend the rest of my life reassuring him, then so be it.

"Great. I'll bring food. Anything you're in the mood for?" he asked, sounding more relaxed now that I've agreed to his plans.

"I'd kill for some Chinese. Sweet and sour chicken to be precise. Think you can arrange that?" I inquired coyly.

"Me hunter. Go kill food and bring it to woman," he joked and I laughed. Who knew Garrett had such a sense of humor?

And that's how I found myself three hours later, a bundle of jangled nerves and sweaty palms.

"When did Banana Republic Barbie move in?" Maysie asked coming to a stop as she walked passed my open bedroom door.

I held up my hand, stopping her. "Don't. Just don't. I feel like I'm going to vomit as it is. I don't need your well intentioned jokes about my clothes." Glancing at my reflection in the mirror I did look a little green.

"Woah, Riley. You're uncharacteristic freak out is *freaking* me out," Maysie said, looking unsure as to whether she should venture into my bedroom.

I watched with dread as understanding dawned on her face. "Garrett's coming over," she stated. When I didn't answer she clapped her hands together like a seal and made a loud whooping noise.

"Ugh. Okay. You guessed it. Garrett's coming over and my panties are officially in a bunch," I told her with a healthy dose of scathing sarcasm.

"Come on, Riley. This is Garrett we're talking about here. You'll be lucky if he remembered to wear matching socks. No sense in getting so worked up about it," she placated. But I wasn't feeling the calm down vibes.

I couldn't explain why I was so nervous. Maysie was right. Garrett was the most laid back person I knew. But this was different. This was the beginning of something new. Garrett and I were finally walking together into that place we had been dancing around since that night all those months ago when I had woken up naked and mortified in his bed.

Maysie's face softened and she came in and gave me a hug. "I've never seen you like this, Riley. It's so damn cute," she couldn't help but add. I gave her a punch on the arm, and none too lightly. She winced around a smile.

The doorbell rang and she looked at me, a mischievous twinkle in her eye and took off running for the front of the apartment. I took off after her.

"I will kick your ass, Maysie Ardin! Don't think I won't!" I threatened, practically tackling her as she reached the door.

"I just want to let him in. Give him the safe sex talk, oh wait. Too late for that one," she joked, clearly pleased with herself.

I groaned and reached around her to open the door and wished I could run for the hills. Because Garrett was on the doorstep, with Jordan. Both of them were carrying bags of food and Jordan held a couple of movies. Obviously our "alone time" was turning into a double date.

But Garrett…he looked amazing. I did a double take when I finally took him in. His hair was pushing back off his face and his eyes were bright and lucid. He wore a faded but comfortable pair of jeans and button up tan and green plaid shirt, tucked in I might add, and rolled up to his elbows. He had traded in his customary Vans for a brown pair of Dr. Martins.

I couldn't stop the grin that spread across my face and I forgot all about sharing our night with Maysie and Jordan. All I cared about was this guy standing in my doorway with a shy smile on his uncertain face.

His eyes raked me from toe to head and he clearly liked what he saw. "You look beautiful, Ri," he said with such intensity that it made me blush.

"You clean up pretty well yourself," I told him, wishing he'd reach out and touch me already.

"You both look downright fuckable. Now, move Riley, this bag is heavy," Jordan complained, pushing passed me so he could suck on his girlfriend's face before heading to the kitchen.

I looked over my shoulder at Maysie who gave me an apologetic smile. "I didn't know you wanted the apartment. I invited Jordan for dinner and a movie. He's staying over. Is that okay? Because if it's a problem, we can go out." She sounded so worried that I couldn't tell her what I was really thinking. Which was, *hell yeah, get out!*

"Nooo," I dragged out. "It's fine. I just hope you don't expect us to sit through another round of *The Notebook*," I warned, closing the door behind Garrett who seemed awkward standing in my living room.

Jordan tossed a DVD case in my direction. "Sorry guys," he said with an apologetic smile. Damned if it wasn't The freaking Notebook. "She's got me by the balls, what can I say?" he explained as Maysie wrapped her arms around his neck and pressed a kiss on his upturned mouth. He turned into her so that his lips were on hers and I was forced to look away. An eyeful of *that* would not help with the crazy nerves unleashing their fury in my stomach.

"I really hope you don't have anything against trite romantic dramas full of enough clichés to make you want to rip your hair out," I said to Garrett, who gave me a cute little half smile.

"I don't care what we watch," he told me, reaching out to take my hand. He laced his fingers between mine and the feel of his warm palm had me suppressing a shiver. This guy's flipping *palm* had me turning myself inside out. How could I have been so blind to the way I felt about him?

I guess I wore idiocy well.

"Well that's good, because Tweedle Dumb and Dumber over here are monopolizing the television with their crap," I teased, earning me a glare from my best friend. Garrett and Jordan laughed, clearly in agreement about the movie selection.

Jordan and Maysie went into the kitchen to put their dinner on some plates, leaving Garrett and me alone in the living room. "We might as well get the good spots on the couch," I said, perching in the corner of our beat up sofa.

Garrett pulled cartons of Chinese food out of the bag he carried and handed me my favorite sweet and sour chicken. I grabbed a pair of chop sticks and started eating. Not that I had much of an appetite given the full flight of birds that had taken up residence in my stomach.

I moved the throw pillows to the floor and Garrett sat down beside me. He leaned back, draping his arm across the back of the couch, his fingers lightly running along the sensitive skin of my nape.

"You're not going to eat anything?" I asked him after forcing down a mouth full of chicken.

Garrett shook his head. "Not really hungry. Maybe later," he said and I wondered if he was suffering from an attack of the killer stomach birds as well.

Eating as much as I was able, I finally put the mostly full carton of food down on the coffee table.

"How was your visit with Gracie?" he asked me.

"It was good. We're good," I said with more than a little relief.

"I'm glad," he replied, not elaborating and simply leaving it at that basic truth.

"Me too," I agreed. Our eyes met and I felt like I was suddenly living in one of those annoying romantic dramas Maysie was addicted to. Only this time I didn't want to turn the channel in protest.

Hell no. This time I was enjoying every glorious, cheesy, and sentimental moment of it.

"Are you going to kiss me or just thinking about it?" I asked him a little breathlessly. The build up was killing me.

Garrett's lips quirked up in a grin. The grin that lit his face up and made it impossible to look away. "You can't let a guy do his thing can you? Always needing to take control," he admonished, his hand gripping the nape of neck in his strong grip and giving me a hard tug towards him.

And then he kissed me. And I mean really kissed me. We're talking the end of the world is tonight and you only have minutes to live kiss.

It was the sort of kiss that you felt from the tips of your fingers to the bottoms of your feet. There wasn't an inch of my body that wasn't affected by the feel of his mouth.

But before we could properly get into the way our lips melded and our tongues searched each other out, we were rudely interrupted.

"It's about fucking time!" Jordan hollered from the kitchen and I could hear Maysie giggling uncontrollably. They were beaming at us as though we had just won the gold for Olympic tonsil hockey.

Garrett pulled back and rolled his eyes, confirming that here was a guy after my own heart. "We'll start charging admission if you don't stop gawking," he called back, his eyes never leaving mine. He touched his forehead against mine, his breathing as labored as my own.

"Do you think we'd get too much shit if we left? I really need to be alone with you. I feel like I've been waiting forever to hold you the way I want to." His words melted me and I found myself nodding emphatically.

We both got to our feet and headed to the front door.

"Hey, where are you guys going? We're just getting ready to start the movie. I made kettle corn!" Maysie shook the bowl in her hands and looked a little dejected.

Jordan wrapped his arms around her waist and kissed the top of her head. "Let 'em go, Mays. Besides, the things I want to do to you are for our eyes only," he said, giving his girlfriend a lavicious grin.

Maysie smacked him but flushed in pleasure. I knew that look on her face too well. Meaning Garrett and I had about ten seconds to get out before clothes started to fly.

"Yeah, let's go," I said hurriedly, grabbing Garrett's hand and pulling him out the door.

After getting into Garrett's van I asked him, "Where to?"

He gave me a little smile. "I have an idea."

He didn't say anything more, instead turning on the stereo, the soft strains of an acoustic set filling the van. Garrett started tapping his hands against the steering wheel and singing along with the song. Once again, I was reminded of what an amazing voice he had.

"Why don't you sing for your band? You're pretty great," I gushed a bit. I was surprised to see this laid back, unconcerned guy blush at the compliment.

"Yeah, I don't do singing in front of big crowds," he said in explanation.

"But you sang at that bar for open mic night," I pestered.

"It's more Cole's thing than mine. I'm fine with playing the guitar." He shot me a hot look. "Or I could sing just for you," he suggested, his tongue darting out to wet his bottom lip before turning his attention back to the darkened road.

"Like that song you wrote, the one you sang at the dive bar?" I asked. I had always wanted to ask him about that song Wondering if I was right in who it was about.

"So you figured it out then?" he asked, smirking.

"Figured what out?" I was going to play dumb on this one. I wanted to hear him say it.

"That it was about you," he admitted with a snort.

"I kind of guessed that. You know with the whole ice of your smile and my touch being toxic. I mean, who else could those flattering lyrics be about?" I teased.

"I wrote that from an angry place, Riley. I promise there has been other since then. Much nicer ones," he said, sounding shy.

"I'd love to hear them sometime," I replied with a sultry tone that surprised me. I watched with a keen sense of satisfaction as Garrett's eyes widened and his Adam's apple bobbed up and down as he swallowed.

I hid my smile by looking out the window. I didn't recognize the neighborhoods we were driving through. Bakersville wasn't a large town but I could admit that I hadn't made it a point to learn all of its nooks and crannies in my four years here.

The town slowly disappeared as we drove deeper into the countryside. After fifteen minutes or so the van took a turn onto a gravel drive before parking in an overgrown lot. Garrett pulled a couple of flashlights out of the glove compartment.

"Come on," he said, sounding unusually excited. I got out of the van and waited as he pulled an old blanket and his guitar case off the back seat. Was he expecting us to hang out on a blanket outside in fucking December?

"Uh…" I began, ready to voice my very loud disapproval of this plan. Maybe he was trying to be romantic or something. I was going to tell him not to bother. That he could save his sentiments and take me somewhere warm.

Garrett gave me a wry look, as if reading my mind. "Don't say anything. Just come on." He held out his hand and I reluctantly grabbed it. He gave my arm a little shake. "I won't let you freeze, Ri. Promise," he vowed with a wink.

I grumbled under my breath as my teeth started to chatter but I followed him through an over grown field toward a row of trees. Garrett handed me a flashlight after turning his on. "You'll want to watch where you're walking. There are some holes along here," he said, indicating the uneven ground.

I was all about some good old fashioned outdoor fun. I loved to hike and had spent most of last summer learning the trails in and around the Blue Ridge Mountains. But even I had my limits. And they definitely applied to traipsing through a field in the middle of the night in a short skirt in freezing temperatures.

But I followed Garrett knowing that come hell or high water I was ready to follow him anywhere. Crazy how a few months can change your mindset so completely.

"If I fall and break my ankle, your ass is carrying me out of here," I whispered harshly.

"Why are you whispering? Are you afraid Big Foot will come and eat you?" Garrett joked and I swatted his arm.

We walked into the line of trees and come through in a clearing by a river. There was a fire pit off to the side surrounded by a ring of rocks and some chairs. There was a picnic table and a dock with a boat tied to it.

And most importantly there was a small cabin nestled back in the trees. Garrett pulled me toward the small building, stopping in front of the door. He reached out to rest the flat of his hand against the smooth wood, his head bowed.

I put my hand on his shoulder, not understanding the sudden change in his mood.

"Are you okay?" I asked him softly.

Garrett's shoulders heaved and then he looked up at me. In the gleam of the flashlights I could see that his eyes were wet. "I haven't been here since…they died," he said in a rush and I understood that this place had belonged to his parents. And him taking me here meant something extremely important.

I opened my mouth and then shut it; I didn't know quite what to say. Garrett squeezed my hand before dropping to dig his keys out of his pocket. Fumbling in the dark, he finally found the right one and put it into the lock. With a squeak he pushed the door open and we walked into the heart of his past.

Chapter
25

Wᴇ were met with a blast of stale, musty air. Garrett felt around on the wall until he found a light switch. He flicked it on, illuminating the darkness to reveal a space that looked as though it had been neglected for some time.

The old, worn furniture was covered with a thick layer of dust and grime. There were cobwebs everywhere. I coughed and then fell into a fit of sneezing.

"This place is worse than I thought," Garrett said more to himself. He went and opened a few windows to try and air the place out. The rush of cold filled the room and I was shivering all over again.

Garrett caught sight of me with my arms wrapped around myself and cursed. "Shit, I shouldn't have brought you here. I don't know what I was thinking." He sounded so dejected that I forced myself to unwrap my arms and unclench my legs so I could walk over to him.

"Well, why did you bring me here?" I asked him.

Garrett lifted his shoulders in a sad shrug. "I was thinking about this place the other day and how much I loved being here when I was younger. Mom and Dad bought it when I was ten and we spent a lot of weekends fishing, swimming, doing your typical family stuff." He walked over to the fireplace and picked up a framed picture that was covered in so much filth that you couldn't see the picture beneath the glass. He pulled his sleeve down over his hand and wiped at the frame, slowly revealing the picture of a family smiling together in this very room.

The man and woman were the same people in the picture at Garrett's house. And the boy smiling a full, happy smile with a head full of unmanageable blond hair was a younger, more content version of the man who stood beside me.

Garrett placed the picture back on the mantle and braced a hand on the wood as he peered down into the cold and empty hearth. "After they died, I couldn't come back here. So I closed it up. Tried to forget about it. I kept the electricity on for some reason even if I never planned to come here again."

He stood up straight and backed away. "But lately, the memories have been harder to ignore." Garrett looked over at me as though I were the reason he was facing some deeply hidden demons.

"And you wanted to bring me here?" I pressed; wanting him to acknowledge what I hoped was the reason behind our late night visit to his family's cabin.

Garrett ran his hands through his hair and gripped his scalp. Then, looking at me, he moved his hands to cradle my face. "Yes. I wanted to bring you here," he stated.

"Why?" I asked.

Garrett let out a noisy breath. "Because very few people know the real me. So many see me as the guitarist of Generation Rejects. The townie that throws the crazy parties. The stoner who fucks around and likes to have a good time. But not you, Riley. Okay, maybe at first that's what you saw." I grimaced at this but Garrett ran his thumb along the bottom curve of my lip as if to stop my guilty thoughts.

"But now, you see *me*. And I want to give you every little piece of the person I am. Of the person I used to be. Because I love you, Riley Walker. And I want you so deep in my life that you can't ever leave," he said softly and I couldn't stop the tears from falling freely. What the hell was it about Garrett that turned me into a pile of hormonal mush?

He kissed me tenderly. Not a sexual action, but one filled with love and devotion. And there wasn't a girl on this planet that could resist the feel of his lips promising the world.

I opened my mouth to admit my own feelings. To bare my soul to the one person who should see it but Garrett pressed his thumb against my lips silencing me.

"You don't need to say anything. Not right now. Right now, I need to be with you…here. Please," he pleaded as if I could deny him anything right now.

I kept quiet and nodded my assent. Garrett leaned in kissed me again and then released me. Quietly, he went about building a fire in the dusty fireplace from wood that had been left from an earlier time. Once the fire was raging, he unrolled the thick blanket he had brought from his van and laid it out on the floor.

Sinking to his knees on the ground, he pulled me down beside him. I fell to my own knees and faced him in the flickering light of the fire. For the first time tonight I wasn't freezing my ass off. I was warm and completely at peace.

Slowly, Garrett pushed my jacket off my shoulders. I wiggled out of the sleeves and tossed the coat onto the couch behind us. I cringed at my overzealousness. But I was totally ready to get naked and sweaty with him. And here he was trying to be all sweet and romantic.

Garrett laughed. "My girl is a little over excited," he teased and I flushed at his endearment. He called me *his girl*. Typically I balked at possessive titles. I was a modern woman after all. But somehow, being Garrett's anything felt like the most wonderful thing in the world.

My trembling hands began to unbutton his shirt. I tried to slow myself. You know, take my time. But I found that I was practically tearing the buttons off in my haste to get him out of his clothing. Garrett couldn't stop laughing as I pulled his belt off in one rambunctious tug.

"You really can't let me take control of anything, can you?" he asked and I wondered if that bothered him. Garrett grabbed my face and kissed me soundly. "And I love you for it. I wouldn't have you any other way," he responded firmly, grabbing the hem of overly girly blue blouse and pulled it up over my head.

We were still on our knees facing each other. Garret only in his jeans, me in my bra and skirt. And suddenly my haste to get naked faded and I just wanted to spend an eternity staring at this man who had somehow, someway become the most beautiful thing I had ever seen.

"You are so fucking gorgeous, Riley." He traced the line of my collarbone, his finger dipping into the crevice between my breasts, unleashing a wave of chills over my skin.

"I'm scared as hell you'll wake up tomorrow and realize you can do a lot better than me. That you and me, we're too different and this can never work." Garrett bent low and replaced his finger in the valley between my breasts with his mouth, suckling the skin and eliciting a throaty moan from my throat.

"Please don't wake up thinking that. Because you and me could be something wonderful. I swear to God I'll spend the rest of my life proving it to you," he said into my skin as he kissed a line up chest and up the side of my neck until he sucked my earlobe between his teeth, making me gasp.

"You don't need to prove anything to me, Garrett," I rasped, finding it hard to talk. Hard to breathe. Hard to think. All I could do was feel his lips on my skin. His fingers now removing my bra from my body in a single fluid motion.

"I already *know* we're something incredible. And I need you in my life, Garrett. I can't imagine my existence without you," I said with such conviction it made Garrett pull back and look me in the eye, as if waiting for me to shout *just kidding!*

"You really mean that?" he asked, sounding so vulnerable it made my heart ache. I wasn't quite ready to declare my love for him but I could share with him how intense my feelings were.

"Yes, I mean it. You and me, on paper we're all wrong. But that's okay, because the reality is we just work. I don't know why. But we do. And I want to take this road with you, wherever it leads us," I said, smiling through the blubbering mess of tears that were wreaking havoc on my face.

Garrett's face lit up and then he kissed me. And he was through with being soft and gentle. Because this time when he touched me, he was all desire and heat and an overpowering need to *consume*.

He laid me down on the blanket, our skin hot from the

pounding lust between us and the fire raging a few feet away. He pulled my skirt down over my hips and I lifted myself up so he could slide it down my legs. His hands slid their way back up until the held my hips and his lips worked a trail to my aching breasts.

He took one nipple in his mouth and arched up to meet him, a loud cry echoing from my lips at the feel of his lips around the sensitive bud. As he worked my flesh, I made short work of the rest of his clothing.

When he was completely naked, I felt him press his hard length between my legs. A thin strip of fabric the only thing separating us. And I was ready for that barrier to take a hike.

"Take my panties off," I breathed into Garrett's mouth. When he didn't move quickly enough for my liking I growled against his lips. "Now!"

Garrett chuckled and immediately complied. Hooking his fingers around the waistband he gave them a vicious yank, tearing them away from body.

"That's what I'm talking about," I purred in satisfaction, watching as he threw the scrap of ruined fabric into the fire. Garrett resumed kissing me and I turned into a liquid puddle as his fingers found my wet center. Stroking, touching, loving every sensitive inch of me.

Thrusting a finger deep inside me, we both groaned in absolute delight at the feel of it. "I love it when you touch me," I whispered, needing to validate all the ways he blew my mind.

Garrett pulled his finger from my body and began to make wet circles around my throbbing clit. I moaned low and deep as he pushed two fingers inside me again. "I love touching you, baby," he whispered back, watching me as I rode the cresting wave he was unleashing on my body.

While his hand worked between my legs, his other hand came up to cup my breast. Rubbing my hard nipple between his thumb and forefinger. When my orgasm hit, it was a violent burst that took me by surprise. I had orgasmed before, but nothing like the complete meltdown I experienced just now with Garrett's fingers deep inside me and his mouth on my breast.

I was a trembling, quivering mess when he finally pulled his fingers out of me and put on a condom. Barely able to wrap my legs around his waist, Garrett put his hand underneath my rear and lifted me up so I could meet him as he thrust deep inside me.

"Oh God!" he groaned, stopping a moment as my body adjusted around him. Feeling him like this I knew I was where I was meant to be.

Reaching around I gave his ass a little smack, startling him. He peered down at me questioningly as he slowly withdrew from my depths and then plunged forward again.

"I'm not gonna break, cowboy. Fuck me like you mean it," I challenged, throwing my head back. And accept my challenge, he did. Garrett fastened his lips to the base of my throat and gripped my hips as he thrust into me as hard as he could. I screamed at the top of my lungs as he screwed my brains out.

Garrett's yells joined my strangled cries. The shadows of our bodies loving each other in a brutally passionate way urging us on and over the edge. And when I came, it was knowing he was right behind me.

Afterwards, we lay in a sweaty, tangled heap. Our legs were pretzeled together, our arms clinging. My ear was pressed against his chest and I could hear the erratic thud of his heart. He was still deep inside me and I knew he needed to dispose of the condom but I didn't want to move. This connection was the most amazing thing I had ever felt.

When we were finally able to breathe again, Garrett slowly pulled out of me and made quick of wrapping the condom in a tissue and putting it out of sight. He was back in my arms before I could complain about missing him.

"Please tell me this is real," he said quietly into my hair, his hand running lazy trails up and down my back.

I looked up at him and kissed his chin. "This is as real as it gets babe. There's no getting rid of me now."

Garrett leaned back and pulled the battered guitar case over. I lay there, completely naked as he started to mess with the strings.

It was such a surreal moment. Garrett Bellows and Riley Walker, in the afterglow of some seriously amazing sex, sitting together in all of their nude glory. And I didn't feel remotely self-conscious. A first for me.

Garrett started to thumb a tune. Just a simple combination of notes but it was amazing. Then looking at me with eyes full of the most beautiful emotion I had ever seen, he began to sing.

My mask means nothing
You see who I am
Breaking me down
on the ground where I stand.
I wanted to lose you
In the face of your pain
Stranded in the dust
Hounded by shame.
You hated
I loved
I was wrong
You were done
If tragedy had a soul
It was mine you took hold
Caught in the vice
It felt so right.
Terrified to lose
What I never could keep
Drowning in regret
Push it down deep.
But the sun does shine
On the wicked and mean
You licked all my tears
Scraped my heart clean
Together we are more
than the sum of it all
Mighty shall stand
While the weak shall fall
My mistakes almost ruined
The place I belong
Beside you, behind you,
For ever how long.
Take this heart

Perfect Regret

That no longer bends
Wrap it up tight
It still needs to mend.
My beautiful girl
My breath
My life
I will love you
Hold you
Whatever the price.
Stay with me now
Until time grows old
And only then
Beautiful girl
Will our story be told.

For about the millionth time since I met Garrett, I was struck speechless. He put his guitar back in the case and leaned over to kiss me.

"I told you I had nicer stuff to sing to you," he said with a grin.

I grabbed the back of his neck and tugged his hair playfully. "You are *so* getting laid again." I bit his bottom lip gently, pulling it into my mouth and smiling as Garrett groaned.

"I knew it would work," he said breathlessly as I pulled myself up to straddle his lap, pressing against his rigid erection.

"Every single time," I agreed, kissing him and letting out a moan as Garrett, after covering himself with a condom, lifted me up and settled me back down on his cock. Taking me deep.

As we moved together I felt nothing but grateful that he had taken another chance on me. To think there was a time I had looked down my nose at him. Thought him beneath me. I had regretted our first night together as the worst mistake I could have made.

What a stupid, stupid fool I had been.

Because if he was my biggest regret then it was the most perfect regret of my life.

Epilogue

"**Y**ou have your plane ticket?" Garrett asked and I could hear his anxiety over the phone. I grinned and rolled my eyes, even though I knew he couldn't see me.

"YES, MR. I have to worry about everything. I will be on the six o'clock flight to St. Louis. Gracie will be here to drive me to the airport in an hour." I dropped my voice down into a sultry whisper. "Which means you'll have me naked and ready in just over four and a half hours. So instead of freaking out about whether I will get on my plane, you need to be thinking of the million and one ways you're going to make me scream once you have me alone."

Christ, I was getting myself all hot and bothered. Not a good thing when I would have to spend over an hour in the car with Gracie and then another two hours on the plane.

Garrett's answering chuckle made me glad I had gone all phone sex operator. He spent entirely too much time waiting for the other shoe to drop. I hated that the way we began still defined so much of who we were now. I knew I had a lot of making up to do for the way I had treated him before. My callous disregard and outright disrespect for him in the early days of knowing each other had unfortunately made Garrett more than a little anxious where I was concerned.

But I was determined to make it up to him. In every way that I could.

"Well shit, baby. I've got a radio interview in forty-five minutes. I'm not sure if that's enough time to take care of this *problem* that's just popped up."

I laughed too. "Well let's see what we can do about that," I purred and then made sure to explain exactly what I would do when we were together again.

I WHEELED my suitcase into the living room and looked around, making sure I had turned off lights and emptied the trash. It was spring break and instead of heading off to a beach somewhere, I was jumping on a plane to St. Louis to see my suddenly very popular boyfriend and his band while they were on tour.

AFTER THAT night Garrett and I had made love in his family's cabin by the river, we had thrown ourselves into building a relationship that *mattered.* And as we fell more and more into the world we were creating together I knew without a doubt that this was the life with meaning that my dad had wanted me to have.

It wasn't just about doing well in school and having the right career. It was about having all that *and* sharing it with someone who was willing to have all of that with you. And I had found that with Garrett. Because my goals, my dreams, they only made sense if he was there, living his own dream too.

And that's what he was doing.

He came with me to Maryland over Christmas, helping me to make new traditions with my mother, brother and sister after my dad's death. And I knew it meant a lot to him to be included in a family again. My mother welcomed him into the fold as though he had always been there.

She made sure to tell me before I left to return to school that my father would definitely have approved of Garrett. And with the release of tension I hadn't known I was carrying, I realized that my Dad's approval would always matter, whether he was here to give it to me or not.

Returning to Bakersville was bittersweet. I was ready to begin my last semester at Rinard and Maysie and Garrett were leaving.

Saying goodbye to my best friend was as hard as I thought it would be. She had cried a lot, I gave her tissues and made a show of being strong. But in the end I had lost it as badly as she had. There was a lot wailing. A lot of snot and blubbering. But in the end I sent her off to the next chapter of her life without judgment, without a list of reasons she was making a bad choice. I simply gave her my support.

I'd come a long way fellas.

Rinard would be an empty place without her crazy energy and our apartment was way too quiet without her incessant chatter. It wasn't until she had left that I realized how much I appreciated her drama. Hell, it had kept things interesting.

But she was off with Jordan and the rest of the guys, including my new boyfriend, touring the country, exposing the masses to Generation Rejects' brand of ear destroying mayhem.

Garrett leaving took pain to a whole new level. It was ridiculous how attached I had become in such a short amount of time. I had spent so long refusing to admit how much I cared about him, now with the flood gates open it was borderline debilitating. Love sucks when it goes badly but when it's good... damn it's amazing.

While I had tried like hell to hold it together when saying goodbye to Maysie, I fucking lost it when Garrett left. I didn't even try to stop the tears and total emotional meltdown that ensued.

Garrett held me and kissed me and whispered a thousand beautiful things for my ears alone. He told me he loved me over and over again and even though I hadn't yet said it back, I promised him we'd talk every single day and I would see him for spring break.

At the time I hadn't been sure how I'd last for three months. But between classes and finishing up my internship, the time had gone faster than I anticipated.

At the beginning of March, I got the letter that I had been accepted to my top choice grad school in Massachusetts. I was hesitantly excited, not sure what that would mean for my future with Garrett. But after telling him and hearing his own enthusiasm, I knew that no matter what, we'd get through anything. And he promised we'd make it work, no matter if we were together or apart. That my dreams, my goals, were important to both of us.

And if I hadn't been sure I loved him before, I most definitely was now.

Generation Rejects were a hit. Their shows, which in the beginning were selling minimal tickets, were now selling out. Mitch's cousin had gotten them radio interviews and their venues were getting bigger and bigger.

I had no doubt the day would come when they would be signed to a major label. And then Garrett's dreams would be realized as well. And even though I was a little freaked out by the thought, I wanted it for him more than anything. He deserved to have his dreams come true. Even if he swore to me daily that his dreams began and ended with me.

"Knock, knock!" Gracie's high-pitched voice called out as she pushed open the door. She was looking much healthier. She had gained some weight and no longer looked washed out and tired. Her eyes sparkled with that mischievous twinkle that always made me a little bit nervous.

She hadn't returned to school yet and was now saying she wasn't sure she wanted to. I tried talking sense into her, pointing out she only had a semester left until she earned her degree. But she wasn't ready to make definitive decisions about her future and I didn't want to push it. Even if it was in my nature to push.

"You ready?" she asked and I nodded, grabbing my suitcase. Following her out into the hallway, I locked up the apartment. We walked down the stairs, passing Maysie's ex, Eli Bray, who was sitting on the steps strumming a guitar.

At one time I would have made a nasty remark as I passed. I would have looked at him like he was a loser, judging him unfairly. I hated that thinking those thoughts would have been second nature to me.

But not anymore.

"Hey, Eli," I said, walking around him.

Eli looked up at me in surprise and placed his hand on his guitar almost protectively.

"Uh, hey Riley," he said haltingly. He took in my suitcase and raised an eyebrow. "Off on spring break, huh?" he asked, getting to his feet and taking my overstuffed bag. He carried it down the steps for me and I gave him a genuine smile. He was a nice guy and I felt like an ass for never giving him the credit he probably deserved.

"Yep. Off to St. Louis," I said.

Eli crossed his arms over his chest. "St. Louis? There aren't any beaches there. Isn't' spring break supposed to be about getting drunk, showing your tits, and getting a sun burn?"

I laughed at his crude description. "Not for me. I'm going to see my boyfriend's band."

Eli nodded but didn't ask any more questions and I knew we were at an end of our brief civil exchange.

"Okay then, well have fun. Later," he said, sticking a pick in his mouth as he leaned down to turn the tuning pegs of his guitar.

"Later, Eli," I responded, hefting up my bag and carrying it to Gracie's car.

"WAS THAT Maysie's Eli?" Gracie asked, watching Eli sit back down on the stoop and start playing again.

"Yep," I answered, getting into the passenger seat.

"Huh. I don't remember him being so cute," she mused and I almost groaned. I recognized the hunting light in my friend's eyes.

"Don't even think about it, G," I warned and she giggled.

"Is Vivian already gone?" I asked her. Gracie nodded.

"She flew out this morning. She's only going to be out for the weekend. She has to be back on Monday for work. But you know she has to keep tabs on Cole one way or another," Gracie said and I rolled my eyes hoping the Vivian and Cole sideshow wouldn't create too much drama while I was out seeing Garrett. I was determined to keep away of all things angst related.

"I really wish they'd get their acts together or go their separate ways. It's like watching a train wreck. Or a cow dying," I muttered, making Gracie laugh.

"Preaching to the choir, girlfriend," she said.

I looked over at her as she pulled onto the highway, heading toward Dulles Airport. "I hear through the grapevine that Mitch asked you to fly out. So why aren't you coming?" I asked her and was surprised to see her tense up at the mention of Generation Rejects' bassist.

It was common knowledge that Mitch had serious feelings for my dear, clueless friend, who I was beginning to think wasn't as clueless as she let on. Poor Mitch. He was a good guy and it was now painfully obvious the feelings were not reciprocated.

"Yeah, I've got group and a meeting with my therapist that I can't miss. I can't really be around that scene yet anyway," she said and I knew that while she was telling me the truth, there was more there than she was letting on.

"Okay, well you'll be missed," I told her and she smiled.

There was no more talk about Mitch. For the rest of the ride, Gracie and I talked about school and my plans to move to Massachusetts. And when she dropped me off at the airport, I gave her a hug and told her I'd call her once I got back to Bakersville.

"Tell Maysie I miss her. And tell the guys hello. And tell Garrett-" she cut off and looked at me as though she wasn't sure she should continue.

"That you miss him?" I asked. Gracie flushed but nodded.

"He was a good friend to me when I needed it. Just tell him I said hi. The missing you part might be a little awkward. You know since he's in love with my best friend," she joked but I felt that momentary flare of guilt that always popped up when I thought about the feelings I trampled on to have the guy I wanted.

"I'll tell him," I insisted before heading through security.

The flight was delayed for a couple of hours due to thunderstorms in St Louis. I was going out of my skin by the time the plane boarded and we were in the air.

It had been three long months since Garrett held me. And I could barely stomach another moment without him.

Once the plane touched down and I gathered my suitcase, I practically ran to the arrivals terminal. When I saw his messy blond hair and blue eyes scanning the crowd looking for me, I thought my heart would burst out of my chest.

When he finally found me, I dropped my suitcase and took off running toward him. He met me half way and grabbed me up in his arms, holding me tight as though he would never let go again.

This was it. This was home. This was my life of purpose.

"I love you," I said against his mouth and I felt him smile under my lips.

"I love you too," he told me fiercely.
No matter what happened in the future, we would be okay.
No bending hearts because ours would never be broken.
And together, just like this, we were perfect.

Coming in Early 2014

THE NEW Adult romance from A. Meredith Walters, the author of Find You in the Dark and Light in the Shadows.

A story of pain, redemption and discovering yourself at whatever the cost.

Reclaiming the Sand

"I WAS an ugly person. I did ugly things. I thought ugly thoughts…then my world was blown apart by the only person who could change me."

Bully and victim.

Tormenter and tormented.

Villain and hero.

Some people are meant to be the predator while others live their lives as the prey. Ellie Mccallum was the bully. The Tormenter. The Villain. Taking what she wanted, stomping over anyone that got in her way. Feelings, futures and relationships be damned. As long as it wasn't *her* feelings or future, Ellie didn't care about the destruction she left in her wake. She didn't know how to empathize, feeling no emotional connection to anyone or anything. A sad and lonely existence for a young woman who had come to expect nothing more for herself. Her only happiness coming from making others miserable.

Particularly *Freaky Flynn.*

Growing up, Flynn Hendrick was only known to his peers as "Freaky Flynn." He lived a life in solitude. Completely disconnected even as he struggled to define himself as something more than *that* boy with Asperger's. He was taunted and teased, bearing the brunt of systematic and calculated cruelty, ultimately culminating in a catastrophic turn of events that brought Ellie and Flynn's worlds crashing down.

But then Flynn and Ellie grew up.

And moved on.

Until years later when their paths unexpectedly cross again.

The bully and the freak are face to face once more.

When labels come to define you, finding yourself feels impossible.

Particularly for two people disconnected from the world who inexplicably find a connection in each other.

And out of the wreckage of their tragic beginnings, an unlikely love story unfolds.

But a painful past doesn't always want to let go. And old wounds are never truly healed…and sometimes the farther you run from yourself the closer you come to who you really are.

Acknowledgements

IN SOME ways, this is the most special part of writing any book. Listing the people that have made all of this possible. My amazing husband and beautiful daughter are at the top each and every time. Without the two of you, my life wouldn't mean a thing. Ian, you support and love me no matter what and you aren't afraid to give me the swift kick in the ass when I need it. You are unapologetic, have a low bullshit tolerance with a major phobia for stupid. There's a reason we've been together for twelve years. Gwyn, you are beyond fantastic in all of your pink, girlie, sparkly fabulousness. You insist on reading where I thank you for being my daughter in each of my books- so here you go darling.

Claire, girl, the fact that you read my stuff and give me constructive feedback (even if you worry about hurting my feelings) is amazing. When you tell me it's good, damn it I believe you. You're awesome!!!

Tanya Keetch, my super editor. Thank you for squeezing me in when my deadline got pushed back. You are always so positive about my stories and it means the world.

Emily Mah Tippetts-your formatting and interior design on this book (and all of my other ones) is amazing. I'm beyond glad I "met" you! I can't wait to meet you IRL in Louisville!!!

Sarah Hansen, you make each of my covers kick serious ass. You are a talent unlike any other.

For my family and friends who have been my constant cheerleaders. I love each and every one of you.

To the amazing blogs who have pimped out my books and have shown me such an incredible amount of love and support.

I could never do this without you! And most importantly thank you to Kristy Garbutt, Kim Box Person, Denise Tung, Cris Hardarly, Holly Malgieri who are my go to gals for everything and are always there to help me when I ask. Love you ladies!

And to you, my fantastic readers. The fact that you are reading my books and love them means the world to me. You humble me with your support and love and without you I'd only be a gal with a dream. THANK YOU!!!!!!!

About The Author

A. MEREDITH WALTERS is a New York Times and USA Today bestselling author who has been writing since childhood. She is also the author of the contemporary romance, Find You in the Dark, its sequel, Light in the Shadows, the novella, Cloud Walking and the New Adult romance Bad Rep. She is currently working on a Find You in the Dark Christmas novella entitled Warmth in Ice as well as the upcoming New Adult book, Reclaiming the Sand to be released in early 2014.

Before becoming a full-time writer, Meredith spent over a decade as a children's counselor at both a Domestic/Sexual violence shelter and later at an outpatient program for at risk children with severe mental health and behavioral issues. Her clients and their stories continue to influence ever aspect of her writing.

Meredith would love to hear from her fans! Follow her on Facebook, Goodreads or Twitter. Or you can email her at ameredithwalters@gmail.com

If you liked this book, please take the time to leave a review where you purchased it. Thank you so much!

This paperback interior was designed and formatted by

www.emtippettsbookdesigns.blogspot.com

Artisan interiors for discerning authors and publishers.

9791832R00152

Printed in Great Britain
by Amazon.co.uk, Ltd.,
Marston Gate.